VIRAGO
MODERN CLASSICS
589

Angela Thirkell

Angela Thirkell (1890–1961) was the eldest daughter of John William Mackail, a Scottish classical scholar and civil servant, and Margaret Burne-Jones. Her relatives included the pre-Raphaelite artist Edward Burne-Jones, Rudyard Kipling and Stanley Baldwin, and her godfather was J. M. Barrie. She was educated in London and Paris, and began publishing articles and stories in the 1920s. In 1931 she brought out her first book, a memoir entitled *Three Houses*, and in 1933 her comic novel *High Rising* – set in the fictional county of Barsetshire, borrowed from Trollope – met with great success. She went on to write nearly thirty Barsetshire novels, as well as several further works of fiction and non-fiction. She was twice married, and had four children.

By Angela Thirkell

Barsetshire novels

High Rising
Wild Strawberries
The Demon in the House
August Folly
Summer Half
Pomfret Towers
The Brandons
Before Lunch
Cheerfulness Breaks In
Northbridge Rectory
Marling Hall
Growing Up
The Headmistress
Miss Bunting
Peace Breaks Out
Private Enterprise
Love Among the Ruins
The Old Bank House
County Chronicle
The Duke's Daughter
Happy Returns
Jutland Cottage
What Did it Mean?
Enter Sir Robert
Never Too Late
A Double Affair
Close Quarters
Love at All Ages
Three Score and Ten

Non-fiction

Three Houses

Collected stories

Christmas at High Rising

POMFRET TOWERS

Angela Thirkell

virago

VIRAGO

First published in Great Britain in 1938
This edition published in 2013 by Virago Press

A CIP catalogue record for this book is available from the British Library.

ISBN 978-1-84408-971-0

Typeset in Goudy by M Rules
Printed and bound in Great Britain by
Clays Ltd, St Ives plc

Papers used by Virago are from well-managed forests and other responsible sources.

MIX
FSC C104740

Virago Press
An imprint of
Little, Brown Book Group
100 Victoria Embankment
EC4Y 0DY

An Hachette UK Company
www.hachette.co.uk

www.virago.co.uk

I

Invitation to the Towers

Nutfield is quite the most delightful town in that part of England. Most of the land round it is owned by families who have remained rich enough not to be obliged to sell their estates, so the speculative builder has been kept at bay and the town is very little larger than it was in the eighteenth century. In 1847 a branch line of the railway was indeed, after terrific opposition, brought to Nutfield, but the station is so inconveniently situated, far away on the north side of the rising ground upon which the town is built, and has so poor a train service, that it is hardly ever used by the townspeople, who prefer to drive to the junction.

The town itself is on the estate of the seventh Earl of Pomfret, who refuses to allow chain stores or cinemas, and exercises a personal and terrifying supervision over the exterior of shops and garages. The principal inhabitants of Nutfield are occasionally invited to dine at Pomfret Towers, but without their wives, as Lady Pomfret, who is an invalid, mostly lives abroad. These evenings are celebrated for their appalling tedium, but no one has been known to refuse an invitation. Respectable heads of families have been heard comparing notes about his lordship's dullness and rudeness, even boasting with some complacence when he has singled out one of them by some special neglect, or deliberate want of courtesy. Anything that is one's own property tends to acquire lustre in one's eyes. People can find a matter for pride, and even boasting, in a set of false teeth, or an artificial leg, while a glass eye can make them almost unbearable. So did the inhabitants of Nutfield boast about Lord Pomfret's rudeness, looking down with condescending pity upon their less fortunate neighbours.

Nutfield High Street is a wide thoroughfare, running gently downhill southwards to the river, with fine elms on each side. The red brick Georgian houses lie back from the pavement behind walls or handsome iron grilles, and all have large gardens at the back. At the bottom of the hill the road makes a sweeping curve to the right and crosses the river on a fine stone bridge, dating from the fifteenth century. The turn of the road and the narrowness of the high-arched bridge are distinctly dangerous, but Lord Pomfret, to the great inconvenience and yet greater pride of his loyal tenants, has so far successfully resisted all efforts to have the corner straightened out or the bridge widened.

In the large, irregular piece of land between the turn of the road and the river stands Mellings, once a dower house of the Pomfrets, now tenanted by a prosperous local architect, Mr Barton, senior partner in the firm of Barton and Wicklow, which has an excellent county connection and a good reputation for handling old buildings with care and discretion. The only fault that a critic can find with Mellings is that it is so near the water, but the foundations and cellars are in excellent condition, and the river-bank along the south front is so strongly embanked and terraced that no complaint of damp has ever been heard, and the house is excellently heated.

Mr Barton had had a hard struggle with Lord Pomfret before he could install central heating, his lordship having the firm conviction that only foreigners liked their houses warm. When Mr Barton had at last overruled these patriotic objections, his lordship brought forward the unanswerable argument that his grandfather never did that sort of thing. Mr Barton had enough self-control not to point out to his landlord that the fifth earl's early death at twenty-one, due to drinking damnation to his trustees for a week on end when, after a long minority, he came of age, had hardly given him a chance to show his feelings about central heating, a science then in its infancy. He bided his time. A month later Lord Pomfret, growling with fury, was ordered abroad for his rheumatism. His agent, Mr Hoare, was empowered to act for him in his absence; Roddy Wicklow, son of Mr Barton's partner, had just gone into Mr Hoare's office, and Mr Barton got his way.

When once the heating was installed, Mr Barton had no fault at all to find in his house. The fine original Jacobean building on the north, where the kitchen and servants were now housed, the large dignified south front which was added about 1760, were described in every guide book, though not all of them mentioned what was perhaps in its master's eyes its most peculiar beauty. This was a two-storey gardener's cottage which the genius of Repton had changed, in or about 1803, from an uncompromising but comfortable brick house to a small-scale model of the Parthenon, with pillars and portico that cut off all light and air from the interior. Of all this Mr Barton was a passionate lover and faithful guardian, finding it of infinite comfort when his wife seemed farther away than usual.

Mrs Barton was well known as the author of several learned historical novels about the more obscure bastards of Popes and Cardinals, with a wealth of documentation that overawed reviewers. Owing to living so much in the fifteenth and sixteenth centuries, she sometimes found it difficult to remember where she was. She was an excellent housekeeper, who never failed to care for her family and give them good food, and all servants adored her, but though she never obtruded her work, or spoke of it as if it mattered, she only had to go into her sitting-room and take up a paper or a book, to be at once engulfed in the ocean of the past, re-living with intensity the lives of people about whom little was known and whose very existence was dubious. When the tide ebbed, leaving her stranded upon the shores of everyday life, she would emerge in a dazed condition to preside at her own table, or take a fitful interest in her neighbours. Her own son and daughter she treated rather as amusing guests who happened to be making a prolonged stay, though her anxiety for Alice, a delicate girl, the younger by several years, pursued her even among her books and research.

Her husband had long ago given up any hope of competing

with the illegitimate offspring of poisoners and intriguers. He was a successful and busy man and his life was a full one. When, at rare intervals, he allowed himself to feel that something was wanting, he took refuge in the beauty of his house. If Mrs Barton had been abroad too long collecting material, her husband might be found at odd times in the drawing-room, filling his eyes with the charm of the exquisitely proportioned white panels, or on the stairs, affectionately fingering the carved balustrade, absorbing from their quiet beauty something that restored him to his usual outward calm.

On a cold morning in January, as Mr Barton sat at breakfast in his warm dining-room, he congratulated himself for the hundredth time on having got the better of Lord Pomfret in the matter of the heating. On the previous night he had been dining at the Towers and had listened unmoved to his host's gloomy though hopeful prediction that a beam would begin smouldering and the whole Barton family be burnt to death.

He was joined almost immediately by his son Guy, a junior partner in his own firm, who had narrowly escaped being christened Ippolito. Guy, who had inherited his mother's good looks, together with his father's peaceful temperament, found life a very straightforward, pleasant affair.

'Morning, Father,' he said, helping himself to a large bowl of porridge and walking about professionally while he ate it. 'Hideously cold, isn't it? Mother's on her way. She said something about Pirandello or Piranesi or something and said she'd be down in a moment,' said Guy, who like most children made fun of his mother's work and was genuinely surprised when he found that real people in London spoke of her books with respect. That she earned a good deal of money by them seemed to him quite fantastic and a little unfair, but he bore her no grudge.

'If you must walk round the table, do speak to me when I can see you,' said his father good-naturedly. 'I can't eat my breakfast with my head twisted round and I can't speak out of the back of my neck.'

'Sorry, Father. It's a kind of affectation that I have to do. I got it in Scotland last autumn and it hasn't quite worn off. It will soon though. Did you have the usual hilarious evening at the Towers?' said Guy, at last sitting down with a plate of eggs and bacon.

'Much as usual,' said his father. 'Hoare and I were the only guests. Pomfret was not quite so rude as usual, because Lady Pomfret was there for once. I don't wonder she prefers living in Florence. She looks more of an invalid than ever, and the Towers is bitterly cold. I've got some news for you and Alice. They want you to come for a weekend before the hunting is over.'

'Well, well, well,' said Guy. 'When you think that we, by which I mean you, have been paying rent regular for the last seven years, and it's the first time our landlord has asked me and Alice to his hospitable board it comes as a bit of a shock. Alice,' he said to his sister as she came in, 'what do you think of staying at the Towers?'

'At the Towers,' said Alice. 'Why?'

'Because Lord Pomfret asked you,' said her father. 'Lady Pomfret is down, and they are having a big house party and want some young people.'

'Oh, I shouldn't feel safe,' said Alice, backing nervously against the sideboard.

'Safe about what, you great silly?' asked her affectionate brother. 'Old Pomfret chucking you under the chin in the corridor? Here, get yourself some breakfast and you'll feel better.'

'No, not Lord Pomfret,' said Alice. 'I don't think he knows me. I meant nightgowns and housemaids and tips and all that sort of thing. I'd be terrified.'

Mr Barton considered his daughter with a mixture of concern and affectionate annoyance. A delicate child, she had never been able to go regularly to school, so that a natural timidity had been fostered by her semi-invalid life. Her health had improved so much of late that there was no longer cause for anxiety, and her father hoped that she would make friends among the young people of her own age in Nutfield, but she held aloof, painfully conscious that she could not compete in their sports and interests. The wish of her heart had been to study architecture and go into her father's office. Failing this she found solace in painting. The old nursery from being her sitting-room gradually became her studio. There she worked happily by herself, but if anyone asked to look at her work she went through such agonies of shyness that she could not paint for several days. Her father and mother, understanding something of her difficulties, never came to her studio without an invitation. Guy's usual criticism of 'Top hole, but a bit queer, isn't it,' she did not mind. The only other visitors welcomed in the studio were Roddy Wicklow and his sister Sally, who felt the combined kindly contempt and almost superstitious respect that the sporting have for the artist. Of her own want of good looks she was fully conscious, accepting this with the humility which was almost a vice in her. A thin girl, with a sallow complexion and dark, lifeless hair, no stranger would have looked at her twice, though her father's eye could see in her a certain grace of movement and elegance of bone which gave promise for the future. Her only assets at present were her long sensitive hands, her large anxious brown eyes, and a smile whose sudden brilliance flashed in gratitude for any kindness shown to her. At this moment the mere thought of two nights away from home with strangers was making her suffer such anticipatory pangs of homesickness as none of her family could quite understand.

'Tips, I admit, are terrifying,' said Mr Barton, 'but why nightgowns?'

'Oh, they despise one,' said Alice. 'I mean the house-maids despite the kind of nightgowns one has, and they hide all one's things. Oh Father, need I?'

'Well, ask your mother,' said Mr Barton in a cowardly way. 'Here she is. Susan, Pomfret has asked Guy and Alice to the Towers. Alice doesn't much want to go. What do you think?'

Mrs Barton laid a heap of letters on the table and sat down.

'I haven't seen Lady Pomfret for years,' she said. 'Not for years,' she added reflectively.

'Well, darling, none of us have,' said Guy, kissing the top of her head, 'because she hasn't been there. If I brought you some coffee and some food, do you think you could concentrate for a moment. Lord Pomfret has asked us for a weekend. Lady Pomfret hasn't, but I don't suppose that matters. I do want to go. Alice doesn't. Father says ask you.'

'But Lady Pomfret *has* asked you,' said Mrs Barton. 'Don't give me eggs, because I ordered fish cakes as well, and I want to show that we eat them. I brought Lady Pomfret's letter down to show you all. It is somewhere among my post. Oh, here it is. I haven't seen her since Florence before the War. She had a German doctor, which annoyed the Italians so much. I don't suppose they would mind so much today, but really I don't know, because they are so very, very insular, though that can't be exactly what I mean. She writes to me that she has been seeing the Skinners in Florence, who sent all kinds of messages to us, Walter, and would like to have my young people to stay. I do detest the phrase young people.'

'Well, say Giovinezza, darling,' said Guy, 'and here are the fish cakes, and I'm glad you drew my attention to them, because I just felt I needed a little something to fill in the gaps, and they will do admirably. Who are the Skinners?'

'People we used to know,' said Mr Barton vaguely. 'People you would never have heard of, too dull to explain. It is a remarkable thing that when people know people in Florence they are always English. I've never been there myself, but I've never met anyone who knows an Italian there, and I imagine it as consisting entirely of Skinners.'

'You are perfectly right, Walter,' said Mrs Barton, turning her beautiful eyes upon her husband. 'Perfectly right. That is why people like Florence. They could never find so many concentrated Skinners in England. Alice had better have a new frock and go.'

'It isn't frocks, darling, it's nightgowns,' said Guy. 'She thinks the housemaids will despise her.'

'Oh I know they will,' said Alice, flushing darkly with misery. 'Please, please need I?'

Mr Barton and Guy very basely said goodbye and went off to their work, leaving Mrs Barton to deal with her daughter. Mrs Barton did not at all wish to be unkind to her, but she felt it was really high time that Alice began to get about and learn to meet people. Her suggestion of a little coming out dance had been received with a frightened resignation that entirely wrecked her plans. It was impossible to invite guests to a party when the heroine of the evening was losing weight at the mere thought, and every day had darker circles under her eyes. Mrs Barton then suggested that the ball should be changed to a small evening party, at which Alice's relief was so great that she could only cry. As she looked like tears every time the party was mentioned, her mother again abandoned her plans, and said a little dinner party would be nice. Alice falteringly said that it would be very nice, but she supposed she would have to speak to the people on each side of her, and looked so abjectedly wretched that her mother gave up the idea altogether. Alice could hardly believe her good fortune and went about for several days with terrified eyes, shrinking from everyone, but she had now recovered her spirits and relapsed into her usual routine, painting in her studio, occasionally taking tea with Sally Wicklow, or visiting the kennels in a timid way with Roddy Wicklow. Not that she particularly liked dogs, whose loud, indiscriminating hospitality she found rather overpowering, but Roddy was so large that no one ever noticed her when she was with him, which gave her a safe feeling.

Alice sat in miserable silence, twisting her legs round her chair and fiddling with her cup and saucer, while her mother considered how best to persuade her unhappy daughter that two days at Pomfret Towers would not last for ever, and that far from all eyes being critically fixed upon her, it was probable that no one would notice her. It was true devotion on Mrs Barton's part to take so much trouble, for she was burning to get back to Ganimede, a vicious but artistic little hunchback, whose exact position in an illegitimate branch of the Borgia family was still undefined.

'Alice,' said her mother.

Alice dropped her cup onto her saucer with a crash and looked wildly round for help. As none was forthcoming she twisted her hands desperately together and said 'Yes, Mother.'

'I don't think the Towers would be so bad,' said her mother, with a carelessness that did not deceive herself or Alice in the least. 'It isn't as if Lord Pomfret were a stranger, and it's only for two days, and Guy will be with you. It might be rather fun.'

Emboldened by despair Alice at last gave voice to the awful fear that had been haunting her ever since the plan was mentioned.

'Do you think there would be any other girls there?' she asked, hopelessly.

'Oh, I should think so, certainly,' said Mrs Barton, glad that Alice was for once showing a little interest in people of her own age. 'And I daresay there will be some dancing, or games, in the evening.'

This was almost more than Alice could bear. Her own mother had entirely misunderstood her, and was pushing her helpless offspring with all her might into the lion's den. A weekend at the Towers might just, just be bearable if no one else were there, or if under cover of a crowd of grown-ups one could stay in a corner, restfully ignored. But if there were to be girls, Alice thought she had better die. They would all have wonderful dresses and exquisite shoes, and be permanently waved and made up, and be frightfully clever and know all about people and theatres and films, and despise one, and why couldn't Mother understand that girls of one's own age were simply the most awful thing one could be asked to face.

'I see,' she said, in a voice whose want of enthusiasm her mother decided to ignore.

'So it won't be awful after all,' continued Mrs Barton with monstrous want of tact, 'and it will be such fun for you and Guy to go together. I must go and see cook now. Don't go out this morning, will you, darling? There's such an east wind, and it won't do you any good.'

She collected her letters, kissed Alice, and left the room. Alice, who had been toying with the idea of walking very slowly by the river till she was frozen to death, obediently got up and went to her studio. She was designing a dust jacket and end-papers for her mother's new book. These were to be a surprise, and though she humbly felt that her clever, beautiful mother would probably find them quite inadequate, she took a great deal of pleasure in the work. From time to time she stopped working to look out of the window at the bitter, frostbound world and thought that even Pomfret Towers might be better than walking in the cold wind till one died, though if any warm and painless kind of death were handy she would much prefer it to Pomfret Towers. She had her mother's way of becoming completely absorbed in what she was doing, and by lunch-time had almost forgotten the impending doom. Mr Barton and Guy, who came home for lunch, were full of a fifteenth-century manor house which its new owner wanted reconditioning, and could talk of nothing else. Mrs Barton, lost in the mazes of Ganimede's family, who had very careless views about marriage, sat in a kind of trance, eating her lunch abstractedly, though with a good appetite, and not hearing anything her family said. So nothing was said about the visit, and Alice went off to have the afternoon rest, which was still part of her regime, in fairly good spirits.

When she came down at tea-time the cold world outside was safely shut away. In the drawing-room a huge log fire threw a golden light on the panelling, the heavy curtains were drawn, and Mrs Barton, looking a little tired, but triumphant, was lying back in a big chair beside the fire.

'Will you pour out for me, darling,' she said to Alice. 'I am quite exhausted.'

'Was it your book?' asked Alice, whose attitude to her mother was worshipping awe that anyone could look so nice and yet be so clever.

'Yes. It's rather stupid of me to take it seriously, and we'll talk about something else.'

Alice, afraid that the something might be Pomfret Towers, set herself to make her mother talk about her work, but this was always difficult, and they sank into a warm, comfortable silence. This was suddenly broken by a deafening noise of barking in the hall.

'Sally and her horrible dogs, I suppose,' said Mrs Barton, sitting up and pushing her hair back. 'I do wish—'

But what she wished, and the butler's announcement of Miss Wicklow, were equally drowned in the noise of three dogs who came bouncing into the room under the false assumption that they were all welcome and honoured guests, paying no attention to their mistress's loud commands of silence.

'Sorry,' said Sally Wicklow, picking up a fox terrier, half throttling a large lurcher, and kicking in a friendly way an excitable Airedale. 'They must have smelt Penny. They're as quiet as angels as a rule. How do you do, Mrs Barton. Any more books lately? I always tell Roddy I can't think how you do it. Hullo, Alice, I didn't see you. How's art.'

Without waiting for any replies Miss Wicklow sank into a chair and stretched out her long legs in riding breeches towards the fire. From under her chair a hoarse subterranean growl arose and all the dogs began to bark again.

'Hullo, it's Penny,' said Miss Wicklow, feeling under the chair and dragging out an old Scotch terrier with a face as large as an elephant's. 'Isn't he a clever dog to know his Aunt Sally is here? And weren't Aunt Sally's dogs clever children to smell Penny?'

'No, they weren't, Sally,' said Mrs Barton rather sharply. 'Anyone could smell Penny. I have told Walter again and again that he ought to be destroyed, and Penny knows he isn't supposed to be in the drawing-room. Ring, Alice.'

The butler came almost at once and Mrs Barton delivered Penny to him.

'And take Miss Wicklow's dogs into the hall, Horton,' she said. 'No, Sally, I will not have dogs in the drawing-room, and you know it. Horton can look after them.'

Miss Wicklow accepted the situation calmly and began to make a very substantial tea, explaining that she had been riding with her brother and had forgotten to have any lunch.

'Roddy'll be along in a moment,' she said. 'He had to go up to the Towers for Mr Hoare about something. I say, I hope Horton isn't feeding those dogs, Mrs Barton. Hadn't I better go and bring them in again? They won't make a sound now, or if they do I'll give Wuffy a good beating – he's the one that always sets them off.'

'I'm sure Horton wouldn't feed them,' said Alice, who knew that Sally, a martinet in the field or the kennels, was incapable of controlling her dogs indoors.

'Well, I'll just bring Wuffy in,' said Sally.

'No, don't,' said Alice, dreading another outburst of barking. 'I'll go and see. I'm sure they are all right.'

She slipped out of the room. At first the dimly lighted hall seemed empty and she thought Horton had taken Sally's dogs away with Penny. Then she saw Sally's three dogs lying as neatly as if they were on tombstones, perfectly silent, each with ears cocked and eyes lovingly turned in the same direction. Alice, following their gaze, saw in the darkest corner of the hall under the staircase a kind of heaving mountain which she at once recognised as Roddy Wicklow taking off his coat.

'Hullo,' said Roddy, advancing towards the light. 'Those dogs of Sally's were giving Horton hell in the pantry, when I got here. Did they bother you?'

'Only in the drawing-room,' said Alice holding out her hand.

'I really oughtn't to shake hands,' said Roddy. 'It's freezing like blinking outside and I hadn't my gloves on. By Jove, your hand's as cold as mine. Have you been out on a day like this?'

He towered over and almost enveloped Alice with his great height and breadth and his loose shabby tweeds, but Alice found it comfortable and reassuring.

'I'm always cold,' she said.

'You look a bit peaked, I must say,' said Roddy. 'Anything up?'

'Oh, a most *awful* thing,' said Alice, suddenly remembering the weekend. 'Something mother wants me to do, and I don't want to, and I know it's silly of me, but I think I'll die if I do, and I oughtn't to tell you about it, but I couldn't help it.'

To her great mortification her voice failed and she had to sniff.

'Well, that's all right,' said Roddy in his matter of fact way. 'One doesn't die of doing things one doesn't want to. Cheer up and blow your nose. I'd wipe your eyes for you only my handkerchief's too dirty. I had to tie up a dog's foot in it and forgot to change it. Do you think Horton could raise an egg if your mother doesn't mind? I've had no lunch. Now, you dogs, quiet till I come back, or you'll hear of it.'

'Oh,' breathed Alice, horrified, and forgetting her own troubles again she dragged Roddy into the drawing-room. 'Could Roddy have an egg?' she asked.

Mrs Barton rang the bell and gave the order.

'Thanks awfully. And now,' said Roddy, who never beat about the bush, 'what's the matter with Alice? She says there's something awful she's got to do and she'll die if she does it.'

'She never told *me*,' said Sally indignantly. 'And what's more no one thought of getting *me* an egg.'

'Well, what is it?' said Roddy, taking no notice of his sister's interjection, and toasting his back as he stood in front of the fire, thus cutting off all warmth from his hostess.

'You are like the great San Philip that of something thousand tons,' said Mrs Barton, to Roddy's great mystification, but she put him at his ease again by asking him not to keep all the fire off everyone.

'I *am* sorry,' said Roddy. 'Oh, good man,' he added as Horton came in with three eggs on a tray. 'Three eggs! I could do with them.'

'Excuse me, sir, but one is for Miss Sally,' said Horton. 'I understood that she had not lunched, neither.'

Sally snatched at an egg, and after a friendly struggle with her brother, they both set to at their meal. Mrs Barton regarded them with tolerance and a vague feeling that so would the Medici have fed their retainers when they returned late from some expedition. Alice made herself as small as possible in a corner by the fire and hoped that Roddy would not ask what the matter was again. She knew her mother wanted her to go, and she very much wanted to please her mother, and perhaps Roddy was right when he said one didn't die of doing things one didn't like, and oh, if only she hadn't told Roddy about it in the hall, but perhaps he would forget.

The conversation was kept up antiphonally by the Wicklows, who gave an account of how they had been to Thatcher's End about the cottages, and over to Pomfret Madrigal about the draining, and down to Little Misfit about the lambs, and Alice felt quite safe again.

Just as they had got to the sad story of the ewe who, having unlike her fellows a faint glimmering of sense, had deduced that the lamb supplied to her in a great coat made of her own dead lamb's skin was not one of the family, and had trampled it to death, sounds were heard in the hall, and Horton, in a voice that would have done credit to a toast master and really deserved a better audience, announced, 'Lord Pomfret, madam.'

His lordship stopped on the threshold and glared suspiciously about him, annoyed to find that Mrs Barton was not alone. He was a tall elderly man with a soldierly carriage. His head was almost bald and his eyebrows very bushy. He had a heavy, old-fashioned moustache of a pale sandy colour. His eyes were small and often looked very angry. It was so long since his only son, Lord Mellings, had been killed in a frontier skirmish and his wife had decided to be an invalid, that very few people remembered what he used to be like. On the rare occasions when he chose to behave well, no one could be more charming, but these occasions grew rarer every year. His heir was a cousin whom he had seldom seen, and had expressed the hope never to set eyes on again till he, Lord Pomfret, was screwed down in his coffin.

The young Wicklows, as employee and employee's sister, stood up when he came in. Alice looked despairingly at Roddy and remained rooted to her seat.

'Sit down, sit down,' said his lordship impatiently. 'How de do, Mrs Barton. What's that there? Your girl, eh? Consumptive or something, isn't she?'

He shook hand with his hostess, took no notice of the rest of the party, and sat down in the seat nearest Mrs Barton, whom he secretly rather admired. Her fine figure, the pleasant air of attention which veiled her wandering thoughts, and her occasional peremptory manner, reminded him of some of the great ladies he had known before motors came in. As for Mrs Barton she was neither frightened nor impressed by Lord Pomfret, and spiked his guns by ignoring his breaches of good manners. The Catholic branch of his family had lived in Italy since 1689, and it was owing to his connections that she had had access to historical papers that she could not otherwise have seen. She was always pleased to see him, and it is probable that Lord Pomfret was more at his ease with her than anywhere else outside his own house.

'Can't you send all these people away?' he said to his hostess, in a voice that could have been and was heard by Horton, who came back with the whisky and soda that was his lordship's usual drink at tea-time.

'Certainly not,' said Mrs Barton. 'Certainly not. Roddy and Sally have been riding about all day doing your business. Did you know they were having to deepen the drain at Pomfret Madrigal?'

'Of course I didn't,' said Lord Pomfret. 'The fools never tell me anything. If they deepen the drain they'll flood Starveacres, that's all.'

'I don't think so, sir,' said Roddy. 'If you remember, we changed those sluices at Starveacres Hatches last year, and the water escapes above the end of the drain.'

'That's young Pickford in Hoare's office, isn't it?' said Lord Pomfret to his hostess, after bestowing a baleful stare on the unperturbed Roddy.

'It is Mr Wicklow, if that is what you mean,' said Mrs Barton severely.

Lord Pomfret made a hideous noise with which it was his habit to hold up conversation till he was ready to plunge into it again.

'Well, Wickford?' he began.

'Mr Wicklow,' said Mrs Barton.

'Oh well, Wicklow, if you like,' said Lord Pomfret. 'There's a fellow called Wickfield in Dickens, stoopid sort of fellow that can't manage his own affairs. Must have been thinking of that. Well, Wicklow, or whatever your name is, what's that you said about the sluices?'

Roddy, with perfect patience and good-humour, repeated what he had previously said. Lord Pomfret, who knew every inch of his estates even better than Mr Hoare the old agent, listened attentively.

'Well, you young men know everything,' he remarked. 'I shall be at the office at nine tomorrow and we'll ride over. You'll have to get up early for once. That your wife, eh?' he added, looking ferociously at Sally, who was having great difficulty in suppressing her feelings while her brother was badgered.

'No, sir, my sister,' said Roddy.

'Same thing,' said his lordship.

'No, Lord Pomfret, it is *not*,' put in Mrs Barton. 'This is *not* Ancient Egypt.'

At this his lordship suddenly laughed in a disconcerting way. He then got up and Alice, who had been holding her breath all the time, saw safety ahead and relaxed a little, when to her horror he turned to her mother and said, 'Are your young people coming to us on the twenty-third, Mrs Barton? My wife isn't often here, and I would like her to have the pleasure of getting to know your children.'

Mrs Barton, always touched when Lord Pomfret allowed his innate courtesy to get the better of the unprepossessing manner which had become second nature, took his hand.

'They would love to,' she said. 'And I hope I shall see your wife while she is here. She was very kind to me in Florence, years ago.'

Alice could bear this no longer. For half an hour she had been frightened out of her wits by Lord Pomfret and now her mother was throwing her alive into his jaws. Despair lent her courage. She stood up and said timidly, 'Oh, Mother . . .'

Lord Pomfret looked in the direction of the sound and saw what he mentally described as a scraggy little piece of goods looking as if he were going to wring her neck. But he was not a stupid man.

'Your girl doesn't want to come, eh?' he said to Mrs

Barton. 'Shy, and that sort of thing? Tell her to do what she likes. Here,' he added, turning to Roddy, 'you'd better come and bring your sister with you. I'll tell my wife to send you a proper invitation.'

Roddy thanked his employer and said they would love to come. Mrs Barton, who with real kindness had not sent a reproachful look, and hardly even a reproachful thought in her daughter's direction, asked if it was to be a big party.

'Twenty or thirty. I don't know,' said Lord Pomfret. 'I hope my wife will enjoy it. I shan't. She has asked that woman that married my poor cousin.'

'Do you mean Mrs Rivers?' said Mrs Barton, who had often been favoured with a list of the relatives by blood or marriage that his lordship particularly disliked.

'I do,' said the earl, 'and I wish I didn't. She's driven poor George nearly demented with her airs. Can't talk about anything but her books. Won't stay with George in Herefordshire. Always gadding about being literary. George is thankful to be rid of her, I think. He'd pay anything to get a little peace. I can't stand those literary women. Now you're not literary, and that's what I like about you. You don't plague a man by gabbling about books as Hermione Rivers does. Glad to have seen you. Don't forget, Wicklow, you and your sister, Friday to Monday.'

While this conversation had been going on, Alice had had time to form a resolution. She was ashamed of her childish outcry, she knew that her mother would be disappointed, she remembered that Guy would like to have her with him. When Lord Pomfret had invited the Wicklows, everything was made easy. Sally, who feared nothing, would strengthen her against housemaids, and if Roddy were there everything must be all right. If anything so awful as dancing or games took place, Roddy would surely protect her. Without waiting for her resolution to cool, she very bravely came forward and holding out her hand said, 'Thank you very much, Lord Pomfret, and I'd like to come very much indeed.'

'What's that?' said his lordship who was rapidly reverting to his usual mood. 'Oh, yes, come along, you and your brother. Don't blame me if you don't enjoy yourself.'

He then allowed Horton to help him on with his coat, asked if that filthy dog had been killed yet, repeated his prediction that the whole household would be burned to death one night, and went away.

The Wicklows also took their departure, and shortly afterwards Mr Barton and Guy came home. As Alice's father and brother had both taken it for granted that she would really be sensible and go to the Towers, the subject was hardly mentioned again. Mrs Barton refrained from any comment upon her daughter's behaviour and retired into her own world, while Alice spent the evening partly in regretting that she had accepted, partly in telling herself that if Roddy and Sally were there it would be all right.

2

Arrival at the Towers

Pomfret Towers was the successor of Pomfret Castle, the Norman fortress built by Giles de Pomfret in the twelfth century, partially destroyed in the Wars of the Roses, rebuilt under Henry VII and battered by Cromwell. The first earl was created in 1689 for services rendered to the Prince of Orange, and in the same year a younger brother, who had rashly adopted the Roman Catholic faith, found it convenient to go to Italy where his descendants still lived. In the eighteenth century the family, much impoverished by the third earl's losses at play, moved into the dower house of Mellings, adding the south wing. The castle was allowed to fall into complete ruin, except for the old buttery where a hermit was kept to attract visitors. The fourth earl, suddenly enriched by the discovery of coal under a northern property, had planned to build a Palladian mansion, and had gone so far as to pull down most of what remained of the old buildings, when he died from a fall when hunting, leaving an infant son, the fifth earl, whose premature death has already been mentioned. As this unlucky young man had already married a neighbouring heiress, their son, born after his father's death, also came into a vast accumulation of wealth, which he increased by marriage. The sixth Earl of Pomfret was an affectionate husband and father, an excellent landlord, and one of the most insufferable prigs that Queen Victoria's reign produced. While at Oxford he came under the influence of the Gothic revival. His first sight of St Pancras station, when on his way north for some shooting, was a revelation, and a family mansion was erected from plans prepared in the office of Sir Gilbert Scott. This pile, for no less a name is worthy of this vast medley of steep roofs, turrets, gables, and chimney stacks, crowned by a Victorian clock tower, took four years to build and is said to have cost its owner first and last as many hundred thousand pounds. The interior decorations are of a richness that vies with the exterior. The walls of the great hall are painted in imitation of Gobelin tapestry. The various drawing-rooms are hung and in some cases roofed with the richest silks. Workmen from Italy were employed upon the carved marble of the balustrades and the plaster of the ceilings, while the copper utensils for the kitchen are estimated to have cost hundreds of pounds alone. Lord Pomfret had one son, the present earl, and two daughters, one of whom had died young, and the other, Lady Emily, was married to Mr Leslie, a landowner in the next county.

In this magnificent home, where it was computed that an under footman might walk ten miles a day in the course of his duties, and the dining-room was separated from the kitchen by a serving room, a flight of stone steps, and a dark passage nearly fifty yards long containing several sharp corners, the sixth Lord Pomfret's children had passed their childhood, and in it the present Lord Pomfret had lived for nearly eighty years. On his father's death he succeeded to an estate that still had a very large rent-roll, in spite of the previous owner's building extravagances, and had spent most of his life looking after it.

For many years the state-rooms had not been used, except on the rare occasions when Lord Pomfret, as Lord Lieutenant, entertained Royalty, for Lady Pomfret lived much abroad. So Lord Pomfret lived in the smallest and warmest corner he could find, and the rest of the rooms remained shut up, dismally sheeted, with shutters closed and curtains put away. Neither the young Bartons nor the young Wicklows had ever seen them in use, and professional curiosity was certainly part of Guy Barton's reason for accepting. Roddy Wicklow, owing to his position in Mr Hoare's office, had occasion to visit the Towers more than once during the ensuing fortnight, and brought back all kinds of interesting news.

Two days before the great weekend Alice was having tea with her friend Sally Wicklow. The Wicklows lived in one of the Georgian houses half-way up Nutfield High Street. Mr and Mrs Wicklow were very sensible parents who knew their place. Sally had a delightful sitting-room of her own looking onto the street, so that she could shout to her friends about dogs or horses as they went by, and the use of the old stables at the back for her dogs and their puppies. Roddy always dropped into his sister's room if he was back by tea-time, and his father and mother never came unless invited. But the young Wicklows were well-disposed towards their parents and made no objection to partaking of breakfast, lunch, and dinner with them when not more amusingly engaged, or to spending the evening in the drawing-room if Sally's wireless was out of action.

'Of course the old earl didn't think of bathrooms,' said Roddy, who had just joined Sally and Alice. 'At least he did put in one, but it was in the bachelors' wing and ladies never used it.'

'What do we do then?' asked Sally. 'Hip baths in front of the fire?'

'You could if you liked,' said Roddy. 'I counted eighteen myself this morning in the Pink Room where they were stored, and ten of those funny flat ones.'

'I don't know those,' said Alice.

'You poor little rich girl,' said Sally. 'Fancy being so young that you've never seen a flat bath. Is that all, Roddy?'

'Not at all. There are two more bathrooms now, at the end of the West wing. The housekeeper showed them to me this morning. Lord Pomfret had them put in for the hunting men before his son died, but they're a bit communist. I mean he just cut one room in two and ran a partition up, but it doesn't go up to the ceiling for some reason, and anyway it's only a quarter of an inch thick, so you have a pretty good guess who's next door.'

'Shall I have to go there?' asked Alice.

'Well, there are two or three rooms that have baths built into them,' said Roddy. 'They were really meant for dressing-rooms, but they use them for bedrooms when the house is full. Seems a bit queer to sleep in your bathroom, but I daresay it's all right. Get down, Wuffy.'

He pushed his sister's Airedale, which was pawing his legs with a view to cake, down again.

'Poor old Wuffy,' said Sally. 'Come up by mother then.'

She patted the sofa invitingly and Wuffy jumped up and settled himself. The fox terrier, seeing his rival exalted, began to growl. Wuffy barked contemptuously and Alice shrank into the far corner of the sofa. Roddy strode to the door, giving the whistle that meant he was going for a walk. Both dogs hurried after him and he opened the door and herded them out.

'Now they'll go and scratch at the drawing-room door and annoy the parents,' said Sally. 'You'd much better have left them here.'

'I don't understand you, my girl,' said her brother. 'A young woman like you that helps the huntsman and runs the beagles ought to know how to handle dogs. Think of others. Here is poor Alice practically having hydrophobia.'

'Oh no, I'm not,' said Alice, who had hoped that her evident dislike of Wuffy and the fox terrier was not noticeable. 'I really like them very much, if only they wouldn't bark and didn't try to climb up me. I am really getting quite friendly with—'

'There's Chloe,' said Sally, as a scratching and whining which had been going on ever since the dogs left the room was succeeded by several loud flaps against the door. 'Isn't she a lamb? She has taught herself to knock on the door with her tail. Come in, angel.'

She opened the door to the lurcher, who entered with a

smile and stood waving her tail fatuously, then came straight up to Alice, put her forepaws on her lap and breathed affection into her face.

'Nice Chloe,' said Alice, in such a fainting voice that Roddy and Sally couldn't help laughing. Overcome with dislike of the loving dog and shame of her own cowardice, Alice's eyes began to swim. Roddy quietly removed Chloe and pushed her out of the room.

'Roddy, you really *are*,' said Sally indignantly. 'Turning Chloe out of her own mother's sitting-room.'

'Mothers who can't bring children up properly don't deserve to have them,' said Roddy, adding in a low voice to his sister as he got up to put more wood on the fire, 'Remember Hero.' This referred to a Great Dane which Sally had bought the year before, and which had so frightened Alice by putting its head over her shoulder when she was sitting in a low chair in Sally's sitting-room that she had actually fainted. Sally, who could not understand Alice's feelings in the least, had nevertheless been extremely remorseful and sold the dog within the week at a very good profit.

'Sorry, Roddy,' she murmured, and her brother gave her a friendly squeeze.

Alice, mortified but relieved, asked Roddy several more questions about the Towers, but conversation became difficult because the maid came to take the tea away, which meant several journeys, and at each opening of the door dogs burst in like long-lost relations, or were cajoled, kicked, and cuffed out into the hall again. Roddy then said that he must go back to the office, and offered to see Alice home.

'Will it be very grand, do you think?' asked Alice as they went down the High Street.

'I shouldn't think so,' said Roddy cheerfully. 'One party's much like another. I'll tell you what, though,' he added hopefully, 'there may be a few good bust-ups. Lord Pomfret hates that Mrs Rivers he was talking about like hell, and her son and daughter are coming too. I met them once. The daughter's all right, she acts or something, but the son's a stinker. He's an artist,' said Roddy with fine contempt.

'Don't you like artists?' said Alice, rather dashed.

'I don't mean you, you're all right,' said Roddy, 'and anyway you don't go about looking like a scarecrow, or a haystack, and you don't expect one to look at your stuff. Julian Rivers is one of those stuck-up blokes. I mean he *needn't* be an artist – they're all quite well off and he could easily do some decent job – but he goes and lives in a studio and makes a song about it. Oh, and I believe the heir is coming.'

'Who?' asked Alice, not quite sure whether she ought to say which or what.

'The heir. You know, the man who will succeed Lord Pomfret. At least not him, because Lord Pomfret won't have him, but his son. I must say it must be jolly hard to see your place go to someone you don't like.'

'But Lord Pomfret won't actually see it go, will he?' asked Alice. 'I mean he'll be dead when it does.'

'You never know what they'll see,' said Roddy, to propitiate any Unseen Powers that might be about.

'Perhaps he wouldn't care by then,' said Alice hopefully.

'I bet he'd care, wherever he was,' said Roddy. 'But

anyway this man is coming and I suppose Mrs Rivers will make a set at him for her girl. I think I ought to write him an anonymous letter and warn him. Are you sure Chloe didn't frighten you?'

'Oh no. I like her very much,' said Alice politely, 'if only she wouldn't breathe.'

'Well, if she breathes again I'll jolly well tie her up,' said Roddy, pushing the wrought iron gate of Mellings open for Alice. 'Good night. I must hare down to the office. We've no end to do before Friday.'

Thursday passed with nightmare swiftness as far as Alice was concerned. She lay awake most of Thursday night imagining all the horrible things that might happen, such as forgetting to take a toothbrush, packing the stockings that had been darned instead of her best ones, whether to put the tip into the housemaid's hand and say 'Thank you' or leave it on the dressing-table, and worst of all the probability, nay the certainty, that she would have to talk to the people next to her at dinner. She had a faint hope that on Friday morning she might see in *The Times* that Pomfret Towers had been burned down the night before, though such an interesting piece of news would certainly have reached Mellings by the milk or the odd man long before the paper arrived, or that Lord Pomfret would ring up to say that Lady Pomfret had gone back to Italy and the party had been cancelled, or that by inconceivable good luck she herself might suddenly have a temperature or spots. None of these things happened. She and Guy were to arrive at the Towers in time for dinner, picking up the Wicklows on the way, so after tea she finished her packing in a kind of stupor, unpacked most of it to see if her golden shoes were really there, and packed it again, not quite so well. She looked at the tear-off calendar that hung over her writing-table and wondered if it would be tempting Providence to tear off today, Saturday and Sunday, so that Monday would seem nearer, but the risk of Providence's taking offence and protracting the weekend indefinitely seemed too great. There was nothing else to be done, so she went downstairs to wait for the car. Her mother called her into the drawing-room, gazed piercingly at her and said she looked very nice. She then gave her a parcel which Alice was not to open till she was dressing for dinner.

'Something to cheer you up, darling,' said Mrs Barton.

Alice was very grateful and hugged her mother, feeling secretly that a good breakfast before one was hanged wasn't really of much use.

Then Mr Barton came in, asking where Guy was. Horton was sent to look for Mr Guy in his room, and meanwhile Guy came into the drawing-room by the other door from his father's study, where he had been helping himself to some cigarettes and stamps, and everything was confusion. When Horton had been reclaimed, showing well-bred umbrage at his vain errand, Mr Barton had forgotten what he wanted Guy for.

'You can ring up if it's anything important, Walter,' said Mrs Barton. 'And Guy, darling, please ask Lord Pomfret if he can lend me that book by his Italian cousin. He'll know the one I mean. It was privately printed and I can't remember the name, but tell him it's about Ferrara and he'll know the one I mean, because it's very rare and I think he's got the only copy in England. He doesn't like lending books as a rule, but tell him I'll be very careful with it, and ask for a piece of brown paper to put round it.'

'I say, Mother,' said Guy, appalled at the prospect of having to face Lord Pomfret with this vague and probably unwelcome request, 'couldn't you write to Lord Pomfret? I mean I daresay I shan't be seeing him much. It's rather a big party.'

'Do as your mother asks, my boy,' said Mr Barton, laying his hand on Guy's arm.

Guy could willingly have killed both his parents on the spot, though he would have regretted it afterwards, but Horton, still registering umbrage, said the car was at the door and the luggage in, so they all said goodbye. Alice clung to her mother with the tenacity of a drowning man. Mrs Barton, giving her an extra hug, unhooked her kindly and pushed her into the hall. Hardly had the car started, when Horton came running after them. Carter, the chauffeur, stopped.

'What's the matter?' asked Guy, putting down the window.

'Mr Barton wishes to speak to you, sir,' said Horton.

Guy got out and went back to the front door.

'Do you want me, Father?' he said.

'It's all right,' said Mr Barton. 'I only wanted to say I thought I'd remembered what I wanted to say, but it's gone again. You'd better hurry, or you'll be late.'

Guy, amused and annoyed, ran back to the car and told Carter to go on. Horton went back to the house and relieved his feelings by treating his master for the rest of the evening with a supercilious contempt which no one took for anything but his usual manner.

When Guy and Alice got to the Wicklows' house the young Wicklows were ready. Sally got in, followed by Roddy, and before Carter could shut the door, a wild yelp from the house was followed by the fox terrier, who hurled himself like a catapult into the car and stood barking at Carter, as a social inferior.

'Naughty Chips,' said Sally. 'Isn't he a clever boy to know where mother is?'

'Instink, miss,' said Carter. 'He saw you getting into the car, miss, and came after you.'

'Well, now he can go back,' said Roddy. 'Here, Carter, take him in, will you.'

'Oh, Roddy, you can't send him back,' said Sally. 'Look, he's asking to come.'

As Chips was still barking furiously at Carter, his meaning was not so clear to others as it was to his mistress. Roddy, taking no notice of his sister's plea, hauled Chips by the collar out of the car, carried him up the path, opened the front door and pushed him inside. For the rest of the journey Sally and her brother argued in a friendly way about dogs in cars, with Guy dropping in an argument on either side as it amused him. Half an hour later the car drove up the immense ramp in front of the Towers (for even to this detail had Scott's masterpiece been imitated) and stopped under the portico. Guy, Sally and Roddy, still arguing loudly, got out, followed by Alice clutching her mother's parcel. Carter whirled away and left them to their fate.

'Sally,' said Alice suddenly, while the men were giving their hats and coats to the footman, 'Carter's gone away with the luggage! What shall we do!'

'What's that?' said Roddy. 'The luggage? He's taken it round to the service entrance. Come on.'

'That'll be all right, miss,' said the footman, who was young and not yet trained to frighten guests. 'He's taken it round to the service door. You'll find it in your room all right, miss.'

'Oh, thank you so much,' said Alice, who would willingly have given him ten shillings for the relief. The young footman stood aside for the butler who, waiting with lofty patience at the inner door, had evidently heard the whole conversation. Alice looked round and felt rather than saw that Guy was ashamed of her. Roddy and Sally were taking it as a joke, but Guy evidently felt that she had let him down before the butler at the very outset of their visit. There was no time for explanations. The butler was moving before them in the direction of the drawing-room, and Alice followed with the rest. At the door the butler paused.

'Miss Wicklow and Mr Rodney Wicklow, I think, miss,' he said, 'and Miss Barton and Mr Guy Barton. And shall I take your parcel, miss?'

Alice was too terrified to say anything but yes. The butler took her parcel, which she was immediately convinced she would never see again, and announced the whole party.

In the large yellow drawing-room about twenty people of various ages and sexes were talking, playing games, embroidering, reading, or otherwise occupying themselves. To Alice there appeared to be at least a hundred, all very noble, rich, smart, and scornful, but she was in no state to judge properly. At the butler's announcement a few heads had been turned in the direction of the newcomers, but as no one seemed to know them the conversations had been resumed, and the little party stood marooned. At least there was safety in numbers, and though Alice knew in her bones that it was she who was the chief object of the other guests' scorn and mockery, she could hide behind her brother and her friends. Suddenly Guy, seeing a girl of his acquaintance, daughter of a neighbouring archdeacon, among the very noisy players at a game of puff-ball, went over to her group, where he was immediately welcomed and absorbed. Roddy and Sally had also seen young friends among the party and tried to take Alice with them, but her shyness had by now so completely overpowered her that she could hardly walk. Just then a miracle happened. The very smartest, most exquisitely dressed girl Alice had ever seen, detached herself from the noisiest group of talkers and came strolling towards the new arrivals. She was tall and dark, with perfectly waved hair and scarlet finger nails. She was wearing the kind of frock technically known as 'little', a name which bears no relation to its price, and had the most elegant legs, the thinnest stockings, and the highest heeled shoes imaginable. Removing a long cigarette holder from her mouth she said in a very attractive deep voice, 'You must be Alice. How do you do. I'm Phoebe.'

'Yes, I am, thank you very much,' said Alice, hardly able to believe her ears. Like the ugly duckling she had bowed her head to await a well-deserved death at those carmined hands, and now the glittering stranger was actually being kind.

'And these are the Wicklows, aren't they,' said the girl, waving her cigarette towards Roddy and Sally with a self-possession for a hundredth part of which Alice would have given her soul. 'I expect they know heaps of people. I've been waiting for you. You'd like to see your room, wouldn't you?'

Taking no further notice of the Wicklows, she led Alice across the great hall, up a very wide staircase of terrifying slipperiness. At the top of the stairs was a wide landing from which one could look down into the hall, round which a corridor ran with bedrooms on one side and Gothic windows onto the hall on the other. Alice's guide turned to her right and went down a short passage, at the end of which Alice could see a bright fire burning through the open door.

'Here you are,' said the girl, switching on the light. 'They were putting you in the Pink Room, but I thought you'd like this better. I'm next door, and there's a door through to my room but I'm not sure if it works. You never know here. Either you can't bolt your enemies out, or you can't let your friends in. Oh, that one's all right,' she went on, opening it. 'I remember now. Last time I was here I was in your room, and I couldn't bolt the door when I was having a bath and Micky came poking in from next door, and I threw a sponge at him, and he was dressed for dinner and was only looking round out of curiosity, and the sponge hit him bang in the chest, and it was the last night and he hadn't a clean shirt, so he had to borrow one of Julian's and it was much too big for him. Shall I help you to unpack? Blast them, they've not brought your luggage yet. I'll ring.'

She seated herself on the wide fender, put her finger on

the bell push and kept it there, while Alice, too shy to make any inquiries, stood fiddling with the two pens with clean nibs, the quill, and the newly sharpened pencil that lay in a lacquer tray on the writing-table. A large card headed by an engraving of the Towers caught her eye. She picked it up and found it informed visitors of the hours of meals and posts. Below this were the words:

Visitors are requested not to ring for their servants between the hours of twelve and one, or six and seven.

'Did you see this?' said Alice, showing it to her new friend.

'Like their cheek,' said the girl, glancing at it. 'It's some mouldy idea of old Lord Pomfret's. He was a vegetarian or a philanderer or something and that's how it took him.'

Alice, guessing that philanthropist or humanitarian were probably the words in her new friend's mind, asked if it was out of kindness for servants.

'Exhibitionism,' said the girl, still keeping her finger on the bell. 'So that everyone would know how noble he was. Anyway the servants all lived in the kitchen wing then and never heard the bells, and the bells usually didn't work because they were that old kind like telegraph wires, and they had to go round about a hundred corners and usually broke or got stuck. This one seems to have passed out. I'll have to shout.'

Followed by Alice, who was afraid of losing sight for a moment of such a valiant if peculiar ally, the girl went down yet another passage to the head of a stone back stair where, leaning over the iron railing, she shouted 'Hoy!' several times at the top of her voice. Steps were presently heard, and an underling in a kind of porter's waistcoat with sleeves came up the stairs carrying Alice's suitcases which he put down just inside the room.

'You told me to look out for these, Miss Phoebe,' said the underling, grinning.

'That's right, Finch,' said the girl approvingly. 'Is that all your stuff?'

Alice said it was and thanked the underling, who grinned again and vanished.

'Now we'll unpack,' said Alice's mentor shutting the door. 'Wheeler will do your frocks and things. I'll send her in to you as soon as she comes up, but you'd better do your own little bottles and whatnots because she has a mania for hiding small things. And whatever you do, don't let her get at your belts and scarves, or you'll never see them again.'

'Thank you very much,' said Alice. 'It's most awfully kind of you.'

'Not at all,' said the girl. 'Uncle Giles asked me to. He said you were shy, and I know how ghastly it is when you don't know anyone.'

'Do you mean Lord Pomfret?' asked Alice, hardly able to believe what she heard.

'That's the one. Oh, I suppose you don't know who I am. I'm Phoebe Rivers. My father is a kind of cousin of Lord Pomfret's and my mother is Hermione Rivers that writes books. Father always lives in Herefordshire and won't come up to London or anything, and when you see Mother you won't blame him. I say, do you mind if I use your bath? Otherwise I have to walk about a mile, and it's no fun fighting the men for the bathroom after your first season.'

Seeing that Alice looked puzzled, Miss Rivers pulled aside a large screen in the far corner of the room. Behind it was a gigantic bath raised several steps above the ground. Alice remembered what Roddy had said about some of the rooms having baths in them, and could not be sufficiently grateful to her new friend, who had arranged things so well for her.

'Yes, please do use my bath,' she said. 'I am so glad it's here. I'd rather do without than have to walk a mile and fight people. Would you like it now?'

'Well, I will if you don't mind,' said Miss Rivers, turning the taps on and pulling her frock over her head. 'I hear Wheeler in my room,' she continued in a muffled voice, 'I'll send her in.'

She kicked her shoes before her into the next room and disappeared to talk to Wheeler, who turned out to be not, as Alice had feared, a proud ladies' maid, but a pleasant housemaid, who did the rest of the unpacking swiftly and efficiently.

'And what will you wear tonight, miss?' she asked Alice, as Phoebe came back in a ravishing apricot-coloured Shetland dressing-gown.

'Hi, Wheeler, let's look,' said Phoebe. 'What's she got? Red, white, black. Red's your colour, so we'll have that tomorrow. White tonight, and black on Sunday.'

'Yes, miss,' said Wheeler.

Miss Rivers then plunged into her bath and from behind the screen shouted instructions to Wheeler about her own clothes. In a very short time she was out again and Wheeler began to get the bath ready for Alice.

'It's most awfully kind of you,' said Alice, as Phoebe ran

an expert's eye over the things that Wheeler had laid out.

'That's all right. Fellow-feeling, you know,' said Phoebe, throwing the rest of her clothes into her own room.

'Do you mean—?' Alice began.

'Lord, yes,' said Miss Rivers. 'I'm as frightened as you are.'

'But—' said Alice.

'It's all put on, camouflage, you know,' said Phoebe. 'When you're on the stage you have to put on side a bit, or no one notices you. The servants here are old friends. Mother brings us here every year, whether Cousin Giles likes it or not, so Wheeler and Finch and Peters – that's the butler – know me quite well.'

'Do you really act?' asked Alice.

'Yes, I've appeared in several dirty Sunday night shows,' said Phoebe, whose air of detachment hardly masked a bitterness. 'Anyway it's a way of getting away from Mother. Hurry up and I'll come and give you the once-over.'

She slammed the door and Alice got into her bath, hoping that she hadn't offended her next-door neighbour, but on the whole much happier than she had ever hoped to be. Lord Pomfret had actually remembered her and asked Phoebe Rivers to take care of her. The luggage had not been lost. Miss Rivers had approved her evening dresses and perhaps she would have Roddy, or someone kind, next to her. The white frock and gold shoes would make her feel safe. She had remembered her gold belt and her gold bag and—And then she was struck to stone. She had given her mother's parcel to the butler, and where was it? Her mother had said she was to open it when she was dressing to cheer her up, and the awful thing was she had been so excited and interested by Phoebe's ways that she had forgotten that she needed cheering up. In fact she had forgotten about her mother and a judgment had fallen upon her. She would probably never see the parcel again. How could she ever get it back from the butler? He would be far too busy pouring out champagne and handing cigars for her ever to approach him. It would have been kicked into some corner by now. How could she ever face her mother? These and other miserable thoughts passed through her mind as she swiftly dried herself and began dressing. As soon as she had on what she hoped Miss Rivers would think a suitable amount of clothes, she knocked at the door and went in.

'Oh, Miss Rivers,' she began, 'a most awful thing has happened.'

Phoebe, all in glistening black, looking more elegant than ever, turned round.

'That's very nice,' she said, eyeing Alice's scanty garb, 'but you'd better get a move on. Here, I'll help you.'

She hustled Alice back into her own room and held up her white dress for her to slip into.

'And now, what's the trouble?' she asked, lighting a cigarette. 'And don't say Miss Rivers.'

Alice explained the awful thing. Phoebe appeared to think very lightly of the misfortune. It was no good ringing now, she said, but she'd send someone to find it. Accordingly she went down the passage and banged on the next door but one. Alice, standing fearfully in the background, saw the door open a little way and a man's voice said what was it.

'Look here, Gillie,' said Phoebe Rivers. 'Miss Barton here

has lost a parcel. Peters has got it somewhere. Be an angel and go and find it.'

'I haven't tied my tie,' said a gentle voice.

'I can see that,' said Phoebe. 'Go and get the parcel and bring it back. There's plenty of time for your tie.'

As Phoebe's envoy set out on his mission, Alice shrank back into her room, not wishing him to hate her, and so did not see what he was like. Phoebe returned and gave Alice a final inspection.

'Anyone ever told you what nice teeth you've got?' she asked.

Alice said they hadn't.

'I'll make you up a bit tomorrow,' said Phoebe, whose own eyebrows, cheeks, and lips were as much a work of art as her finger nails. 'You won't look bad at all in that red dress. It's just as well it's got a coat. You look a bit skinny in that white. I wish I had something to give you, but I haven't. I'd give you this fur,' she said, alluding to her own wrap, 'but it's the wrong colour. It would look filthy on your dress. You haven't got a scarf or anything, have you?'

Alice said she hadn't and felt rather dashed again, when a gentle knock was heard at the door and a hand with a parcel came round the corner.

'Here it is,' said the gentle voice of what must be Gillie.

'OK,' said Miss Rivers. 'And now you can do your tie.'

The hand withdrew, and Alice fell upon the parcel. What was in it, but a charming white rabbit-skin cape, lined with very soft apricot velvet.

'That's the spirit,' said Miss Rivers approvingly. 'Put it on. Now you look twice the man. Your mother knows what's what. No rat's tails dipped in ink to make it look like ermine. Now, my girl, you listen to me. No one's going to look at you: but if they do they won't think about you, because you look just right. Come on.'

Full of humble gratitude, Alice followed her benefactress downstairs to a smaller drawing-room, decorated with green brocade and hung with pictures bought by the sixth earl from contemporary artists. The furniture was in the highest style of Pre-Raphaelite discomfort: sofas apparently hewn from solid blocks of wood and armchairs suited to no known human frame, both with thin velvet cushions of extreme hardness. All was of the very best workmanship, and it was so obvious that the brocade on the walls, the velvet on the chairs, and the heavy olive green curtains that hid the windows would never wear out, that Lord Pomfret had long ago given up any idea of altering them. It was a room that Lady Pomfret particularly disliked, but as she had never had the energy to say this aloud, no one knew it.

Phoebe introduced Alice to four or five young men and women, and then left her, evidently considering that she had done enough for the time being. The young people looked incuriously at her, and went on with their own conversation, which was, Alice thought, very dashing but rather dull, being chiefly about the chances for Monday. What kind of chances they were, she didn't know, so she tried to look interested and intelligent, succeeding so well that Guy, who had repented his unkindness, and meant to be specially nice to his sister, had a relapse, and talked very loudly with the archdeacon's daughter, so that no one should suspect him of having a sister who wasn't being a success.

'Heard the latest?' said one of the men. 'They're deepening the drain at Pomfret Madrigal. That means the Monday country will go to hell.'

'They'll flood Starveacres, just as they did in '23,' said a slightly older man with a brick red face. 'Drowned half the vixens in the country.'

The rest of the group shook their heads and said according to their various sexes and mental capacities that it was a damned shame, or too sickening, or a bit over the odds. Gloomy silence then fell on everyone.

'Didn't they change the sluice at Starveacres Hatches last year?' said Alice.

Though her voice was not loud, and she stammered slightly at finding herself talking alone, her announcement could not have caused a greater sensation. The man with the brick red face said, 'Gad! you're right, Miss Er,' thus proving to Alice's intense interest that people said Gad in real life, while the rest of the chorus said Of course they had heard it, or How stupid of them, or Gosh, fancy my forgetting that, or Damn good thing too. The waves of their conversation then flowed over Alice again, but she felt that she was one of them, even though she still didn't know what the chances for Monday were, or could possibly be.

'How did you know that?' said a voice at her elbow, and turning she saw Roddy.

'You told Lord Pomfret the other day when he came to tea,' said Alice.

'So I did,' said Roddy, 'but I didn't think you noticed things like that.'

He smiled at her, not displeased that his words about

Starveacres Hatches should have made such an impression.

'Well, you see,' said Alice, 'I was so terrified that Lord Pomfret was going to say something about my coming for the weekend that I noticed *everything*. Do you think I'll be next to you at dinner, Roddy?'

But at this moment Lord Pomfret came up, glared, shook hands, and without a word took her away, steering her uncomfortably by the upper part of her arm, while Roddy was left to the chastening reflection that Alice's interest in Starveacres Hatches had been caused more by fear of Lord Pomfret than regard for himself.

'Enjoying yourself, eh?' said Lord Pomfret, continuing to push Alice through his guests. 'Never mind. I want my wife to meet you. Hope she's enjoying all this fuss. I'm not.'

Alice realised with a shock that she had quite forgotten her hostess's existence and looked anxiously about for her. A tall woman, with fine eyes and a discontented, eager expression, stopped them. 'Oh, there you are,' she said to Lord Pomfret, taking no notice of Alice. 'I want to speak to you.'

Alice felt sorry that Lady Pomfret was like this and thought she would have been rather older and perhaps kinder looking, but to her relief Lord Pomfret continued to urge his way through his guests, saying to the tall woman, 'All right, all right, another time.' Alice had an uncomfortable impression that the tall woman was looking with hatred at her back, but her rabbit cape protected her. At last Lord Pomfret got to the far end of the room and stopped before what was so obviously Lady Pomfret that no one could have thought she was anything else. She was wearing jewels and must once have been very lovely, though it was now a sad, declining beauty. A pleasant-faced woman was standing beside her, listening to what she said. Lord Pomfret waited till his wife had finished speaking and then introduced Alice to her.

'She doesn't quite know what to make of all this,' said his lordship. 'It's her first party, Edith, so I want her to have a friend.'

Lady Pomfret smiled very kindly at Alice and gave her a thin hand covered with rings, saying that she had known her mother very well in Florence.

'Dinner will be ready soon, I suppose,' said Lord Pomfret. 'Are we waiting for anyone?'

'Only for Mr Johns,' said the pleasant-faced woman.

'Hermione again,' said his lordship angrily. 'Why does she want to have that fellow down here? She's after me about something or other, tried to buttonhole me just now.'

'Mrs Rivers wanted to sit next to Mr Johns,' said the pleasant-faced woman, 'but Lady Pomfret had made a different arrangement and I'm afraid we can't alter all the name cards now.'

'Of course not,' said Lord Pomfret. 'Have your own guests where you want them, Edith. There's Peters at last.'

The butler came up and announced dinner and Lady Pomfret rose, saying that they would go in as they were as it was an informal party. She then drifted off with some older women. Alice moved nervously after them, feeling that as the most insignificant and perhaps the youngest person there, she ought to go in after all the older women, yet terrified at the idea of getting mixed up with the men.

The handsome, discontented woman whom she had by now discovered to be Mrs Rivers, and therefore Phoebe's mother, was also lingering behind, and Alice almost knocking into her apologised humbly and was told it didn't matter in a way that annihilated her. Just then she was rescued by the pleasant-faced woman who took her arm and led her in the wake of the other women towards the dining-room.

'You are Miss Barton, aren't you?' said the pleasant-faced woman. 'My name is Merriman; but everyone calls me Merry. I'm Lady Pomfret's secretary. I hope you are comfortable in your room. Let me know if you aren't.'

'Oh yes,' said Alice. 'Miss Rivers – Phoebe – was very kind to me.'

'Let's see,' said Miss Merriman, looking at a card she was holding, 'you are between Mr Rivers and Mr Foster. Mr Rivers is an artist; you know his mother and his sister. Mr Foster is very nice. He is—'

But now they were all in the dining-room, and what with the guests all talking and the sight of a long table stretching away to infinity, covered with what looked to Alice like six thousand shining knives and forks and spoons, and more carnations in more silver vases than she had ever seen in her life, she was unable to concentrate on what Miss Merriman had said. A man smiled at her which made her jib, but it turned out to be Mr Hoare, the agent, whom she really knew quite well; Peters approached her saying, 'At the far end on the left, miss.' Phoebe gave her a kindly shove, and somehow she found herself sitting in her place with a card in front of her which bore her own name. She realised that a man was sitting on each side of her and then became unconscious, alternately hoping and fearing that she would wake up at Mellings.

She was brought to again by soup being placed in front of her in a silver plate. She had often heard and read of such things, but here it was, actually happening. She, Alice Barton, was sitting in Pomfret Towers, wearing a white rabbit cape, among hundreds of people who were evidently very interesting and important, about to eat soup from a silver plate. She looked for Guy and Roddy and Sally, thought she saw them far away, and decided that from this moment, deserted as she was by her brother and her friends, she must make a new life of her own. Accordingly she looked cautiously to her left. Her neighbour on this side was a very tall young man; if his legs were as tall as the rest of him he must be very tall indeed, though of course sometimes when people stood up it made them quite short again. All she could see of his face was a hawk-like profile and a mop of untidy, wavy black hair. By craning her neck she was able to see the name Mr Rivers on the card. This was then the son of the terrifying Mrs Rivers, the young man who was an artist, of whom Roddy had spoken in slighting terms as a stuck-up bloke. Alice's whole being revolted against stuck-up blokes. On the other hand, this Mr Rivers was an artist, and Alice, struggling alone with her paints, had an admiration approaching awe for anyone who was a real artist and had exhibitions, and was disposed to make large allowances for genius. But if Mr Rivers were going to look straight in front of him and say nothing, she would never know what he was really like.

'Excuse me,' said a voice on her right, very diffidently, 'I think you dropped this,' and a hand pushed her gold bag at her.

'Oh, thank you so much,' said Alice, taking the bag nervously. 'It must have fallen off my lap.'

'Yes, it must,' agreed her neighbour, a fair, rather delicate-looking young man, who as he was not Mr Rivers must be the unknown Mr Foster. 'They will starch the table napkins, and then everything falls off.'

'Mother is always trying to make them put less starch in,' said Alice, feeling on safe ground, but Mr Foster seemed to have nothing more to say, so Alice, feeling that he was nearly as shy as she was, made an effort and asked him where he lived. He said he had a flat in London, but had lived abroad a good deal. Alice said her mother had lived abroad too, but that was a long time ago. Perhaps, said Mr Foster, that was before he went abroad. Alice said she thought perhaps it was, and they both drank some water and crumbled some bread. This slight refection revived them to that extent that they both began to speak at once, both said they were sorry, and both forgot what they were going to say. By the time Alice had recovered her wits she was being handed vegetables, and when this was over Mr Foster had been claimed by the guest on his other side, so she was again reduced to looking at Mr Rivers's profile and wondering what she could say to him. Mr Rivers himself shortly saved her any further trouble by turning towards her and remarking that his sister had told him to look out for her.

'You are Miss Barton, aren't you?' he asked, looking intently at her.

On hearing these remarkable words Alice at once fell in

love. It had never happened to her before except with people like Charles I, or Sydney Carton, but she knew at once that it was the real thing. As Julian Rivers turned his face towards her, gazing with deep-set dark blue eyes into her very soul, his delicate mouth twitching, only that was not quite the right word, with sensitiveness, his black locks flung recklessly and very untidily above his marble brow, a romantically dark shade on his cheeks, upper lip and chin, because he had told his mother before dinner that he was hanged if he would shave twice a day to please anyone, as those staggering phenomena met her eyes, Alice felt that the culminating point of her whole visit had been reached in one blinding, searing moment. In that flash of ecstasy she suddenly knew what all poetry, all music, all sculpture, except things like winged Assyrian bulls, or the very broken pieces in the British Museum, meant.

'Your sister was very kind to me,' she said.

'Oh, she's all right,' said Julian Rivers, adding, 'I could make a picture of you, you know. I was looking at you in the drawing-room before dinner. Your face is all out of drawing, and I like that purple tint under your jawbone, and there's a splendid green bit under your eyes. God! how I could put in your nose with my thumb. I must do it.'

He sketched a face in the air while he spoke, fingers lightly crooked, an expressive thumb modelling imaginary planes. From this Alice was able to deduce that his remark about her nose was not so much a personal threat as an artist's manner of speech. She felt tremendously flattered by his kind words, and began to wonder what she really looked like. Guy sometimes called her walnut-face, and Sally had once told her as a compliment that she looked like a liver cocker spaniel to whom Sally was at the time much attached. Phoebe had just told her that she had nice teeth, but no one had ever told her that her face was green and purple and out of drawing, and she knew she had never been really understood before.

'Do you mean paint me?' she asked.

'Paint!' said Julian contemptuously. 'I want to use you as the means of expression for an idea. "Green Hell" I might call it. I'd put your eyes on quite a different plane, to help the idea, and get some rose madder into the eyelids. We'll get on well together.'

'Would it take long?' asked Alice, pleased at the thought of inspiring an artist, but wondering what her mother would say.

'You can't tell,' said Julian, suddenly becoming sombre in a very marked way. 'It might all come in half an hour, or it might take weeks, months, years. Did you ever know Bolikoff?'

Alice said she didn't.

'Practically no one does,' said Julian. 'He lives in Camden Town and never goes out. His art is entirely subjective. He had a model called Billy.'

Here he paused, partly for effect, partly to catch up with his food before someone took his plate away.

'Was he a good model?' Alice asked, fascinated by this story of Bohemia.

'It wasn't a he. Billie, I said. I believe she was wonderful. She did everything for Bolikoff, cooked, mended, went out as a model to earn money for him.'

'But how did she have time to sit for him?' said Alice.

'She didn't,' said Julian. 'She hadn't time. But he spent years over a picture that was to represent her emotional effect upon him. Years.'

'Was it good?' asked Alice.

'Oh, good!' said Julian, rather impatiently. 'Good and bad have nothing to do with it. It was a pure abstraction. He put a sewing machine in one of her eyes and a kidney in the other. Of course her eyes weren't in her face, you understand, because he hardly ever looked at her and wasn't sure what her eyes were like; in fact he didn't want to know; he could get nearer the truth by intuition than by actual physical vision.'

'Then what was her face like if her eyes weren't in it?' said Alice.

'There wasn't any face. I told you, it was only a representation of the emotional effect she had on him. But he painted a broken egg with a hand coming out of it. The hand had only three fingers, and the thumb was full of worms,' said Julian in a voice of devout worship.

'Did Billie mind?' asked Alice, feeling that a portrait of herself on those lines would hardly give her acute pleasure.

'She was dead, long before he had finished,' said Julian. 'It was just as well. She interfered with his mental concept of her. But it all shows you how impossible it is to say how long any picture will take. When shall we begin?'

'Well, I'm only here till Monday,' said Alice.

'One couldn't do anything here,' said Julian. 'The whole feeling is wrong, and Mother would want to interfere. You don't know what that means. Just because she has written some novels she thinks she can understand me. Understand!' and Julian laughed mirthlessly.

Alice said she knew Mrs Rivers's books were very good, but she hadn't read any of them.

'I read her first novel,' said Julian. 'One had to. It's about a middle-aged woman who goes on a cruise to Norway and has a terrific comeback with a young professor. Wish fulfilment, of course. And there was a lot about fiords and salmon fishing. Where she gets her ideas from I can't think. I couldn't read any of the others. And she writes funny things about her friends and gets their backs up. You don't know what it is to have a literary mother. Literary!'

'But I do,' said Alice, roused in defence of her mother. 'My mother writes books. But she never interferes at all. She and Daddy let me have a studio of my own, and they are very sweet about always waiting to be asked before they come up.'

'Oh, have you a studio?' said Julian. 'Then I'll come and start work next week. Say on Tuesday.'

Alice hardly knew whether to be relieved or hurt that he took not the faintest interest in the fact that she painted. She said it would be very nice, but she must ask her mother if it would be all right. Her attention was then distracted by the difficulty of cutting some grapes from the bunch that was being handed to her. The gold grape scissors twisted and mangled the stalk, but cut they would not. Alice, too shy to give up the task she had begun, uneasily conscious that she was holding up the traffic of the table, was almost in tears, when Mr Foster's gentle voice said to the footman:

'Bring the grapes to me, please. I'll cut them.'

The footman withdrew the dish from the thankful Miss Barton and handed it to Mr Foster who pulled a little cluster from the bunch and told the footman to hand it again.

'Thank you very much,' said Alice, when the grapes were safely on her plate. 'Those scissors are so very lovely, but they don't cut at all.'

'I was so sorry for you,' said Mr Foster. 'Those gold scissors never cut, and I saw Julian couldn't help you. The footman was between you and he couldn't see what was happening. I hope I didn't interrupt your talk.'

'Oh, no,' said Alice. 'Do you know Mr Rivers much?'

'Fairly well,' said Mr Foster. 'His father's a kind of relation of mine. He has a place in Herefordshire and never goes anywhere. I suppose you've read Julian's mother's books.'

Alice said she hadn't and were they nice?

'Quite nice I should think,' said Mr Foster, 'but I've only read one. It was about a woman who had a husband and family but she thought they didn't understand her, so she went with a travelling party to Northern Africa and had a very motherly affair with a young Moor who had a French mother. Of course it all came right in the end, and there was some very highbrow stuff about Roman ruins. I think she rather fancied herself as the heroine.'

'Miss Rivers is very nice too, isn't she?' said Alice.

'Yes, Phoebe is a splendid girl, but a bit of a bully,' said Mr Foster. 'She came banging at my door before I had finished dressing just now, and made me go and find a parcel that one of the guests had lost. Of course I didn't mind doing it a bit,' he added hastily, 'because I know how awful it is when you lose anything in a strange house, but she wouldn't even let me wait to get my tie straight.'

As he finished speaking the ladies were already leaving the room, so Alice had no time to thank him for his chivalrous rescue of her rabbit cape. She had been sympathetically attracted by his diffident manner when he first spoke to her, and now she was full of admiration for his courage in speaking to a footman and his kindness in fetching a parcel for a stranger. Although Julian Rivers was undoubtedly her ideal man, she felt she would very much like to make friends with Mr Foster.

3

Amusing the Guests

When the ladies had reached the yellow drawing-room, Alice was joined by Sally Wicklow, full of the delightful time she had had at dinner. She had, it appeared, been seated between an M.F.H. in whose country she had once hunted and a man in the diplomatic. The M.F.H. had been so struck by her account of how she had helped a young mare who had been frightened by a motor-lorry to recover her nerve that he had offered to mount her whenever she liked, an offer that Sally, who had only one horse, had at once accepted, naming the day when she would first like to go out. Flushed with this success she had turned to her neighbour, who said he had heard her talking about horses, and did she know anything about dogs. He had, he said, brought back from the Near East a couple of rare dogs called Bazoukis. They were specially trained for running down partridges and were always rewarded by being allowed to eat a couple of birds alive. Owing to this injudicious method of life they refused all food except live chickens. This was possible in Sussex, where his mother lived, but almost impracticable in his flat in Jermyn Street, as his man drew the line at clearing up the claws and feathers. Sally by great good luck had met a Bazouki at the home of one of her dog-breeding friends and was able to suggest to her neighbour a change in diet that her friend had found helpful. The owner of the dogs had then promised to let her have a puppy if her advice was successful, and they arranged to visit Lord Pomfret's kennels together on the following morning, while the others were shooting.

'Are you going out with the guns?' said Sally to Alice.

'I don't know,' said Alice. 'I can't shoot.'

'Of course you can't,' said Sally. 'I mean are you going to join them at lunch? I wouldn't if I were you. Women are a nuisance at that sort of thing. I say! I've got a word to say to Guy. That brother of yours doesn't run straight. He ought to have stuck to you before dinner and seen that you were all right.'

Alice attempted to defend Guy, saying she had been perfectly happy because Miss Rivers was so kind to her, but Sally, zealous in her timid friend's cause, would hear of no such weakness, calling upon Phoebe, who was near by, to support her.

'Brothers aren't much good,' said Phoebe. 'Julian wouldn't do a thing for me, I know. Who's going out with the guns tomorrow?'

'I'm not,' said Sally, 'and Alice had better not. She gets knocked up at once. I say, Miss Rivers, is it your mother that writes those topping books?'

'I suppose so,' said Phoebe. 'There can't be two like her, thank goodness.'

'Well, I read one,' said Sally, 'and I thought it was splendid. That one about the woman whose husband is in love with his typist, at least he isn't really, but it looks like it, and so she goes off to Danzig and goes off the deep end a bit with a man in the diplomatic, but nothing really happens, only when her husband comes to fetch her he thinks she's looking so jolly young and well, all because of the kick she got out of the man that she nearly went off the deep end about, that he has a kind of reconciliation, and there's a lot of awfully interesting stuff about the history of Danzig and the Polish corridor and the old houses and that sort of stuff, absolutely as good as a guide book only better.'

'Yes, that's Mother's,' said Phoebe. 'Everyone thinks it's herself she's writing about and she thinks so too. She writes bright little articles about country life too, and everyone in Herefordshire thinks it's themselves and takes offence. It's hard on Father.'

Miss Merriman now came over with a message from Lady Pomfret that she would like to talk to Miss Barton and Miss Wicklow. Lady Pomfret, who was sitting near the fire on a sofa, very kindly made Sally sit beside her and offered Alice a low chair. Two or three King Charles spaniels, curled up near their mistress or in the folds of her gown, growled lazily and Alice shrank back.

'You are so like your mother,' said Lady Pomfret to Alice, smiling at her alarm. 'She could never love dogs. She was a great comfort to me in Florence, many years ago, before she married your father. I have read all her books with great interest. Will you tell her that, and say how much I hope she will let me come and see her before I go abroad again?'

Alice, overawed by Lady Pomfret's sad broken beauty and her almost regal way of sending for guests that she wanted to talk to, said something inarticulate. Sally, who never talked unless there was something definite, and preferably four-legged, to talk about, sat pleasantly silent, thinking of the M.F.H.'s offer. Lady Pomfret fell into a dream of her youth and her only son. She had shirked life and duties after his death and knew it. She also knew, not being a self deceiver, that it was too late for her to make any fresh resolutions, that she would never take up the burden that her husband had uncomplainingly – at any rate so far as she was concerned – borne for so many years alone. If she could have died and left him free to marry again and perhaps have heirs for his title and wealth, she would have shrugged her thin elegant shoulders and gone, but death does not come so easily. One of the many reasons for her life abroad had been an unacknowledged distaste for meeting her husband's heir, the middle-aged cousin who had taken her child's place. To please her husband she had consented to spend a few weeks at home and receive not the heir, who always wintered in South Africa, but his son, whom she liked. But she thought of her own son all the more. Abstractedly she gazed at the pearls and jewels she was wearing and wondered who would have them when she was dead. The future earl was a widower, so the jewels would adorn whatever bride this young man might choose. Lady Pomfret had few friends among the young, and looking round the room at so many charming, well-dressed, indistinguishable girls, she saw no future countess. The long silence, which Alice was too shy to break and Sally saw no reason for breaking, was interrupted by Mrs Rivers, who had been talking with friends and now came eagerly towards the sofa.

'What shall we do this evening, Cousin Edith?' she asked. 'We must keep the people amused.'

Lady Pomfret, to whom the idea of amusing her guests was quite foreign, merely looked a question. When she had been a hostess people had talked, or played cards, but certainly had not needed amusing.

'We can't have them all hanging about talking,' said Mrs Rivers. 'There will be a couple of bridge tables I expect and the rest had better play games. I thought we had better organise it before the men come in.'

'I wonder,' said Lady Pomfret, who noticed that Mrs Rivers had behaved as if the two girls were pieces of valueless furniture. 'I wonder, Hermione, what these young people would like.'

'Poker's my best game,' said Sally, 'but I'm pretty good at six-pack bezique.'

'I used to play bezique with my father,' said Lady Pomfret, 'but only with two packs. You must show me your game, Miss Wicklow.'

'That is hardly what I meant,' said Mrs Rivers. 'Something like charades, or clumps, or that game where two people go out and the people inside have to choose something for each of them to say but neither of them knows the other has to say it. It's most amusing if it is properly played. You'd love it, Cousin Edith.'

'I want to have a little talk with Professor Milward,' said

Lady Pomfret, 'and then I expect I shall go to bed. But you young people must do just as you like.'

Mrs Rivers was doubly annoyed, first that the two girls had been consulted and secondly that Cousin Edith had included them all three in the phrase young people. She was convinced that she didn't look her age, but a woman who wrote highly successful novels and brilliantly witty articles was not a young person. Young persons did write novels, but theirs were not like hers. Her heroines always drew back in time, besides being extremely distinguished and a complete walking Baedeker of every country they visited. She was just about to swallow her annoyance in the most disagreeable way she could think of when the men came loudly into the room. Lord Pomfret, who was among the first, walked straight up to his wife and asked how she felt.

'Very well, thank you, Giles,' said her ladyship. 'I have had a pleasant talk with Miss Barton, who must allow me to call her Alice, and Miss Wicklow. Hermione wants to organise some games. I shall go to bed early.'

'Games?' said Lord Pomfret. 'Two tables are enough.'

'Everyone doesn't play contract,' said Mrs Rivers. 'I thought clumps, or that game where you choose a word and each player chooses a person whose name begins with one letter of the word. For instance if we chose Pomfret, I should be—'

She paused for a moment, unable to think of any character beginning with a P.

'Punch,' said Lord Pomfret, with what in a commoner would have been a guffaw. 'Edith, Mr Johns would like to have a little talk with you. Here, Johns, let me introduce you to my wife.' He then added in a loud aside, 'Hermione's publisher fellow, my dear, but you'll find him quite agreeable.'

Sally and Alice were now standing up waiting for orders, and Lady Pomfret graciously made room for Mr Johns on the sofa beside her.

'I shall want you soon, Mr Johns,' said Mrs Rivers. 'We are going to play games. I thought of that game where you choose a well-known character and each person has to say the flower or the scent or the book that reminds them of them. I remember playing it in Rio once, in Spanish. It is most amusing.'

Mr Johns, who had no intention of playing any games at all, made a courteous noncommittal reply, for Mrs Rivers was one of his best sellers, and fell into a conversation about Italy with his hostess, who became almost animated.

'Well, now we'll organise something,' said Mrs Rivers. 'Suppose we get up the spelling game at this table. The box of letters ought to be in the drawer. No, it isn't. Now, where on earth can it have gone? It was here yesterday. Gillie,' she called to Mr Foster, who had drifted towards the fire, 'will you ring? I must ask Peters where the letters are. Thanks so much. We are getting up the spelling game. You'll play on my side, won't you?'

Alice saw the horror in Mr Foster's face and sympathised deeply. She would willingly have rescued him, but was so paralysed at the thought that she and Sally would be forced into some terrifying game by Mrs Rivers that she had turned to stone, vaguely hoping that if she didn't move no one would notice her. But Sally, whose instinct for self-preservation was very strong, had no such inhibitions and asked Mr Foster in a cheerful way if he played bezique. Mr Foster asked if it was six-pack, and on hearing that it was, at once brought a small card-table from a corner, put it in a safe place behind the sofa where Lady Pomfret and Mr Johns were talking, produced the cards from a drawer in a writing-table, placed two chairs at the table, and invited Sally to sit down.

'That was a good piece of work,' said Sally admiringly, as Mr Foster shuffled the cards.

'You gave me the chance,' said Mr Foster. 'You really saved my life. I am terrified of Hermione.'

'A bit of a monster, isn't she?' said Sally, looking unlovingly at Mrs Rivers, who was now talking feverishly to Peters.

'But the letters were in the drawer last night,' she said. 'I put them there myself.'

'Yes madam,' said Peters, who although he disliked and despised Mrs Rivers was not going to let the wife of the Honourable George down in public. 'Doubtless they have been removed.'

'Well, it's most annoying,' said Mrs Rivers. 'Oh, Merry, do you know where the letters have gone? They were in the drawer last night.'

Before Miss Merriman could answer, one of the well-dressed indistinguishable girls screamed, and said she was frightfully sorry, but she and Peter and Micky had taken them for a paper chase in the old wing of the house and forgotten to pick them up. Peters asked Mrs Rivers if anything else was required, gravely received her order to send over to Nutfield for a new box next day and retired with the firm determination to do nothing of the sort. One thing was, he said to the housekeeper, that anyone could see with half an eye that young Mr Foster didn't like Mrs Rivers no more than his lordship did.

Young Mr Foster, warmed by Sally's genial, slapdash manner, was losing a good deal of his shyness. In apology for not being able to talk about hunting or shooting he explained that he had been a stupid delicate kind of boy and had had to live abroad a great deal. On being pressed by Sally as to what he did for a crust, he said even more apologetically that he worked with a firm of picture dealers.

'Good Lord! Then I suppose you know all about the Old Masters and things,' said Sally, waving her hand at the Mid-Victorian paintings with which Lord Pomfret's father had completed the furnishing of the yellow drawing-room.

Mr Foster said he did.

'I think they're ghastly myself,' said Sally. 'I'll tell you what I like; those rum old birds in the dining-room. That's your game.'

'Yes, the ones in the dining-room are pretty good,' said Mr Foster. 'I only hope we'll never have to sell them. Uncle Giles has never sold a family picture yet. I wish he would sell the stuff in this room, but it wouldn't fetch a penny.'

'Look here,' said Sally, laying down the cards she was shuffling, 'what's your name? I mean what are you called?'

'My name is Giles,' said Mr Foster, 'but I'm called Gillie.'

'And Lord Pomfret is your uncle,' said Sally, struggling with an idea.

'Yes, and I suppose I come in for all this some day,' said

Mr Foster mournfully. 'You've no idea how awful it is, knowing nothing about country life. I know Father would never come here. He'll leave all the work to Mr Hoare and your brother – Mr Wicklow is your brother, isn't he? But I do want so much to do the right thing.'

'Well, you listen to me,' said Sally. 'The very first thing you must do, when you can do anything, is to stop up those earths in Hamaker's Spinney. If I've told Mr Hoare that once, I've told him a hundred times, but he had some kind of row with the hunt secretary and he won't do it.'

Forgetting the game, Sally put her elbows on the table and expounded to Mr Foster what she would do on the estate if she had a free hand, while Mr Foster listened with the deepest interest and admiration. When she had reorganised the hunt, the beagles, the otter hounds, the shooting, and most of the farms on the estate, she paused to see what effect her words had made.

'Thanks most awfully,' said Mr Foster. 'Do you think you could sometimes spare time to go round with me a bit and show me things? Uncle Giles wants me to be here a good deal, and my firm will make it easy. I like Hoare very much, but he gets impatient with me.'

Sally said of course she would.

'That's really very kind indeed,' said Mr Foster. 'I find the people here a little alarming. Except Miss Barton, who was next to me at dinner. She was very nice.'

Sally, delighted that Alice had made a conquest, poured out praise of her friend and said she was sure Mr Foster and Alice would be great friends because they had both been delicate and weren't really up to the mark. Mr Foster accepted this pronouncement in the spirit in which it was made, and said he hoped Miss Wicklow would call him Gillie, as it would make him feel more at home. Miss Wicklow said what rot, of course she would, and everyone called her Sally.

Lord Pomfret, having seen his wife provided with entertainment in the shape of Mr Johns, with Professor Milward near by reading a book waiting his turn, laid hands on the three best bridge players in the room and took them off to the library to play in peace. This left the field clear for Mrs Rivers, who bullied some of the guests into playing Corinthian bagatelle, others into a mild gambling game, and about a dozen, including Alice, into one of those games which, she said, are so amusing when well played, which consist chiefly in two players going out and getting lost while the rest wrangle about what they are to do. Guy and the archdeacon's daughter had meant, with a few bosom friends, to play puff billiards, but the charming girl who screamed had taken two of the puffers to squirt water at Peter and Micky over the partition between the two bathrooms, and no one knew where they had been left, so Mrs Rivers had caught them all for her game. Guy took the opportunity of asking his sister if she was having fun, to which Alice, knowing that to say how terrified she was of being asked to take any active part in the game, especially if it was going out of the room and guessing something, would only annoy Guy, replied that she was, so that her brother felt no more responsibility.

'What a noise,' said Lady Pomfret to Mr Johns. 'Hermione Rivers cannot be happy unless she is moving people about. You publish her books, I believe, Mr Johns. They do quite well, I hear.'

Even Mr Johns, the very successful and enterprising senior partner in the well-known publishing firm of Johns & Fairfield, whose advertisements in the Sunday papers were in such gigantic type that most readers never saw them at all, was subdued by Lady Pomfret's perfect want of interest in such a burning fact as sales. That Mrs Rivers's books did quite well was an under-statement that he could never explain to his hostess. Something told him that the mention of so many thousand copies, or so many hundred pounds, would make no impression on her at all.

'I once looked at one,' Lady Pomfret continued, 'about people in Rome. A woman with a grown-up son who lets herself have a kind of affair with a young American writer. When the characters spoke Italian it was not very correct. Of course the heroine was meant to be herself, but that was so foolish. Everyone knows that although she has made her husband's – Lord Pomfret's cousin you know – life a perfect burden by her airs, she is a most faithful wife. In fact I don't think any man has ever looked at her, so she has hardly had much chance.'

These remarks were balm to Mr Johns, who often said to Mr Fairfield that the Baedeker Bitch, for so he discourteously called his most successful novelist behind her back, in allusion to the amount of local colour that she piled into each of her books, was so grasping and conceited that the large sums of money that they made by her books were indeed hardly earned. But he was too cautious to give more than a qualified assent to Lady Pomfret's statement.

'After all, Lady Pomfret,' he replied, 'an author's chief aim is probably to make money. Mrs Rivers has gauged, in a most remarkable way I may say, the mental needs of the library subscribers. The enormous bulk of our reading public are women of forty and over. To each of these Mrs Rivers gives the pleasing assurance that, given the same chances, she could have a love affair with an attractive and cultivated man of her own age or younger. Again, travel is now so cheap and easy that most of these women have been abroad at some time. In her books they find the places that they have visited, they can recognise the towns they have seen, the scenery in which they have, in their own words, rambled. It gives them a feeling of cosmopolitanism. And when you add to this the delightful self-deception that each of them has a charming young admirer waiting for her, you must agree that Mrs Rivers brings happiness to many drab lives.'

'I must say I never thought of Hermione as a public benefactor,' said Lady Pomfret. 'And I believe she writes for magazines too. It is all very peculiar and slightly unpleasant. Do you know Mrs Barton's books?'

'We have had the pleasure of publishing them all,' said Mr Johns, again hopelessly overawed by Lady Pomfret's thorough want of interest in his profession, 'but I do not know her personally.'

'She is quite different,' said Lady Pomfret. 'You must meet her. Her daughter, by the way, is staying here. Her books are always accurate and she never talks about them. I have enjoyed our talk so much, Mr Johns. Now you will forgive me if I have a little time with Professor Milward.'

Mr Johns accepted his congé and avoiding Mrs Rivers's eye made his way to the gambling game where he made more noise than anybody and won seven and sixpence. Lady Pomfret had her talk with Professor Milward, who to your surprise was not an old man with a beard, but an agreeable young historian who had come with an introduction from an old friend of her son's, and wanted to browse among the Pomfret papers in the library. Shortly after this she left the drawing-room with Miss Merriman in attendance, on her way to her room. In the hall she passed Phoebe Rivers and Guy Barton, dancing to a portable gramophone, and asked if they were enjoying themselves.

'Thanks awfully, Cousin Edith,' said Phoebe, 'we are having a lovely time. Mother sent us out to guess something or other, and we have been here for half an hour while they make up their minds what it is they want us to guess. With any luck they'll keep us out here till bed-time.'

Lady Pomfret smiled vaguely, said good night and went on her way. The gramophone wailed down a chromatic scale and stopped.

'Here, hang on a moment,' said Phoebe to Guy, who was winding it up again. 'I've something to say to you. Is your little sister enjoying herself?'

'Of course she is,' said Guy. 'Why I asked her before we began that rotten game of your mother's if she was having a good time, and she said yes.'

'Of course she did,' said Phoebe. 'She's a nice child and wants to save other people trouble. You might look after her a bit, though. Just see if she looks lonely. She's scared stiff unless people are nice to her.'

'Good Lord! One doesn't have to be a nurse to one's sister,' said Guy indignantly.

'All right,' said Phoebe. 'We'll be dancing tomorrow night, I expect, and you must see that some of the men ask Alice. If you don't, I will. Stick the record on again.'

Guy rather sulkily started the gramophone and swung out into the hall with Phoebe. He thought it pretty good cheek for a girl who hardly knew him to lecture him about Alice. If Alice weren't such a silly little ass it would be all right, but dash it all, fellows didn't want to dance with a girl who looked scared. He would dearly have liked to tell Phoebe what he felt about her interference, but he was secretly a little in awe of her. Really she was just like any other girl, but somehow she got away with it; it was probably being an actress.

As they danced past the drawing-room door Mr Foster and Sally came out.

'Hullo!' said Mr Foster. 'Your mother unfortunately caught us between two games, Phoebe, and has sent us out with a message for you. You each have to pretend to be some historical person and then go in and talk and they are to guess who you are.'

'Good God!' said Phoebe. 'Oh, look here, Gillie, I don't think you and my partner have met. This is Guy Barton, Alice's brother, and this one,' she said, speaking to Guy, 'is Gillie Foster, my sort of cousin.'

The young men shook hands, Guy a little hurt at being made known as Alice's brother.

'Mother would like me to marry him and be the future Lady Pomfret,' said Phoebe, 'but that's where her toes turn in, isn't it, Gillie?'

'I do like Phoebe immensely,' said Mr Foster, appealing in his diffident way to everyone, 'but she doesn't feel like it.'

'Besides,' said Phoebe, with the bitterness which the mention of the stage always brought into her voice, 'there's my profession. But I don't mind dancing with you. Come on.'

Guy and Sally joined them, to the strains of the gramophone, and pleasure was taken seriously till Sally exclaimed, 'Oh Lord! what about the historical characters?'

All four young people stopped dead and became speechless. After a decent interval they all spoke at once, making various suggestions which were in their turn countered, again everyone speaking at once, by such objections as No one knows if he ever existed, How can you talk like a person when you don't know anything about her, The archdeacon would have fits if you did Hitler, Do you remember the time we did Canova and no one had heard of him except the man that thought we meant Casanova? At last they all laughed so much that they could do nothing but point helplessly at each other. As some fifteen minutes had passed in this intellectual exercise, and Guy and Phoebe had already been waiting for half an hour in the hall before the messengers came out, there now seemed to be a fair prospect of shelving the game indefinitely.

'I say,' said Sally, powdering her face, 'let's choose someone Alice can guess. It'll be fun for her.'

This kind thought led to a further discussion as to what characters Alice was likely to know. Guy said why bother about that. Sally, at once up in arms, said he hadn't been a bit kind to Alice that evening, and what about it. As she and Guy were on the footing of brother and sister a very acrimonious conversation followed, and Guy was getting sulkier and Sally more heated, when the drawing-room door was opened and Mrs Rivers looked out. In a carefully veiled voice of exacerbation she said she did hope they would *soon* make up their minds, as Peters was just coming in with the drinks and that always broke the party up.

'Sorry, Mrs Rivers,' said Sally. 'It was Gillie's and my fault really, because we made Guy and Phoebe laugh. We'd really settled it, only we hadn't quite decided what they were to say.'

Mrs Rivers withdrew, annoyed that Miss Wicklow, whose brother was only an assistant to Mr Hoare, should already be on such easy terms with the future Lord Pomfret. Guy, quickly restored to his usual careless good humour, said,

'I say, I've got an idea. Let's be Aunt Sally and Guy Fawkes.'

This brilliant thought made everyone weak with laughing again. It was agreed that, the conversational powers of these celebrated characters being unknown, Guy and Phoebe should talk about anything they liked and let the audience do the guessing. Accordingly they all returned to the drawing-room where, in spite of Mrs Rivers's utmost exertions, her party had repeatedly broken up into gossiping knots and had to be harshly reassembled. The gamblers, who had just finished their last game, came up with lemonades or whiskies and soda and stood behind the circle which Guy and Phoebe were to entertain. By this time the two impersonators were feeling so silly that they could only giggle and make a few inane remarks. Phoebe's repeated references to her pipe inclined the more serious part of the audience to say 'Baldwin' to each other, while Guy's insistence on the destruction of the Houses of Parliament led others to say 'Socialist. What's the fellow's name, you know the one I mean.'

After a few minutes Mrs Rivers, who had been getting more and more on edge, said that was enough, and now everyone must guess, one at a time. The usual debacle of intelligence then took place. Those who were first asked to speak, though they had been shouting at the tops of their voices a moment earlier, were struck with almost half-witted shyness. One or two people who hadn't yet grasped what the game was about said was that the first syllable or the whole word. Others said that Mr Barton and Miss Rivers, or if on more intimate terms, Guy and Phoebe, were too marvellous and they simply couldn't *imagine* who they were acting, and wandered off in a very cowardly way to other parts of the room. While this was going on Alice had been sitting in a trance of terror, her feet and hands as cold as ice, her head hot, the drawing-room dancing before her eyes, seeing the awful moment when she would have to say something coming remorselessly nearer and nearer. At last, as from an immense distance she heard Mrs Rivers's voice saying 'Now, Miss Barton, what is your guess? We really must get on with the game.'

Guy, who had a kind heart and had only disowned Alice from the proper snobbishness of a brother, had privately acknowledged to himself that Phoebe and Sally, though they had no business to interfere, were not entirely wrong. He saw his young sister looking like a trapped rabbit, he heard Mrs Rivers speaking to her in a not very kind voice, and though he could have wished she did him more credit he was sorry for her, and determined to make up for his previous neglect. Alice had opened and shut her mouth several times without making any sound, and was twisting her fingers miserably. Mrs Rivers tapped her foot in an impatient way.

'Come on, Alice,' said Guy. 'Have a shot at it.'

Encouraged by these kind words Alice shut her eyes and said, 'Hengist and Horsa.'

'I say,' said Guy, hitting Phoebe violently with his elbow, 'that's jolly good. She's got it in one.'

Phoebe, whose theatrical experience, slight though it was, had made her quick at taking a cue, was completely equal to the occasion.

'Anyone could see you were Hengist,' she said loudly, 'but how she guessed I was Horsa I can't think. Come on, let's get some drinks.'

The few members of the audience who were still taking any interest said Of *course*, and How *awfully* well they'd done it. Mrs Rivers, deeply suspicious, tried to explain to Guy that he hadn't played the game properly, but was swept onwards by the tide and overpowered. All she could do was to shepherd the ladies towards the door and bed. On her way she stopped to say good night to Mr Johns.

'I simply hadn't a moment to talk to you this evening,' she said. 'Someone must amuse the young people, and when Lady Pomfret isn't here I really feel it is up to me. But tomorrow I shall pin you down for a real good talk, while the others are out shooting. I have an idea about advertising that I want to discuss with you.'

Mr Johns expressed his pleasure at the prospect, and Mrs

Rivers again collected her flock and began herding them into the hall. To her annoyance her daughter Phoebe, with the archdeacon's daughter and the screaming girl, showed no signs of following her, but remained talking noisily with some of the men. Much as Mrs Rivers would have liked to reclaim them, she dared not leave her other charges, who had already shown unequivocal symptoms of wanting to scatter.

'Miss Barton,' she said, making Alice jump, 'please tell Phoebe I want her.'

Alice, relieved to find that Mrs Rivers was not going to scold her for anything, obediently went back to the other end of the room and delivered to Phoebe her mother's message.

'Oh, all right,' said Phoebe. 'Sorry,' she said to the little group. 'When Mother gets a good fit of exhibitionism she goes all out. She's doing the Good Hostess, mindful that young girls need their beauty sleep. Oh, my God!'

The whole group began to move towards the door. Alice, who had been afraid that Phoebe would defy her mother and send some message which would expose her to Mrs Rivers's displeasure, followed them. Finding herself near Guy she asked him in a whisper if it was really Hengist and Horsa.

'Of course not,' said Guy. 'I thought you needed bucking up a bit, so I said it was.'

If he could have seen how Alice's heart immediately swelled to six times its natural size with admiration and gratitude for his noble lie, he would have thought it foolish, but quite suitable.

Meanwhile Sally, bored by waiting, had rewound the

gramophone. On hearing it Mr Johns seized the screaming girl and began to waltz in the style of the nineties and with great skill and bravura. Before Mrs Rivers knew where she was her party had again melted in her hands and were fox-trotting round the hall, and in several cases singing the words of the record.

'Come on,' said Sally to Mr Foster.

'I would love to,' said Mr Foster, 'but there's Miss Barton. She's the only one not dancing and my cousin Hermione is quite capable of being unpleasant to her because she's annoyed with us.'

'Quite right,' said Sally, taking a quick look at Alice. 'She looks tired. Look here, you can easily find someone to dance with. I'll go up with Alice.'

'That's really awfully good of you,' said Mr Foster gratefully.

Sally went over to her friend, bade a cheerful good night to Mrs Rivers, and had Alice half-way up the great staircase before anything could be said. As they paused at the turn to look back at the cheerful scene, a voice from below said, 'I say, Miss Barton.'

They looked down. The part of the hall just below them was in comparative darkness. Julian Rivers was standing there, his upturned face white against the gloom, his hair wilder than ever.

'I didn't know you were one of us, Miss Barton,' he said. 'It was splendid.'

Alice was flattered, but so completely at a loss for his meaning that she didn't know what to answer, and it was Sally who asked Mr Rivers what the dickens he meant.

'That Hengist and Horsa,' continued Mr Rivers, taking no notice of Sally. 'A bit of pure surrealism. You and your brother were marvellous. The perfect inevitable-incongruous with a Royal Family complex. I can't tell you how profoundly significant it was. My whole conception of my picture will have to be altered.'

'That's the best news I've heard since Roddy's mare won the point to point,' said Sally aloud to herself. Mr Rivers would doubtless have taken up the challenge, but his mother called him so imperiously that he had to shrug his shoulders, a gesture whose expressiveness loses a good deal when performed in semi-darkness for the benefit of an audience several feet above one, and go over to her. Sally dragged Alice rapidly upstairs and into her bedroom, where she flung herself into a chair before the blazing wood fire.

'What a lovely evening it was!' said Alice.

'That last bit was no joke,' said Sally. 'I can't stick artists, nor can Roddy.'

Alice, who had forgotten during the evening that she was in love, had suddenly been recalled to her better self by Julian Rivers's apostrophe, and was now feeling all the suitable feelings. He had stood below her – (below, which was so wonderful) – in the half-light – (a lovely word, like Yeats's poetry) – and looked upwards – (upwards, which was pure romance) – and said that she was marvellous. Oh, lyric love, half angel and half bird, she thought. Not that Julian was really like a bird; but he was certainly like an angel, like Lucifer if it was not a little unkind to say so, darkest and noblest of the archangels.

'Pretty grim,' Sally continued, quite unaware what her

friend's silence meant. 'It was quite a decent evening though, if only Roddy hadn't had to go and talk business with Mr Hoare. I call that the limit, don't you?'

Alice, thus appealed to, had to ask Sally what she was saying, and to confess that she had never noticed that Roddy hadn't joined them after dinner. What with love and terror it had been very difficult to see anything.

'You're half asleep,' said Sally, with affectionate tolerance. 'Hurry up and get into bed. I'm going down to dance again and Old Mother Rivers won't bother you here. She's got a first-class hate on because I made friends with Gillie. I'm sorry for the chap. It must be ghastly to be delicate and then come into a place like this.'

'Why didn't he say he couldn't come then?' asked Alice.

'I told you you were half asleep,' said Sally. 'When I say come into it, I mean come into it. Listen, my lamb. His father comes into all this when his Uncle Giles, that's Lord Pomfret, dies. And he'll be Lord Pomfret some day. He likes you awfully, and that's just as well,' said Sally with her usual candour, 'because if you are pals with him you can put in a good word for Roddy when old Hoare retires.'

Sally kissed her friend and ran downstairs.

Alice stood bewildered before the fire. What a day it had been. The events of the last five hours flitted confusedly through her mind. The terrifying arrival, Guy's desertion, Phoebe's kindness, the dinner, Julian Rivers who would always mean more to her than anyone in the world. Mr Foster, who was so very nice and kind about the grapes and had fetched her parcel for her though he hadn't known it, which was really rather romantic, and turned out to be the heir to Lord Pomfret's name and possessions. Mrs Rivers's horridness. Guy's kindness about Hengist and Horsa. Again Mrs Rivers's horridness. And last of all Julian, looking up at her through the gloom, dark Romeo, speaking such words as she had never thought to hear. With a sigh she turned to the business of going to bed. Her hairbrush and toothbrush she found without too much difficulty, but the housemaid had hidden her nightgown completely. After opening and shutting every drawer and cupboard in the room three or four times, she was forced to the wretched conclusion that she hadn't packed it, though she distinctly remembered doing so, because she had to take it out again when she remembered that she had forgotten to put her black slip in, and had to rearrange everything. She did not dare to ring, and it was not until she had miserably put on some of her underclothes as a temporary nightgown, and got into bed that she found the nightgown wrapped round a hot water bottle. With a grateful heart she put it on and soon fell asleep, lulled by the gramophone from below, and the thought of Julian (Julian! that name!) and the morrow, which was a much more beautiful word than tomorrow. Her last conscious thought was of gratitude that she had found her nightgown, for to face the housemaid in the morning in an obvious substitute would have been more than she could bear.

4

Trials of a Publisher

After a peaceful night Alice was woken by the housemaid's tap at her door. The nightgown complex rose in her mind, but in a flash she remembered how she had found it safely and was now wearing it. When the housemaid had drawn the curtains and brought in a jug of hot water she approached the bed.

'Would you like your fire lighted, miss?' she said.

Alice thought it sounded nicer than anything she could possibly imagine. To lie luxuriously in bed, looking out on a cold, bleak day, and watch a housemaid rouse those grey ashes in the fireplace to a glowing flame, would be as good as the Decline of the Roman Empire. But as usual she had to find a dark thought to take her own happiness away. Was it thinking of others to lie in bed and have the fire lighted for one? Wasn't it rather awful to be snug under soft blankets and silk eiderdowns while Wheeler, who was quite old enough to be her mother, and even her mother and a half, was down on her knees in the cold, sweeping up ashes, laying paper and sticks, putting on logs, kindling the warm fire from which she would get no benefit? And Wheeler was wearing a cotton dress.

'Would you like the fire lighted, miss?' said Wheeler again, thinking that the young lady wasn't properly awake yet. 'Miss Phoebe told me to be sure to ask you. It's very cold this morning.'

'Oh, yes please if you don't mind,' said Alice. 'I mean if it really isn't a bother.'

Wheeler paid no attention to Alice after her first three words, for she had noticed in a long and respectable career, during which she had risen from seventh to second housemaid, that young ladies talked a lot of rubbish and standing listening to them wouldn't get your rooms done, so she went down on her knees, as indeed she had always meant to, her question being merely rhetorical, swept up the ashes, laid paper and sticks, put on logs and finally lit a fire which gleamed and danced half-way up the chimney. Then she moved quietly about the room, folding up Alice's evening things and putting them away, while Alice watched her, like a wild animal peering from its burrow, trying to remember in which of some three dozen drawers her evening stockings and her silk slip had been put. Wheeler then approached the bed again.

'Will you be coming down to breakfast, miss, or should I bring you up a tray?' she said.

Again Alice was dumb, longing for a friend who would tell her what to do. If she had breakfast in bed, which sounded too heavenly, would everyone despise her? Would they go out on their own business or amusement while she was idly guzzling in bed, so that when she came down she would find an empty house. Or if she came down, would she be the only girl, and be hated by the men as a forward, designing intruder on their meal?

'What do you think I ought to do?' she faltered, throwing herself on Wheeler's compassion.

Wheeler, who was quite used to having her advice asked and not taken, answered whichever Miss Barton wished, which threw Miss Barton into paroxysms of despair, till she added that Miss Phoebe always had hers in bed.

'Oh, in bed then, please, if it isn't too much bother,' said Alice with an effort.

She then lay back and shut her eyes, feeling that two such decisions in one day were all she could manage.

'Tea or coffee, miss?' said Wheeler, who was quite used to their going to sleep again, and wished to get her instructions first.

'Tea, please,' said Alice, at once wishing she had said coffee.

'Miss Phoebe always has coffee,' said Wheeler. 'And India or China, miss?'

'Oh, India, I mean China. Or if Miss Rivers is having coffee perhaps I'd better have it too, if it wouldn't be a trouble.'

'Yes, miss,' said Wheeler. 'And do you take cooked breakfast?'

'I – I don't know,' faltered Alice.

'Eggs, or fish, or anything like that, miss,' continued the remorseless inquisitor.

'Oh, yes please. Just anything, it doesn't matter what,' said Alice, wishing she had courage enough to add, 'and please go away and don't let me ever see you again.'

'And some fruit, miss? And what will you be wearing today?'

'Oh, I don't know, I mean yes please fruit, but I could find what I want to wear myself if you don't mind,' said Alice.

Wheeler appeared content and went away. In a surprisingly short time she came back with a tray which she held poised with a pitying expression while Alice quickly sat up in bed and prepared her knees to receive her breakfast.

'You'd better have a wrap or something, miss,' said Wheeler, when she had put the tray on Alice's legs. 'It's a cold day and the fire hasn't burnt up yet.'

She fetched Alice's dressing-gown and put it round her shoulders, brought a cushion from the big chair, stuffed it behind Alice's back and left her victim in peace.

It was indeed a fascinating prospect upon which Alice now gazed. On her tray was a gay flowered breakfast set. Coffee and hot milk were in twin jugs with covered tops. There were three plates with covers on them, a little toast-rack, two kinds of jam, about a dozen little balls of butter, sugar brown and white. There were an apple, an orange and a small bunch of grapes, with a gold knife and fork, and a napkin as fine as Alice's best handkerchiefs was folded by her plate. She cautiously lifted the three lids. Under the first was a piece of grilled fish, under the second a fried egg on fried bread among crisp rashers of bacon, under the third little hot rolls of various kinds. Accustomed though she was to excellent food at home, Alice had never seen so lavish a display, arranged with such art, for the benefit of one person, and found it almost impossible to believe that that person should be herself. However she managed to make a very tolerable breakfast of coffee, eggs and bacon, one piece of toast, two little rolls, some butter and strawberry jam, and the grapes, after which she supposed she had better get up. The thought of the fish, and the rest of the toast and rolls and the fruit oppressed her, for it seemed terrible that so much trouble should have been taken over food that she had not touched. She thought it possible that Wheeler and the cook might be offended, and seriously contemplated trying to hide or burn some of it. But on reflection she decided to brave the matter out, for the half-burnt corpse of a fish would give her away hopelessly.

So she got up and by great good luck found all her clothes. When she was dressed she knocked at Phoebe's door. No answer came, so she opened the door cautiously and looked in, but the bed and the room were empty. This was a shattering blow. With Phoebe Alice would not have minded facing a drawing-room full of people. Alone she feared a dragon at every corner. She might meet Peters, or one of the footmen, in the hall, and they might wonder what she was doing. If, on the other hand, she stayed in her bedroom and wrote letters, as people did in novels and in memoirs, the housemaids would come to make her bed and hate her for interfering with their work. This seemed on the whole the more awful prospect of the two, so Alice went downstairs. There was no one on the staircase, no one in the hall. She was suddenly seized with terror of all the shut doors round the hall. Which was the right one to open?

Would people be in the green drawing-room where they had assembled last night, or in the yellow drawing-room where they had played that dreadful game after dinner, or in the library, or in one of the other rooms that she hadn't yet seen? Just then she saw Miss Merriman coming out of a door at the far end, so she went quickly back to the foot of the stairs and began walking across the hall again, so that Miss Merriman should think she had only just come down.

'Good morning. You look rather lost,' said Miss Merriman, thus shattering her hopes that she would be taken for a hard-boiled, self-possessed society girl. 'You'll find it warm in the yellow drawing-room.'

She led the way briskly to the other side of the hall, opened the door, almost pushed Alice in, and went off on one of her many household errands. Alice advanced timidly into the room. A large fire was crackling cheerfully at the further end, but no other sound could be heard and she could see no one. She looked at the bookshelves, turned over a heap of magazines on a table, chose one and sat down in a huge armchair before the fire. She would have much liked to have known where Sally and Roddy and Guy and that kind Mr Foster were, but did not know how to find out, so she curled up in her chair and began to read about the doings of Society, of which she too, at any rate till Monday, was a part. A slight noise made her look up once, but seeing that it was a man whom she didn't know, and that he had settled himself at a writing-table, she went on with her reading, thankful that she had not been seen.

Mr Johns, for it was he, had come into the drawing-room to write his letters because the library was full of Professor

Milward and the archdeacon arguing about Neville de Pomfret who, having benefited largely by the dissolution of the monasteries, had subsequently died in a very sudden way, his death being attributed by his friends to poison administered by an ex-abbot disguised as an apothecary, and by his enemies to the Wrath of God which had caused him to indulge in intemperance of every kind to his own destruction. As both the archdeacon and the professor only wrote immensely learned books which were published by various University Presses, rarely selling more than two hundred and fifty copies, Mr Johns had no professional interest in them, so he had slipped away, and was delighted to find the drawing-room empty. He also had to make an important decision: whether or not he would stay over the weekend. When he had been invited to Pomfret Towers he had accepted with alacrity, taking the invitation as a personal distinction from the earl, whom he knew slightly. But on the previous evening he had discovered that it was Mrs Rivers who had caused him to be invited, with the intention of cornering him for a business talk. Though Mr Johns had the greatest respect for Mrs Rivers as a best seller, both he and his partner disliked her more cordially than any other of their authors. From the first moment of her success she had taken herself with devastating seriousness, speaking of My Work, ringing her publishers up almost daily to inquire how sales were going, reading every press cutting she could get and rushing into Johns & Fairfield's office to demand libel actions against unfavourable reviews, haggling for terms that even her sales hardly justified. Gladly would her publishers have parted with her to any of their rivals, making a grateful sacrifice of the handsome income she brought them, but so far no other offer had been quite large enough to tempt Mrs Rivers's voracity, and she made a merit of remaining faithful to the house which had helped to make her name, with an attitude of condescension, as to old and tried family servants, which was almost more than they could bear.

It was Mr Johns's practice, whenever he went away to a strange house, to have a telegram sent to him every day from his office, containing the words 'Return if possible urgent'. This telegram he tore up if he was enjoying himself, but if he was bored he was able to exhibit it mournfully to his host and ask if he could be sent to the station in time for the best afternoon train. If his presence was really needed his office would send him quite another telegram explaining what the business was. The telegram might now be expected at any moment, and he would have to decide what he wished to do. From a few words that Lord Pomfret had dropped on the preceding evening Mr Johns had gathered that his lordship had been committing to paper some account of his life as a sportsman and landowner. If this were so, and no other publisher had got wind of it, Mr Johns was ready to stay until he had pinned the earl down to some kind of agreement. A good deal of his work for his firm had been done under uncomfortable conditions. More than one brilliant young writer had been caught by Mr Johns on stormy passages to and from America, when such men as were not laid low had gathered round the bar, some in a spirit of bravado which they subsequently repented, others, among whom luckily for himself was Mr Johns, because they looked upon the Atlantic as an ill mannered but ineffectual bore whom they preferred to ignore. The well-known American novelist Abner Croke had been carried away by Mr Johns right under the eyes of a rival firm because Mr Johns, with his firm's interests in view, had sat through an interminable tête-à-tête dinner in Mr Croke's private suite at the Savoy, sympathised with Mr Croke's physical inability to drink anything but barley water, listened to all Mr Croke had to say about his President, and finally assisted him to his Louis XV bed, there to sleep off the effects of a very gallant defiance of his nonalcoholic regime.

As for Mrs Rivers, he had met her at lunch and gathered from her with no difficulty that she was thinking of writing a novel about her cruise up the Amazon. Thinking that a first novel by a good-looking clever woman might be well worth a gamble, he had asked her to lunch with him, listened with courteously veiled want of interest to all she had to say about herself, written at frequent intervals to inquire how her work was getting on, and within a few weeks had given her a contract for her first novel with an option on two more. His gamble had been a complete success. Mrs Rivers, as he had told Lady Pomfret, had a gift amounting to genius for writing books which, as his American partner observed, got the middle-aged women right where they lived. Mrs Rivers had produced a book a year, her royalties in England and America were mounting steadily, and the firm of Johns & Fairfield, as also their opposite number in New York, Vandemeer & Apfelbaum Inc., were reaping a rich reward for Mr Johns's work. But for all that, Johns & Fairfield, as we have said, would willingly have forgone their profits, or at any rate a part of them, for a little respite from their client's trying ways. Messrs Vandemeer & Apfelbaum would not so willingly have forgone them, but Mrs Rivers had only once visited New York and her American publishers had almost recovered from it, with the trifling exception that each was determined to be on vacation when next the English authoress came, and let his partner do the entertaining.

Mr Johns, having written two or three letters, began to consider seriously what he would do. Mrs Rivers, not content with plaguing his life out at his office, personally, by telephone, and by letter, had bullied her cousin – only her cousin by marriage though – the Earl of Pomfret to invite Mr Johns to Pomfret Towers, so that she might further bully and plague him to her heart's content, in a place where he had no secretary, no sham telephone messages, to save him from her. His blood boiled as he thought of her, and he determined to go as soon as the telegram came. Then he thought of the earl's memoirs, and how he had never yet shirked any unpleasant duty that might help the firm, and he determined to stay. Just as he made this decision, Mrs Rivers came in.

There was on the writing-table at which Mr Johns was sitting a monstrous erection which had once been a receptacle for knives, tall, wide and sloping upwards to the back. This case had been gutted and refitted and now contained four different sizes of notepaper of a hideous grey colour with what looked like hundreds of hairs mangled into it and the address stamped in heavy Gothic characters, coroneted envelopes to match, postcards, telegraph forms, and gummed wrappers for newspapers. As Mr Johns had been using some of the notepaper, and very much enjoying the coroneted envelopes, the lid was open and made a screen nearly two feet high in front of him. Bending his head low over the blotter, which was of massive chased silver and must have weighed at least half a stone, he hastily picked up one of the eight different pens that lay on a silver pen tray before him and began to pretend to write, taking however great care not to touch the paper with the nib, lest the noise should betray him. In vain does the ostrich hide his head in the sand. Mrs Rivers, looking about her, saw Mr Johns's legs under the table and came graciously though eagerly forward.

'Good morning, Mr Johns,' she said.

Mr Johns, every inch a gentleman, rose.

'Don't get up,' said Mrs Rivers, taking a chair on the opposite side of the table, in a position where the stationery holder was not between herself and her publisher. 'Have you a cigarette?'

Mr Johns handed her his case.

'Match?' said Mrs Rivers. 'Oh, here they are.'

She opened the lid of an elephant's foot mounted in silver which contained about a hundred wax matches with different coloured heads, struck one, lit her cigarette and put the match in a silver ashtray heavily embossed with the Pomfret arms, an ashtray which Peters used as a trap for the third footman whose duty it was to clean it, finding remains of plate polish on the under surface with grim and unfailing regularity.

'Oh, do *you* want one?' she said, as Mr Johns helped himself to one of his own cigarettes.

But Mr Johns had a little lighter in his pocket and used that.

'This is splendid,' said Mrs Rivers. 'I thought you wouldn't be going out with the guns, so I determined to run you to earth. I couldn't get a word with you last night. My cousin Edith isn't up to organising her parties and I really have to do the work of hostess, and these young people need so much amusing. I assure you it is no joke to have to run the whole house party. If only the young people would play with *intelligence*. All those games can be *so* amusing when they are played intelligently. We were playing that game of choosing characters and guessing who they are by what they say at Lord Stoke's last summer and it was most amusing. I chose Hypatia, and Lord Stoke was Disraeli, and we kept everyone in fits of laughter.'

Mr Johns, who had been privileged to hear from his old acquaintance Mrs Morland, whose successful novels he did not publish, exactly what Lord Stoke had said afterwards, and how devoutly the whole company had wished that Mrs Rivers might at an early date share her character's fate, and how willingly they would have taken the path of the Athenian mob themselves, but that the conventions of Society forbade, said he was sure they did.

'But really if they only make fun of it all,' continued Mrs Rivers, 'I feel I am only wasting the time I should be giving to My Work. I know you want to hear how I am getting on, but I simply can't talk about it just now, till this weekend is over. I have trained myself to work at odd times, one must you know when one has a family, and as a rule I get up early and get through at least five hundred words before breakfast, so that I can be free for my children. But you know all that, Mr Johns. But here I really cannot concentrate on My Work when I have the whole burden of the house party on my shoulders. Now take last night. Phoebe and that young Mr Barton went out together and it took them at least half an hour to decide who they were. Phoebe *can* be so trying. And when they came back they talked such nonsense that everyone was laughing,' said Mrs Rivers indignantly.

Mr Johns, thinking privately of how Mrs Rivers as Hypatia had kept everyone in fits of laughter, said it was too bad.

'And I should have been working,' said Mrs Rivers. 'I had a chapter mapped out in my mind and was *longing* to get the rough idea down on paper, but Cousin Edith looked so lost—'

And at this point Mrs Rivers almost tripped over her own tongue in her anxiety to explain simultaneously how she always gave so many hours a day to her work, how Cousin Edith relied on her for everything, and how stupid the young people had been last night.

Mr Johns abstracted his mind till she should have talked herself to a temporary standstill. His attention was attracted by the paper-cutter, an outsize elephant's tusk with an earl's coronet carved on the handle, and he was trying to balance it on one finger.

Alice who, absorbed in the doings of Society, had not noticed Mrs Rivers come in, gradually became aware that someone was talking in the room. The words 'Phoebe' and 'young Mr Barton' struck her ear. She looked round the back of her large armchair and saw that the terrifying Mrs

Rivers was talking to the man at the writing-table. At the same moment she became aware that they didn't know she was in the room, and that they were already so far embarked on their conversation which appeared to be, one-sidedly at least, a good deal about the other guests, that she would find it extremely awkward to make her presence known. Sally, the fearless, would probably have called out loudly that she was here, but from this course Alice shrank back appalled. She was trying to screw her courage to the sticking point when her own name rang like a thunderbolt in her ears.

'... and when that little Miss Barton said Hengist and Horsa,' Mrs Rivers continued, 'I realised how stupid I had been to take so much trouble. Why Cousin Giles asked her I don't know.'

Alice went into a mental swoon of terror and missed Mrs Rivers's next remarks. By the time she had recovered, Mrs Rivers was asking Mr Johns why on earth Cousin Giles had asked the Wicklows.

'Mr Wicklow is in the estate office, so that is reasonable,' she said, 'but why ask his sister? She was boring poor Gillie stiff last night, first with cards, then with talking about dogs and foxes. Gillie doesn't know one animal from another. He is only interested in art and music and books – the sort of things Julian and Phoebe like. But I didn't come here to bother you about myself. I only wanted to have a few words with you about My Work. I feel I must have more advertising for this book. Everyone says you don't advertise me enough.'

Mr Johns, who had heard this statement more than once, showed no annoyance and went on balancing the elephant's tusk.

'Look at Bungay,' said Mrs Rivers, naming a publishing firm of great activity, 'they give their authors two whole pages on Sundays.'

Mr Johns put the elephant's tusk down and pointed out to Mrs Rivers, as he had often done before, that the methods of Bungay were not the methods of Johns & Fairfield. Mrs Rivers repeated that all her friends said her books ought to be more advertised. Mr John, restraining an impulse to hit her with the elephant's tusk, or an even stronger impulse to tell her to go to hell, tried to suggest to her that his firm knew, on the whole, what they were doing, and that advertising on a large scale would not be of great benefit with her kind of public.

'Well, if Mr Bungay tries to have me,' said Mrs Rivers, with a charming smile, or what felt like one inside herself, 'I may fall, you know.'

Luckily for Mr Johns, Peters came in with a telegram which he handed to him. Mr Johns read it in silence and told Peters there was no answer.

'I'm afraid this may mean that I'll have to go to town,' he said.

'What's that about going to town?' asked Lord Pomfret, who had followed his butler into the room.

'Mr Johns wants to leave us, Cousin Giles. Don't let him,' cried Mrs Rivers, sincerely annoyed that her prey appeared to be escaping her.

'Nonsense,' his lordship replied. 'If he's got to go, he's got to go. Do you know where that damned boy of yours is, Hermione?'

'I thought he was out with the guns,' said Mrs Rivers.

'Well, he wasn't. He's painting,' said the earl. '*Painting!* I don't mind his making a fool of himself in his studio or whatever he calls it, but when I found him making one of his filthy daubs on the staircase, I stopped it at once. Stoopid picture too – all crooked. It's my belief the boy can't see properly. Why don't you take him to an oculist? He's probably going blind like old Osbert Rivers. Why don't you send him into the army? Get his hair cut. Go to a decent tailor. Now Phoebe's a nice girl, rides straight and looks smart. Pity she wasn't the boy.'

Mr Johns said he must go and see about his packing, but as no one paid any attention to him he remained. Mrs Rivers, though chagrined at Lord Pomfret's strictures on her son, was pleased by his praise of Phoebe, and determined to make the best of things.

'Phoebe *does* look well just now,' she said, with a burst of mother's candour. 'And she and Gillie seem to get on so well.'

The earl made his formidable noise, a noise which to Mr John's sensitive ear appeared to be the equivalent of the transatlantic 'You're telling me,' but offered no further comment.

'I was thinking,' Mrs Rivers continued, 'that as Cousin Edith is rather tired, perhaps she'd like me to see to the arrangements today. I thought Phoebe and Gillie might ride this morning as they haven't gone with the guns, and then after lunch if Cousin Edith isn't using the car I could take Julian and Gillie over to Rising Castle to see Lord Stoke's pictures. And after dinner I thought we could play games again with only the intelligent people, and the others could play Corinthian bagatelle, or puff ball if they have found the puffers. I'm afraid I shan't get much of My Work done, but I was thinking of Cousin Edith.'

The earl's only comment was to ring the bell, which was answered with a promptitude that spoke volumes for his temper, and demand Miss Merriman. Mrs Rivers went on to say that she was sure Cousin Giles agreed with her that her books weren't advertised enough.

'Eh?' said Lord Pomfret. 'Advertisements? I throw 'em all in the waste-paper basket. Can't think why they spend all that money on advertising Guinness and all those things. If I want a glass of Guinness I have it. Don't need any advertisements for that. Good morning, Merry. Can you tell me what Lady Pomfret is doing today?'

'Yes, Lord Pomfret,' said Miss Merriman, who as usual was carrying a sheaf of papers. 'Mr Foster is with Lady Pomfret now, and at half-past twelve she would like Miss Barton to go for a little walk with her. In the afternoon she is driving over to Rising Castle and taking the archdeacon and Professor Milward, and would like to know if you are coming with her.'

'Certainly not,' said the earl. 'Give her my love and say certainly not. Of all the deaf old bores in the county, Stoke is the worst. I'm going round Six Corners Covert with Mr Wicklow to have a look at the fences.'

'And,' said Miss Merriman, making a note, 'Lady Pomfret said if you don't mind she thinks a small dance would be nice after dinner, and to have the big gramophone moved into the hall. Is there anything else?'

'You'd like to go to Rising Castle, Hermione,' said the

earl, with great courtesy, 'wouldn't you? There'll be plenty of room as I'm not going.'

'I'd love to,' said Mrs Rivers, as amiably as she could, 'but I really must work this afternoon. But Julian would love to go.'

'No, Julian had better not go,' said his lordship. 'Thank you, Merry. Oh, wait a moment though. What's this about your leaving, Mr Johns? Merry knows all the trains.'

'You could get the 11.35 if you haven't much packing,' said Miss Merriman. 'Or there's the 2.30. You could go straight from the lunch-table. Or we could send you to Barchester to get the 3.45.'

'I have been looking at my engagements,' said Mr Johns, 'and I think this telegram isn't really urgent, so I can stay till Monday as we arranged.'

'Very well,' said Miss Merriman, with her usual pleasant expression, and went away.

'Ought to know your own mind,' said the earl reprovingly to Mr Johns. 'Bad plan to change. I made up my mind to go to India once. Changed my mind, stayed at home, and went out by the next boat. Damned hot it was too in the Red Sea.'

'And what happened?' asked Mr Johns, keyed up for the point of this blood-stirring anecdote.

'Happened? Never heard that anything happened,' said the earl with some irritation. 'And I wish you'd tell that boy of yours not to paint in the house, Hermione. There's plenty of room in the racket court if he wants to make a mess.'

These words were so unmistakably a congé that Mrs Rivers, after a word or two of expostulation of which her cousin took no notice at all, went away to sympathise with Julian.

'Damned interfering woman,' said Lord Pomfret, looking after her. 'How d'you get on with her, eh, Johns? I suppose you make a pretty penny out of her, eh? Can't stand that boy of hers, hair like a foreigner. You'd better go to Rising Castle this afternoon with her ladyship. Stoke's an old bore, but he has a good library and some good pictures. And when you come back, come and have a talk with me in the library before dinner.'

With which his lordship took himself off to the estate room and was no more seen.

Mr Johns tore his telegram in two and threw it into the waste-paper basket. His whole being was singing a song of triumph. The Baedeker Bitch had got it in the eye this time, and he wished Mr Fairfield had been there to see. Mr Johns would dearly have liked to know whether Lord Pomfret's thwarting of his cousin's plans had been accidental or deliberate, and came to the conclusion that chance having played into his lordship's hands, he had made the very most of his chances. Now that he had seen Mrs Rivers meet her match, nothing would induce him to leave Pomfret Towers a moment before the appointed time. Humming a tuneless little air he walked towards the door, meaning to go and take a stroll in the Italian garden, when a thought made him turn back. One never knew what happened to the contents of waste-paper baskets. There were rumours that when the housekeeper's room felt dull, it had the drawing-room basket in and played at 'pieces', putting together the fragments of its employer's letters. If this telegram were found and word came to Mrs Rivers's ears through her maid, if she had one, or a housemaid, that after receiving an urgent recall to London he had stayed on at the Towers, especially after witnessing her discomfiture, there might be trouble. So, stooping with a little difficulty, he retrieved the two scraps and walked over to the fire. He dropped them into the flames and was then surprised to hear behind him a very small voice say, 'Oh, I *beg* your pardon, but I really didn't know what to do.'

He turned round and saw a girl with large frightened eyes, looking up at him from a huge armchair. Why she was frightened, or why she should beg his pardon, he couldn't conceive. But human nature was always worth studying, so he sat down and said,

'It's perfectly all right, I assure you. Will you have a cigarette?'

The girl, looking more alarmed than ever, refused in a way that made him feel he was offering her drugged chocolates, adding that she didn't mean to.

'I'm sure you didn't,' said Mr Johns comfortably. 'I don't think we met last night, did we? My name is Johns.'

'Oh, thank you very much,' said the girl, still eyeing him nervously. 'Don't you do Mother's books, or perhaps you're not that one, I *am* so sorry if I was silly.'

'I do publish books,' said Mr Johns. Then remembering his hostess's words the night before he added, 'Are you by any chance Miss Barton?'

'I'm Alice Barton,' said Alice, anxious to be correct.

'I'm so glad to meet you,' said Mr Johns. 'I admire your mother's books very much and didn't know I was to have the pleasure of talking with her daughter.'

Alice could think of nothing to say but 'yes,' a singularly inappropriate remark, which she made in a strangled voice, twisting her hands wretchedly. Luckily Mr Johns was used to every kind of peculiarity in his authors, who varied from blustering bullies to writers who were so shy that they lived in Shropshire and would never come to town, and if visited at home became incapable of speech, so he talked away agreeably about Mrs Barton and how well her books sold and how sorry he was that he had never seen her, because he was in America on the one occasion when she had visited the office, until Alice's eyes got smaller again and her hands quieter.

'Can I tell you an Awful Thing?' asked Alice, suddenly interrupting his flow of words.

Mr Johns begged her to.

'I didn't mean to,' said Alice, 'and I know it's awful, but I was reading here, because I didn't know where anyone was, and you came in to write and I didn't know who you were so I didn't say anything, and then Mrs Rivers came in and I didn't know what to do, and it was awful, but I didn't mean to, and it really wasn't my fault because it gets harder to do a thing all the time if you don't.'

She stopped and stared at Mr Johns as if he were a jury about to bring in their verdict.

'I think I see,' said Mr Johns. 'You mean you heard the beginning of Mrs Rivers's conversation with me and not having made your presence known you found the situation increasingly awkward and felt it wiser on the whole to keep quiet.'

Alice was not sure if this was condemnation or excuse,

but the word 'wiser' gave her courage, and she nodded violently several times.

'Well,' said Mr Johns, 'I think you were very sensible. And I'm glad,' he added in a burst of confidence, 'that you did keep quiet. I wouldn't have had an interruption for a hundred pounds. Do you realise, young lady, that you were privileged to hear an insufferable piece of conceit meeting her match?'

'Do you mean Lord Pomfret?' asked Alice.

'I do.'

'He wasn't rude, was he?' faltered Alice.

'Good God, no! He simply put the lady in her place. I haven't enjoyed anything so much since hansoms went out.'

'But I thought Mrs Rivers was very clever and brilliant,' said Alice, on whom the glorious idea was slowly bursting that she was not the only person to whom the celebrated authoress was offensive.

Mr Johns, throwing caution for once to the winds, let loose his pent-up feelings and told Alice a little of what he thought about Mrs Rivers. 'Miss Rivers is a delightful girl,' said Mr Johns, 'and I'm not surprised she has gone on the stage to get away from her mother. As for Julian he is simply his mother over again.'

'But Lord Pomfret was rather unkind about him, wasn't he?' said Alice. 'I mean an artist *must* paint, and this house would be so lovely to do, and Julian hasn't got a studio here.'

'Have you ever seen any of his pictures?' asked Mr Johns.

'No,' said Alice, 'but he wants to do a portrait of me.'

'Well, I hope it will be a great success,' said Mr Johns kindly, thinking of the exhibitions that Mrs Rivers had forced him to attend. Julian had never yet had a one-man show, but he belonged to a society called The Set of Five, who were apt to exhibit in an out of the way gallery off the Tottenham Court Road. Here Mr Johns had been unwillingly forced to look at Julian's pictures, to him repulsive and inexplicable. He remembered with particular dislike a portrait of Phoebe, or so it was called in the catalogue, her pretty face painted in planes of purple and green, her nose on one side, her neck twisted. There was also a little affair called 'Crabs Go Whence' in which two small crab's claws were glued to a piece of three ply. Above the claws were painted a scalene triangle, an eye, and a child's impression of a railway engine, while below them was nailed a small piece of suet, renewed from time to time during the fortnight for which the exhibition was open. Mr Johns had also once attended a cocktail party in Julian's studio, at which Phoebe's theatrical friends, smart and good-humoured, had talked theatre shop, while Julian's friends, mostly large young men with conspicuous hair, had clustered together, looking angrily at all newcomers. Mr Johns had been introduced to several famous artists in their early twenties, who had been oafish or scornful, according to their temperament, and had gladly gone over to Phoebe's easy-going band. Julian had, after much pressure, exhibited a number of his drawings and paintings. The artists had looked at them in complete silence. Julian, getting sulkier and sulkier every moment, whisked each picture away and banged each new one down, giving his audience very little chance to see what they looked like. When a friend of Phoebe's, feeling genuinely sorry for Julian, had broken the silence by saying how funny it was that pictures always looked nicer in a frame, Julian had banged his last picture on the floor, locked himself into his bedroom, and refused to come out till the party had left, which was not for a long time, the artists being too shy to leave as long as there was any drink left, and the theatricals, most of whom were resting, being only too glad to have somewhere to rest. Mr Johns had left soon after his host's disappearance, feeling extremely sorry for Phoebe.

Thinking of all this he looked at Mrs Barton's girl, who was going to be quite good-looking when she had filled out a bit, and tried to imagine her in Julian's studio. It was not a success.

'Will Julian paint you in London?' he asked.

'Oh no,' said Alice, 'he said he would do me in my studio.'

Mr Johns, interested, inquired about the studio. Alice, thawing under his pleasant manner, told him all about how she had been delicate, and how she loved painting, and how her parents had let her turn the old nursery into a studio, and how she was trying to design a jacket for her mother's next book. Having said this, she felt she had gone too far and wished she were dead, but Mr Johns showed such genuine sympathy that she became almost glad to be alive. Just as they were in the middle of this delightful conversation, Miss Merriman came in.

'Oh, there you are, Miss Barton,' she said. 'Lady Pomfret says if you aren't doing anything else, will you come out with her at half-past twelve? She wants to take the dogs in the Park before lunch.'

'And I must take a walk or I shall be getting fat,' said Mr

Johns optimistically. 'I have enjoyed our talk very much, Miss Barton. Will you ask your mother if she will allow me to call upon her whenever I am next down here, and then you will perhaps show me your work.'

Alice said, with a return of timidity, that it wasn't really work, but of course Mother would like to see Mr Johns very much, and went off to get ready for her walk. She had felt ever since Mr Johns began to talk to her, that such easy, comfortable conditions could not last, and soon this was all too true, for look as she might she could not see her brogue shoes anywhere. With a tremendous effort of courage she gave a timid ring, but no one came. It was almost half-past twelve by the gilded clock on the mantelpiece, and if she were late Lady Pomfret might publicly chide her, or send her home, or make everyone laugh at her. For the third time she went to the door and looked into the passage to see if a housemaid was about, when the door next but one to hers opened and Mr Foster came out of his room.

'Good morning,' he said. 'You are going out with Aunt Edith, aren't you?'

'I don't know,' said Alice miserably. 'I can't find my shoes.'

Mr Foster looked down at her small stockinged feet and his face assumed an expression of concern.

'I suppose you rang the bell and they didn't answer,' he said.

Alice nodded, too near tears to trust herself to speak.

'Most annoying,' said Mr Foster half to himself. He went to the head of the service staircase and called down it in a mild voice. No one answered.

'Dear, dear, dear,' said Mr Foster, and taking a large lump of coal from a box which stood on the landing to replenish the bedroom scuttles, he dropped it down the well. There was a crash and a sound of footsteps below.

'Who is there?' said Mr Foster in the same mild voice.

An indistinguishable answer rose from the kitchen quarters.

'Tell them to bring Miss Barton's walking shoes at once,' said Mr Foster. 'Wait a minute. What are they like?' he asked, turning to Alice. 'Brown brogue shoes with a buckle. At once. Miss Barton is waiting to walk with her ladyship.'

Almost before Alice could begin to say thank you for this gallant rescue, an emissary from the boothole came rushing upstairs with two or three pairs of brown shoes in his green baize apron.

'Are those yours, Miss Barton?' said Mr Foster.

Alice pointed at her pair, which the emissary laid reverently outside her bedroom.

'Get them on,' said Mr Foster, 'and I'll take you down to Aunt Edith. You are Finch, aren't you?' said Mr Foster to the emissary. 'Listen, Finch. If the shoes aren't up by the time the ladies have finished breakfast, I shall have to tell Peters to look into it.'

Finch said he was sorry, but he had been doing the young gent's brushes and things, and seemed to get behind-hand like.

'All right,' said Mr Foster. 'Remember what I said. Now, Miss Barton, we'll find Aunt Edith.'

Alice was indeed grateful for Mr Foster's guidance, for Lady Pomfret's sitting-room was far away in another wing.

In the passage leading to her ladyship's rooms they met Miss Merriman, who took Alice in tow.

'Can I speak to you for a moment, Merry,' said Mr Foster.

Miss Merriman took Alice in to Lady Pomfret and came back into the passage.

'It's about the upstairs bells, Merry,' he said. 'No one answered Miss Barton's bell just now, and Phoebe told me that they had the same trouble last night. And her shoes hadn't been brought up.'

'Dear me,' said Miss Merriman, and going into Lady Pomfret's sitting-room, which her ladyship and Alice had now left by the garden door, she rang the bell.

'Peters,' said Miss Merriman, 'Miss Barton's shoes weren't brought up, and no one answered her bell. I will speak to Mrs Caxton about the housemaid. What was Finch doing?'

'He told me,' said Mr Foster, 'that he had been cleaning brushes for one of the guests. What brushes, do you know?'

'It was probably Mr Julian Rivers's brushes, sir,' said Peters. 'His artistic brushes, sir. His lordship took exception to the smell of turps in Mr Julian Rivers's room, sir, and gave orders that Mr Julian was to do his dirty work, as his lordship phrased it, elsewhere. Now I come to mention it, sir, I did notice a smell of turps coming from Finch's boot-room this morning. I shall Mention it, sir.'

'Yes, please do,' said Miss Merriman.

'I am sorry to have troubled you,' said Mr Foster to Miss Merriman, 'but I didn't quite like to speak to Peters myself. I haven't really any right to report on the servants, but Miss Barton is just the sort to get neglected because she doesn't push.'

'That's all right,' said Miss Merriman. 'I'm very glad to do anything for you, and Peters needs bracing up sometimes. I'll go and see the housekeeper now.'

'Thank you so much, Merry,' said Mr Foster. 'You know, I do feel a bit awkward sometimes here. It's a queer position, and I would hate to do too much, but I must look after the guests a bit. But when you are here it makes all the difference.'

'Thank you,' said Miss Merriman.

Mr Foster then went to the estate room which was empty, as Mr Hoare left at twelve on Saturdays and Roddy was out with the earl looking at the Six Corners Covert. He went over to the opposite wall and pulled down the big estate map which was mounted on linen and flew up with a click. He already knew the country pretty well from his increasingly frequent visits to Pomfret Towers, and had little difficulty in finding Hamaker's Spinney. In that spinney were the earths that Miss Wicklow had ordered him to stop. He had been greatly struck by Miss Wicklow's kindly, efficient manner, and wished Mr Hoare, who always seemed faintly to resent his existence, were as pleasant to deal with.

Mr Foster had known vaguely for many years that his father was the Earl of Pomfret's heir, but as he had lived a great deal abroad for his health and had never cared greatly for his father, he had not thought much about it. His mother had died when he was very young, his father had never taken much notice of him, and he had been chiefly brought up by an aunt, now dead. A few years earlier his health showed such marked improvement that he was able to come back to England, and found a position with a firm of picture dealers to whom his real knowledge of foreign galleries and collectors was of considerable value. But it was only in the last two years that Lord Pomfret had expressed a wish that his heir's son should learn something of the place which he would presumably inherit. Mr Foster had visited Pomfret Towers and made great friends with Lady Pomfret, who when in England was glad to have someone to talk to about her Italian acquaintances, and when in Italy was glad to see her English friends. What Lord Pomfret thought of his young cousin he kept to himself, but it gradually came to be an understood thing among the indoor and outdoor servants and the earl's tenants that Mr Foster was to be obeyed. Mr Hoare, the agent, who managed through twisted loyalty to take the want of a direct heir as an insult to himself, was the only person that disliked Mr Foster, and it had been a great relief to the future earl when Roddy Wicklow with his good sense and imperturbable good humour came into the office.

One reason for Lord Pomfret's wish to have his cousin oftener at the Towers was the bad health of old Major Foster, who might be expected to die at any time. So far he had not come up to his lordship's hopes, but the news of him was steadily worse, which gave Lord Pomfret a satisfaction that he was at no pains to hide. Mr Foster had no particular affection for his father, but he was not anxious for his death, which would put him in a position that might force him to give up his interesting and pleasant life in London. So old Major Foster continued to be on the point of death, and young Mr Foster learned all he could about the Pomfret lands and affairs.

Presently he pulled the green cord that made the map roll

up again and decided to stroll out towards the kennels, where he knew Miss Wicklow and the diplomat had gone. As he went down the beech avenue he saw Lady Pomfret and Alice walking with her ladyship's King Charles spaniels. His aunt had mentioned in the course of their conversation that morning that she liked Susan Barton's girl very much and hoped she would enjoy herself, adding it was a pity she was so shy. Mr Foster, who had also felt sympathetically sorry for Alice from the first moment of speaking to her, had suggested to his aunt that she should take Alice for a walk. His aunt had looked at him with the peculiar expression that he had by now come to recognise as a weighing of girls as possible future countesses, and sent Miss Merriman to ask Alice to accompany her. Mr Foster was pleased at his success and thought, in which he was probably right, that a little consideration would help Miss Barton to get over her shyness. He flushed with annoyance when he remembered how helpless she had been under the inattention of the servants, and determined to keep an eye on her while he was there. That he had shown considerable courage in attacking Finch and Peters on her behalf did not occur to him, for he considered it his duty, as representing their host, to look after the comfort of all guests, and had trained himself to overcome his own natural diffidences where the running of the house and estate were concerned. His uncle's natural gift of command he could never hope to possess, just as he would never acquire his entire indifference to other people's opinion, but he watched and tried to emulate his power of making quick decisions and his confidence in his own judgment.

Presently Sally Wicklow and the diplomat came along the road, turned in at the gate, and met Mr Foster. Mr Foster asked the diplomat what he thought of the kennels and listened with polite interest to all he had to say, Sally occasionally putting in a very sensible word. When they got near the house the diplomat went in, while Sally and Mr Foster took another turn in the Italian garden. In the distance they could see the Countess and Alice returning from their stroll.

'Oh, there is Alice,' said Sally. 'I *am* glad to see her. I couldn't find her anywhere this morning and I feel rather responsible for her. She hasn't been about much, you know, and she is frightfully shy.'

'I think she will be quite happy with my aunt,' said Mr Foster. 'Lady Pomfret likes Alice very much.'

'So do I,' said Sally. 'Do you?' she added, rather threateningly.

'Yes I do,' said Mr Foster. 'It is quite comforting to meet someone who is just as frightened of people as I am.'

Sally stopped and looked at him.

'You do put your ears back a bit,' she said, 'but don't worry, you'll go straight at the fences all right.'

'Thank you very much,' said Mr Foster.

'And if anything worries you, let me know and I'll give you a lead,' said Sally.

Mr Foster thanked her again.

'And I'll tell you what,' said Sally, 'we'll both keep an eye on Alice. Phoebe has been very decent to her, but she's the sort that always gets left out unless someone pulls her in, so let's see that she has a good time here.'

'I would like very much to do that with you,' said Mr Foster.

By this time Lady Pomfret and Alice had come up. Sally, even as she greeted her hostess, cast an appraising eye over the spaniels.

'Do you like dogs?' asked Lady Pomfret politely.

Sally, heroically concealing her feelings about people who talked about liking dogs – one might as well inquire whether one liked people – modestly said that she didn't know much about King Charleses, but she thought the small bitch looked a bit queer. Lady Pomfret said poor Giulia hadn't been very happy for the last few days.

'You see, I am away for months at a time,' she said, 'and I can't take the dogs with me because of quarantine coming back. One of the keepers looks after them very nicely, but I don't think he understands Giulia.'

Hearing her name spoken in a melancholy way, Giulia was immediately overcome with self-pity and lay down on her back, feebly waving her paws. Sally at once went down on her knees and after looking at Giulia gave her a kindly slap which put that hypochondriac on her feet again.

'Wrong feeding,' she said.

'Oh, is that all?' said Lady Pomfret, moving towards the Towers.

'Good Lord, it's everything,' said Sally, accommodating her manly stride to her hostess's stately tread. 'Look here, Lady Pomfret, who feeds your dogs?'

'I do,' said her ladyship, 'and my maid, and they get something in the servants' hall, I believe, but of course they are never allowed in the kitchen. Isn't that enough?'

'Of course if you *want* those dogs to pass out, Lady Pomfret,' said Sally earnestly, 'that's the way to do it. Two meals a day and not too much at either is what they need.'

'I don't quite see how I could manage that,' said her ladyship helplessly.

'Well, I don't mean to interfere of course,' said Sally, properly diffident where a question of someone else's animals was involved, 'but if you'd like me to write out what they ought to have and tell your maid exactly when to feed them, you'll have them as fit as anything in a week.'

'That would be very kind of you,' said Lady Pomfret with evident relief. 'I'm afraid my maid is very stupid, but she can just speak English.'

'That sounds pretty dumb,' said Sally.

'I don't mean that she has any impediment in her speech,' said Lady Pomfret, 'but she is Italian.'

'That's all right,' said Sally. 'I did a bit of Dante once, and anyway "dog-biscuit" must be much the same in Italian. I mean all foreigners use our sporting words. Look at the French.'

5

Trials of an Artist

More than half the party were either shooting or lunching with the guns, so lunch was in the small dining-room at a round table. Alice was between Professor Milward and the archdeacon and would willingly have changed places with the lowest scullery maid. It turned out however that the archdeacon knew her father, who had modernised the interior of the Rectory at Plumstead Episcopi, while Professor Milward, being used to young women at Oxford and much preferring them uneducated, talked to Alice very amusingly about nothing, till her spirits rose and she was able to say no thank you to the wine, which on the previous evening she had been afraid to refuse, though she didn't drink it. Sally, deep in dogs with Lady Pomfret and the diplomat, cast an approving glance at her friend from time to time.

Mr Johns, who found himself next to Mrs Rivers, apologised profoundly for not having been able to find her before lunch. He said, quite untruthfully, that he had heard she had gone out, so he had looked for her in the grounds but in vain. Mrs Rivers, mollified by this attention, said she had been Working.

'But I couldn't Concentrate,' she said. 'I was worried about Julian. I think Cousin Giles is a little unfair to him. I found the poor boy really annoyed. He was doing a really remarkable interior of the hall from the staircase, when Cousin Giles turned him off it. The poor boy was too much upset to talk it over with me. As soon as I came into his room he slammed all his things together and rushed out. So I went back to My Work – I have to, you know,' she added with a gay smile.

Mr Johns, who knew quite well that she hadn't to in the least, except in so far as her earnings made a pleasant addition to the ample allowance that her husband gave her, and that the children had two hundred a year each, expressed sympathy, and said he was sure Julian would be quite happy when he was back in London.

'Ah, but that won't be just yet,' said Mrs Rivers. 'I had such a good offer for my house for the winter that it would have been positively wicked not to take it. Then as soon as I have finished my New Book, I shall perhaps go abroad. I always need a rest after I have finished A Book. You publishers are such brutal taskmasters.'

Mr Johns, who far from being a taskmaster had the greatest difficulty in persuading Mrs Rivers that one book a year was quite enough, made a deprecating noise and asked where Mrs Rivers would be till she went abroad.

'Oh, here, of course,' said Mrs Rivers. 'I felt Cousin Edith really needed someone with her, and Phoebe can hunt, and

Julian must make some kind of studio for himself in one of the unused rooms. It won't be a very gay winter for me, but I shall Work very hard, and as long as the children are happy, that is all that matters. I suppose Julian and Phoebe are having lunch with the guns.'

'Mr Julian has taken his artistic things to the North Attic, madam,' said the voice of the omnipresent and omniscient Peters respectfully at her back. 'He said he did not desire lunch. Miss Phoebe and Mr Guy Barton have taken sandwiches and walked over to Pomfret Madrigal to see the houses Mr Guy Barton's firm is reconditioning, madam.'

'But Mr Julian *must* have lunch,' said Mrs Rivers, her thoughts leaping, as usual, to her son.

'I mentioned to Mr Julian that luncheon was a desideratum, madam,' said Peters, 'but he said no. He hadn't finished his breakfast not till near eleven,' Peters added, tempering the blow.

'I don't know why Phoebe should want to go to Pomfret Madrigal,' said Mrs Rivers. 'What's that young Barton like?'

'Guy Barton?' said the archdeacon who was opposite her, interrupting his own conversation with Lady Pomfret. 'A very capable young man. He was in charge of the work at the Rectory and carried it out admirably. If you want to do up an old house, Mrs Rivers, you won't find anyone better than Guy's father, and this young lady's father,' he added paternally to Alice, 'in the county. But as I was saying, Lady Pomfret,' he continued, addressing himself again to his hostess, 'it seems to me that there is no one who writes now as Scott, or Dickens, or Thackeray used to write.'

The archdeacon, as always when he wished to make a

point, used his pulpit voice to make this remark, with the result that all conversation was momentarily held up. The archdeacon's statement was so incontrovertible that no one spoke.

'You, Mr Johns,' continued the archdeacon, 'who move in the literary world, would you support me in this?'

'You are perfectly right, archdeacon, perfectly right,' said Mr Johns, trying to look sad.

'I was reading a book the other day,' said the archdeacon, 'a book which had, I gather, been chosen to represent the best of current literature for the year, or the month, it is immaterial. It was by an author whose name escapes me. The action took place in Buenos Aires with which I myself am intimately acquainted, having been English chaplain there for two years before I came to Barchester. Not only were the scraps of Spanish in the dialogue far from accurate, but the subject was the illicit passion of a middle-aged woman, an English woman, for a young Spanish landowner.'

A frightful sense of storm hung in the room. Lady Pomfret said she must show the archdeacon her mother-in-law's water-colour drawings of the Alhambra.

'And, although the passion was not consummated,' said the archdeacon, bent on saying his say, 'the moral effect was the same. I sent the book back to the library. I was ashamed that an Englishwoman should have so written.'

The awful use of the word consummated struck the whole company dumb. Mrs Rivers flushed angrily and Mr Johns looked at her with apprehension. Never, in all his tactful career, had he been so entirely at a loss for the helpful thing to say. Professor Milward and Miss Merriman caught each other's eye and had to cough. Sally was the first to recover her wits.

'Well, if she didn't come a cropper, it was all right,' she said. 'I mean no real woman would go on like that and anyway when one's about fifty no one's going to look at one, so whoever it was that wrote it must have made it all up, and I call it jolly clever to think of things, but if I was going in off the deep end I wouldn't pick on a Spaniard!'

At this innocent implication that no one could possibly fall in love with her, Mrs Rivers's atmosphere became more electrical than ever. Mr Johns drank all his whisky at a gulp.

Mr Foster now rallied the conversation by asking the archdeacon, in a perilously shaky voice, whether Dickens had not perhaps gone a little far in the affair of Edith Dombey and Mr Carker. Thackeray, he said, had also allowed Lady Clara Newcome to elope to a life of sin with Lord Highgate, while as for Scott, it was common knowledge that the real tragedy of St Ronan's Well, until the author was dissuaded by Ballantyne, was to have been that Clara Mowbray's marriage with the false Francis Tyrrel had actually been— but the archdeacon, who did not approve of such words in lay mouths, interrupted him and took up the cudgels in defence of the elder novelists with such vigour that the whole party were drawn into the argument. It was generally considered that the archdeacon had the best of it, for to his statement that the books of Scott, Dickens and Thackeray would never be repeated, there appeared to be no answer. A few dissentient voices were drowned in the slight tumult of rising from table, and the party broke up.

Mr Johns with great cunning attached himself to Lady Pomfret, reminding her that she had promised to show him a rare three-volume novel by her mother-in-law, called *A Step Too Far,* which had shocked Mr Gladstone, and was taken away by her to her sitting-room.

The rest of the party had coffee in the hall, and Mrs Rivers was able to tackle the archdeacon about affairs with Spaniards. If, she said, he had lived in Buenos Aires he must have noticed, as she did when she was there, that fair English women were particularly attractive to men of Spanish blood, and if a woman was no longer loved or understood by her husband, she could hardly be blamed for listening to a man who knew, as the cold English hardly knew, what real love meant.

On any other occasion the archdeacon, who stood no nonsense about broadmindedness, would have told her in no uncertain terms what he felt about listening to foreigners, but on hearing that she had lived in Buenos Aires he could hardly wait till she had finished speaking to inquire whether she knew some of his many friends in that city. Mrs Rivers, though she was apt to imply that she had lived dangerously and languorously in Buenos Aires for at least a year, had as a matter of fact been there for three days and had only met the heads of the railway in which her husband had an interest, so she had not known the Ernest Smiths.

'I wish you had,' said the archdeacon. 'He is a delightful man and his wife is very intellectual. I can't think how you missed them. They are quite the centre of social life. But I suppose you knew the Juan Robinsons?'

'What would you say, archdeacon,' said Mrs Rivers, refusing to hear of the Juan Robinsons, 'if I said that I was the author of the book you condemn?'

'Speaking frankly, I should think it in doubtful taste,' said the archdeacon, thus leaving Mrs Rivers, and Professor Milward who had been listening to their conversation, to determine whether the book itself or the possibility of Mrs Rivers's having jokingly called herself the author was what he deprecated.

Baffled by the archdeacon, Mrs Rivers turned to Professor Milward, who at once said that he had read and admired all her books. This was very untruthful of Professor Milward, but he had a gambler's nature and staked his all on Mrs Rivers being so ready to talk about herself that he would have no difficulty in carrying off his ignorance. In this imposture he was perfectly successful, so much so that Mrs Rivers, telling him how devoted her American public were to her, did not notice her son come moodily into the hall and approach Alice Barton.

Alice, who had in the diverse emotions of the morning quite forgotten Julian Rivers, was happily drinking her coffee and listening to Sally telling the archdeacon that it was time something was done about the wiring on the Plumstead side, when she became conscious of two very untidy grey flannel legs standing between her and the world. Looking upwards she saw a bright blue pullover, a green flannel shirt, and above all a dark face with deep-set eyes, which caused her to remember with a jerk that she was in love.

'Did you hear what happened to me this morning?' said

Julian, who inherited his mother's total want of inhibition in talking about himself.

'Do you mean about your painting the staircase?' Alice asked.

'I wish I *had* painted the staircase,' said Julian with suppressed fury. 'I wish I'd put three coats of rose madder all over that frightful Victorian excrescence. I just had an idea of an emotional value that could only be expressed by the line of the stairs, and then Cousin Giles had to turn me off. God! Why do I submit?'

Alice could see no reason why so godlike a being should submit, but feared that if she said so it might be the wrong thing, so she said nothing.

'If Bolikoff had been here, do you know what he would have done?' said Julian. 'He would have taken no notice at all. He painted all through the revolution. He despises everything that comes between him and his art. If I were Bolikoff I would still be sitting on that staircase. Shall I tell you why I am not?'

He paused to throw back his hair.

'Could you sit down, please,' said Alice. 'You are so tall that it makes my neck ache.'

'Oh, I could sit down,' said Julian with a bitter laugh, and folding his legs up with disconcerting suddenness, he collapsed onto a large cushion at Alice's feet. 'You prefer to look down on me, of course. Everyone does. It is all my mother's fault. She sent me to a co-ed school. What was the result?'

He stopped for a moment, stretched out his legs, extracted a battered cardboard box from his trousers pocket and lit a cigarette. Alice, who was discovering that his habit of asking questions didn't at all mean that he expected or wanted an answer, looked with respectful love at his raven locks and wondered if ever he combed them.

'You don't want a cigarette, do you?' said Julian, who had put his cardboard box back into his pocket and folded up his legs. 'Girls!' he exclaimed. 'Like loathsome slugs all over the place. If you had been brought up with them, great hideous things playing hockey, and all pally with the boys, you'd never want to see one again. I shall never have any sex life and I hope Mother will be pleased. After all, what is sex?'

Alice, though thrilled by the very modern turn the conversation was taking, and deeply sorry for Julian, felt that this was a question she could not answer, so she continued to say nothing. Suddenly Julian sprang up like a scissors man, seized Alice by the wrist and pulled her to her feet.

'God! I could do you now!' he said. 'Come up to the North Attic. I've put my painting things there. I'll start on you right away. Come along, the daylight won't last much longer.'

Half flattered, half terrified, Alice followed him across the hall and up the great staircase. Mrs Rivers looked, saw her son disappearing in company with that little Alice Barton, and called his name loudly. Alice, unwilling to offend Mrs Rivers, would have stopped, but Julian, saying he was sick of interference, urged Alice on, across the landing, along the corridor, up another staircase, along another corridor, through a door, up a wooden staircase and into the North Attic.

This room, which had once been the day nursery of Lord

Pomfret and his sisters, was now a kind of lumber room. It had never occurred to Lord Pomfret's father, or to his architect, that a room at the top of the house, facing north, only accessible by a narrow wooden staircase, was in any way unsuitable for a nursery. As a tribute to modern science a fire escape had been installed near the window, consisting of a complicated apparatus of rope and canvas on an iron framework. In case of fire this was supposed to be thrown out of the window, and the inmates of the nursery to slide down a kind of canvas chute to safety, but no one had the faintest idea how it worked. Lord Pomfret's father had once suggested that a rehearsal should be held. Nurse had shown unequivocal signs of disapproval, saying, and doubtless with reason, that the children would catch their deaths of cold going down that thing. Two of the under gardeners, who lived half a mile from the house and would therefore not have been available till everyone was burned to death, had been sent into the nursery to undo the machine. Terrified of Nurse's silent scorn and hate on the one hand, and their master's displeasure on the other, they had bungled the job. Finch, father of the present odd man, had with the courage of despair got into the chute, while Wheeler, whose niece was now second housemaid, stood at the bottom to hold it, and all the housemaids looked out of the bedroom windows. Finch, losing what little presence of mind he had left, forgot to brake himself with his knees and elbows and arrived at lightning speed into Wheeler's chest, knocking him senseless and spraining his own ankle. Nurse, who had surveyed the scene with grim satisfaction, said what had she told his lordship, adding darkly that it wasn't decent. The sixth earl had slunk out of the room. The escape was rolled up and replaced later in the day by the estate carpenter and his mate, and had never again been used. Luckily a fire never did break out, and young Lord Mellings, for such was the title of the eldest son, and his sisters Lady Agnes and Lady Emily, invented a delightfully frightening story that God lived in it, and when the hymn 'God moves in a mysterious way' was sung in church, they knew that it had something to do with the fire escape.

It is improbable that the present Lord Pomfret had ever been in the old nursery since he was a young man, but if he had found his way there he might have recognised the same wallpaper that it had been his pleasure to rub off with a wet finger when Nurse wasn't looking, and the furrows in the linoleum carved by himself with his first pocket-knife, which was at once confiscated by Nurse. Boxes were stacked along one wall. An old dress stand with an hourglass figure, some disused washstands, the ten flat baths in a pile and six of the hip baths that had been ejected from the Pink Room, a nursery screen made of illustrations from newspapers and catalogues, filled a good deal of space. But the part of the room near the window was clear and here Julian had set up his easel.

'Where shall I sit?' asked Alice, seeing no chair.

'Anywhere. It doesn't matter,' said Julian, who was arranging his paints with his back to her.

'Could we get a chair from somewhere?' said Alice.

'I don't need a chair,' said Julian.

'But I mean,' said Alice, 'don't you want me to sit for you?'

Julian cast a look over his shoulder.

'There's a box or something over there,' he said.

Alice looked at the something. It was a large flat dress basket, probably packed with curtains or hangings, and far too heavy for her to move.

'What do you want to move it for?' said Julian, hearing a scuffle.

'To sit on,' said Alice, feeling hopelessly in the wrong as usual.

Julian straightened himself up and faced her, palette in one hand, a tube of paint in the other, a brush in his mouth.

'I don't want to *look* at you,' said Julian, his articulation slightly impeded by the brush. 'I've seen all I want of you. But it's a good thing to have you about while I paint. It keeps the emotional value.'

He turned round and busied himself again with his paints. Alice sat down on the dress basket. The room was cold, the surface of the basket was very nobbly, but Alice minded nothing in the cause of Julian's art.

'I shall scrape out that thing I'd begun this morning when Cousin Giles had to interfere,' said Julian, turning over some canvases. 'God!' he added, holding one up, 'this is good.'

Alice came over to look. It looked marvellous to her and she said so, not quite daring to ask what it was about.

'Marvellous! Bolikoff used to spit when he heard that word,' said Julian contemptuously, but to Alice's relief not imitating his idol. 'But a damn good piece of painting. It has value.'

He held it various ways up, looking at it lovingly.

'I'll show you the lot,' he said generously. 'It'll give you an idea of what the Set of Five are after.'

Alice would have liked to inquire what the Set of Five was, but felt it better not to, so she stood in deep if bewildered admiration while Julian showed her canvas after canvas, expatiating at great length upon their value, rhythm and tonality, and the room grew colder and the light faded, and tea seemed very far away.

Presently the party downstairs broke up. Lady Pomfret and her chosen guests went off to Rising Castle. The diplomat went to sleep. Sally said she was going to talk to Peters about Lady Pomfret's dogs. Mr Foster said he had once been to a bull-fight in Spain, which he was ashamed to say he had enjoyed, and to see Sally tackling Peters in his pantry would be the next best thing, so he went with her. Mrs Rivers, in spite of being a famous authoress, was then left alone till Miss Merriman, who always found time to do everything that ought to be done, asked her if she would come for a little walk and exercise the dogs. This invitation Mrs Rivers was not sorry to accept, for Miss Merriman, with infinite tact and discretion, ruled the whole household and held the fate of the guests in the hollow of her hand, and she thought that by a few judicious hints to her she might have things arranged a little more to her own liking.

Giulia and her friends were collected and the two ladies set off across the park. Mrs Rivers first inquired after Miss Merriman's invalid sister and was glad to hear that she was no worse. Miss Merriman and her family were a mystery which all Lady Pomfret's friends longed to penetrate, but Miss

Merriman by her unfailing good humour, and a faculty of saying things that meant nothing at all, had kept them entirely in the dark. Not that she had anything to conceal, for her family was eminently respectable, but at the outset of her career as the perfect secretary-companion she had decided to have no private life at all, as far as her employer's friends were concerned. The most that Lady Pomfret or any of her friends knew was that Merry had an invalid sister with whom she spent her holidays. Lady Pomfret, who was entirely incurious, had never wished to know more, but everyone who came to her house had been attracted and puzzled by Miss Merriman's sphinx-like attitude, and most of them had tried at one time or another to find out something about her past, her likes and dislikes, her private feelings, and no one had had the faintest success. The only person who knew her Christian name was Lady Pomfret, who wrote it on cheques. Without her Lady Pomfret was helpless. By some secret magic she had made all the servants respect her as if she were their lawful mistress, and without her infinitely tactful collaboration with Peters and the housekeeper, Pomfret Towers would never have been run. And above all, although she was responsible for so much at the Towers, she never annoyed Lord Pomfret.

Mrs Rivers said they might go in the direction of Pomfret Madrigal and perhaps they would meet Phoebe and Guy Barton. Miss Merriman said that would be quite a good idea, so they took the path across the fields. Mrs Rivers said she had not met any Bartons before at the Towers and did Merry know anything about them. Miss Merriman said she had heard that Mr Barton was a very good architect and she understood that Mr Guy Barton was in his father's firm.

'They aren't county people then,' said Mrs Rivers. 'What is Mrs Barton like?'

'I have never met her,' said Miss Merriman, 'but I believe she is very nice. I expect you have read some of her books. I hardly ever have time for reading, but I believe they are very interesting.'

'Oh, *that* Mrs Barton?' said Mrs Rivers. 'I didn't know she lived down here. Her books are terribly highbrow, aren't they?'

Miss Merriman said she didn't know.

'I only pretend to amuse people,' said Mrs Rivers, but as Miss Merriman did not make the proper response, which was that she did far more, Mrs Rivers left the subject for the moment.

'It's a pity the girl – Alice – is so insignificant,' she said. 'She is a very unpleasant mixture of schoolgirl awkwardness and schoolgirl forwardness. She really quite spoilt our games last night.'

'One moment,' said Miss Merriman, 'Giulia has got something in her hair.'

She knelt down and pulled a cluster of burrs from one of Giulia's long silky ears.

'I do think Miss Wicklow is very pushing about Cousin Edith's dogs,' Mrs Rivers continued, when Miss Merriman was ready to go on. 'Peters won't at all like it if she interferes with him.'

Miss Merriman said she believed Miss Wicklow ran the beagles.

'She is just the sort of girl who would,' said Mrs Rivers.

'Yes, I believe she does it very well,' said Miss Merriman.

'I really wanted to talk to you seriously, Merry,' said Mrs Rivers, 'about Gillie. Miss Wicklow seems to be making a dead set at him. Of course it is only to be expected when everyone knows he will be Lord Pomfret, but one does hate to see a young man so blatantly pursued. We must put our heads together and see that he gets the right wife, Merry. It would be frightful if he were caught by a pushing girl like Miss Wicklow, or an ill-bred little thing like Alice Barton. You and I would never feel at home in this house again.'

'But it isn't my home,' said Miss Merriman in a matter of fact way. 'I think we ought to turn back now. Lady Pomfret likes the dogs to be in by four. Miss Rivers and Mr Barton must have gone back the other way, by the hatches.'

More than this Mrs Rivers could not get from the imperturbable Miss Merriman, so she was forced to fall back on the interesting subject of herself and tell Miss Merriman how many signed photographs she gave away last year. If Miss Merriman had had real tact she would have asked whether Mrs Rivers could possibly spare her one, but she merely remarked that she must get one of Mrs Rivers's books from the library as soon as she had time to do some reading, and that Lady Pomfret had had Mrs Rivers's last book on the list ever since it came out but hadn't got it yet. Whether Miss Merriman knew how annoying this was to Mrs Rivers, who would have liked the libraries to buy enough copies for all their subscribers, we are not in a position to say.

Near the Towers they met Lord Pomfret and Roddy Wicklow on their horses, accompanied by Phoebe and Guy on foot. When Phoebe had asked Guy to walk with her, she only wanted an excuse to get away from lunch at the Towers with her mother, or to avoid what to her was the boredom of a shooting lunch. But during their walk she had discovered that Guy's secret and passionate interest was in stage architecture and decor of every period, and had acknowledged to him, in the rather ungracious way that was her armour, that when she wanted a pretext to get away from home she chose the stage because she loved the scenery and lighting, and all the workman's side of it, and wanted to see the apron stage given a proper trial for Shakespeare; but as for acting, she had no opinion of it at all. Guy, enchanted to find a fellow enthusiast, dropped the slightly boorish manner which he saw fit to adopt towards young women, and plunged into technicalities. They then inspected the house that Guy was renovating, ate their lunch in it, talked and smoked, and came back, as Miss Merriman had guessed, by the hatches, where they fell in with Lord Pomfret and Roddy, returning from the Six Corners Covert.

Roddy had risen immensely in his employer's estimation during their ride, both by his real interest in the estate, and the knowledge he had already acquired of land and people, so his lordship was in a less saturnine mood than usual and there was a good deal of laughter between the young people. Phoebe was the first to see Miss Merriman, dragged rather too fast by Giulia who wanted to get home, and her glad shout of 'Hullo, Merry' was taken up, though in the more respectful form of Miss Merriman, by the others. She then caught sight of her mother, who was a little way behind, remarked 'Oh Lord! Mother!' and became her usual bored supercilious self. Guy hung back. Lord Pomfret said 'Had a good walk, Hermione? Better than Rising Castle, eh?' and trotted away to the stables, followed by Roddy, with whom he wanted to inspect a damp stall.

Tea was in the small dining-room where lunch had been. Two huge round tables, each with a gigantic and massive silver tea equipage, almost filled the room. The shooters had just come in and there was a tumult of voices and a bustling about to get places. Mrs Rivers made for the tea kettle at the smaller table. Miss Merriman came up.

'Shall I pour out here?' said Mrs Rivers.

'Thank you so much, Mrs Rivers,' said Miss Merriman pleasantly, 'but I think Lady Pomfret wants the archdeacon's daughter to do this table.'

'Oh, I'll do the big table then,' said Mrs Rivers.

'Thank you so much, but please don't trouble,' said Miss Merriman. 'I think Lady Pomfret wants me to pour out, so will you sit by Mr Foster?'

Mrs Rivers almost shrugged her shoulders, but seeing that the diplomat was on the other side of the seat assigned to her, she took her place quite resignedly.

'Where is Julian?' she asked.

No one took any notice, so she called across the table, 'Merry, where is Julian?'

For once Miss Merriman was at a loss. Mr Foster said in his gentle voice, 'I expect he is in the North Attic. He was going to take his paints there.'

'I saw him go upstairs after lunch,' said the diplomat, 'with Miss Barton.'

Mr Foster frowned slightly.

'I think I had better go and look,' he said. 'Julian forgets all about the time and the North Attic is very cold.'

'I say, Foster,' said Roddy Wicklow, arriving from the stables, 'you haven't seen Alice anywhere, have you? I haven't seen her today and I want to see if she is getting on all right.'

'I think she is in the North Attic with Julian,' said Mr Foster, going towards the door.

'I say, that room is like an icehouse,' said Roddy. 'I was up there yesterday looking for some old maps, and meant to tell you we ought to have fires there to air it.'

Mrs Rivers, already annoyed that her daughter had spent most of the day with a local architect, and that her son, after refusing lunch, had spent most of the afternoon with the local architect's dull little sister, was even more annoyed that Mr Foster, who was sitting next to her, and Mr Wicklow, who was at any rate the probable future estate agent, should find it necessary to go and look for that little Miss Barton. She spoke loudly to Mr Foster to that effect, but Mr Foster, accompanied by Roddy, was already leaving the room, followed by a shout from Sally to bring Alice down at once and pull Julian's hair, which pleasantry brought on her a dry look from Mrs Rivers, of which Sally took no notice at all.

As Mr Foster and Roddy went upstairs they exchanged a few words about Six Corners Covert. Mr Foster said he was so glad to have Sally's advice about the earths, because he knew nothing about them himself.

'You won't go wrong if you take Sally's tips,' said Roddy, gratified by the praise of his sister. 'She really knows the country and the farmers much better than I do, because I was away at school and Cambridge, and then an agricultural course. She would make a much better land agent than I would. I say, Foster, young Rivers can't have much sense.

Alice isn't frightfully strong, I mean she was a delicate kid and all that, and he oughtn't to take her to that attic, without a fire.'

'I don't suppose there's a light either,' said Mr Foster grimly. 'When my uncle had the house wired for electric light he didn't have the top storey done. He said the servants would only use it if he did, and set the house on fire. So they still go on carrying oil lamps and candles about among all this woodwork. Here we are.'

They had now reached the top of the wooden staircase.

'Rivers is alive anyway,' remarked Roddy, as the sound of Julian's voice came booming down the passage. He opened the North Attic door. So little light came from the window that at first the two young men could not see Alice at all.

'Are you there, Miss Barton?' said Mr Foster.

'Hullo, what's up?' said Julian.

'Nothing,' said Roddy, 'except that tea is ready and it's much too cold up here for Alice.'

'I'm not really cold,' said Alice, from the dark corner where she was sitting on her dress basket.

'But you are,' said Mr Foster with some concern, as he took her hand and helped her to get up. 'Your hands are icy. Come down at once. What have you been doing?'

'Of course if you call it cold!' said Julian scornfully. 'I suppose Mother sent you to find me.'

'No,' said Mr Foster mildly. 'We came to find Miss Barton, not you.' Alice sneezed and Mr Foster led her out of the room.

'All right,' said Roddy. 'If you catch cold, Alice, I shall know why.'

'What do you mean?' asked Julian truculently.

'I mean,' said Roddy, turning round and putting his large chest almost up against Julian's, 'that if Alice is ill again, after sitting up there in the cold listening to you gassing, I'll knock your head off.'

The defiant scowl with which Julian treated this announcement was, owing to the gathering darkness, entirely lost on Roddy, who turned his back on the artist and went downstairs. When they reached the dining-room Mr Foster made Alice sit at the smaller table, near the fire, and asked the archdeacon's daughter to give her some tea at once to warm her.

'What has she been doing to get cold?' asked the archdeacon's daughter.

'I went to the North Attic to see Mr Rivers's pictures,' said Alice, anxious to shield her hero, 'and it got rather dark.'

'If that isn't Julian all over,' said the archdeacon's daughter, annoyed that a mere artist should treat so lightly a girl who knew that they had changed the sluices at Starveacres Hatches. 'Selfish as six cats, he is. All artists are. He tried to show me his pictures once, when I was in London, and he asked me to come to his studio. I took one look at his pictures and I said, "Come and have a drink at my club and get it out of your system."'

'Did he?' asked Alice.

'I'll say he did,' said the archdeacon's daughter. 'Three of them he put down, and never a word of thanks. I'll tell you what, Gillie, you ought to put some whisky in Miss Barton's tea. Nothing like whisky to keep off chills, when you're hunting, or any other time.'

Mr Foster thought the idea good. He rang for Peters and asked for whisky which was brought at once. Alice, to whom alcohol was a terrifying and almost unknown experience, begged not to have it, but Mr Foster, reinforced by Sally and Roddy, who had finished their tea and come to look, insisted. Phoebe then came over to their table, followed by Guy, and everyone gave good advice at once, while Alice sipped and choked, and felt a comfortable glow inside her.

'What *is* all that noise?' said Mrs Rivers to Miss Merriman.

Miss Merriman, who observed everything, said it was the archdeacon's daughter giving Miss Barton some whisky in her tea in case she had caught cold in the North Attic.

'Of course if she would keep Julian up there,' said Mrs Rivers. 'Julian, hadn't you better have some whisky, dear? I don't want you to have a chill. Why didn't you come down sooner?'

At this her son put his cup of tea down with a crash, picked up a large piece of cake and left the room.

Alice's supporters now urged her to go and lie down before dinner, and though she did not at all want to be alone, such is the power of mass suggestion that she began to feel rather tired and languid and said perhaps she had better. Accordingly Phoebe volunteered to see her safely bestowed and the two girls left the room, accompanied by sympathetic murmurs from the archdeacon's daughter, the Wicklows, and Mr Foster.

In the hall Julian was playing the piano very loudly to relieve his feelings. Alice felt he was in disgrace on her account and could not bear it. Breaking from Phoebe, she ran over to the piano and said, 'Mr Rivers.'

'Well,' said Julian, crashing more wildly than ever.

'I didn't really get cold at all,' said Alice.

'Of course you didn't,' said the pianist. 'We'll have another go at the portrait, but I'll do it in your studio. Too much blasted interference here.'

Just then the inner door of the hall was opened. Lady Pomfret with her three guests had returned from Rising Castle. Miss Merriman, who always materialised miraculously when her employer needed her, came out of the small dining-room.

'I think you had better play the piano later,' she said softly as she passed Julian. 'Lord Pomfret doesn't like this piano used before dinner.'

'Merry,' said Lady Pomfret, trailing silver foxes as she came, 'what is that dreadful noise? I thought the piano-tuner had been last week. We had a delightful time with Lord Stoke,' and she passed on, accompanied by Miss Merriman, to her own rooms.

Lord Pomfret appeared at the door of the library, where he was having his tea-time whisky and soda.

'Come here, Johns,' he said, taking no notice of the archdeacon or Professor Milward. 'I want to talk to you. And stop that damned noise, whoever it is at the piano. I will *not* have that piano played before dinner.'

Luckily for him the noise that Julian made in slamming the piano lid was drowned by the noise that Lord Pomfret made in slamming the library door. With a white face Julian turned upon his sister and Alice.

'All right,' he said, 'all *right*. Thanks, Alice, you're the only decent one in the house.'

He leapt up on a window seat, opened the casement window and jumped out.

'It's a pity his parents didn't let him go to a University,' said Professor Milward, carefully shutting the window after him. 'They get rid of those tiresome moods so much faster. Now, archdeacon, I'd like to show you some notes I made this morning on Eustace Pomfret, the founder of the Italian cadet branch. They may interest you.'

The professor and the archdeacon passed on into the green drawing-room, in deep converse.

'He'll get cold,' said Alice, on whom Julian's dying words had made an indelible impression.

'Not he,' said Phoebe wearily. 'He's showing off. It's only a four-foot drop onto the grass. He'll come in by another way. Come along, Alice.'

With great kindness Phoebe saw Alice comfortably installed, advising her to put on her dressing-gown and lie in the chaise longue, which she pushed nearer to the fire. This seemed to Alice an almost sinful kind of luxury, but being really a little tired, and a little sleepy after the whisky, she obediently followed Phoebe's advice. Phoebe promised to wake her when she came up to dress, and left her alone in the firelit room. The thought of a white-faced, haggard Julian, possibly lying with a broken leg, in the cold wet night, calling on her name, gave Alice a tremor of love. He had also said she was the only decent one in the house. On this thought she brooded drowsily, watching the light from the fire as it flickered on walls and ceiling.

6

Miss Merriman Intervenes

When the company assembled for dinner, Alice, well rested and really looking quite her best in the red dress, with a very little rouge and lipstick artfully applied by Phoebe, came into the green drawing-room with much more confidence than she had felt on the previous night. Mr Johns had been very nice to her in the morning. Lady Pomfret had been very nice to her when they went for a walk. Julian had given her a wonderful and interesting afternoon in the North Attic, which was not really at all cold. Tea had been even exciting, with whisky in her teacup and everyone fussing. And then Julian, after telling her that she was decent, had practically committed suicide for her sake, and what more could a heroine want.

Roddy Wicklow, talking horses with some of the hunting people, smiled at her across the room and she went over to his group. Here she was received with flattering appreciation by the man with the brick red face and her other sporting friends of the night before.

'By Jove! you put us all in our places last night about those hatches, Miss Er,' said the man with the brick red face.

A generous chorus of Rather, and I should say she did, rose from the party.

The archdeacon's daughter inquired if she felt quite rested. The girl with the scream said she and Peter and Micky had been having a bet about the chances for Monday, and Miss Barton was to decide.

All Alice's confidence fled. She had meant to ask Sally or Phoebe what Monday's chances were, and she had forgotten, and now nemesis had come on her. In her nervousness she dropped her bag. Roddy stooped to pick it up and as he gave it to her said 'Say a bit sticky but not so bad.'

'A bit sticky, but not so bad,' said Alice with a slight stammer.

The girl screamed wildly and hit Peter (or Micky), calling him a Beast.

'I said it would be hard,' she exclaimed, 'and now I've got to give them sixpence each. What a sell!'

The man with the brick red face said if it was hard he wouldn't take his hunters out again for anyone. Everyone began talking horses again and Alice's brief celebrity was over. As she modestly went in behind the other women Roddy caught her up and said she looked very nice.

'It's really Phoebe,' said Alice anxious to give credit to her friend. 'She put some make-up on me. Do you like it?'

'It's awfully nice. Very nice indeed,' said Roddy. 'But I wouldn't do it in the daytime,' he added seriously.

'Oh no, not in the daytime,' said Alice, suddenly realising

what abysms of bad taste had been waiting to engulf her if Roddy hadn't given her a warning.

Peters, by whom the fact that Mr Foster had specially mentioned Miss Barton's shoes had not passed unobserved, marshalled her himself to her seat, which was between Lord Pomfret and Mr Johns. As the guests had not gone in in couples, there was the usual slight difficulty about setting to partners. Mrs Rivers, half-way down the table, had annexed Professor Milward, when the man on her other side had already begun talking to her. The mistake rapidly spread, and Alice found that both her gentlemen had their heads turned to their other partner. Being of a meek disposition she did not feel slighted, and did her best to look as if she preferred not talking. But Lord Pomfret, who noticed a great deal, had no intention of allowing the amenities of his table to be upset.

'Here, that's all wrong,' he said in a voice that stopped all conversation at his end of the table. 'Half of you talking to the wrong people. Hermione! *Hermione!* You talk to Mr Cloves, and let Milward talk to Miss Faraday-Home. That's better.'

Mr Cloves, who was only a shooting man and of no interest, blushed horribly at this sudden notoriety and Mrs Rivers could hardly get a word out of him. However, Professor Milward and Miss Faraday-Home, which turned out to be the name of the screaming girl, fell into a conversation about films which lasted through four courses, and Lord Pomfret turned to Alice.

'You should never let that sort of thing happen,' he said. 'It ruins any dinner. How did you get on with Lady Pomfret?'

Alice said it had been very nice.

'She likes you, you know,' said Lord Pomfret. 'Says your eyes remind her of your mother. You want to eat plenty, you know. You look skinny. Not like your mother.'

'I could never look like Mother,' said Alice.

'She was a very handsome woman when we first knew her,' said the earl. 'My boy was devoted to her. A long time ago. Getting on all right, eh?'

Alice said it was all very nice indeed and Julian – she said the name hesitatingly, thinking that the earl might say My cousin, and Mr Rivers to you, commoner! – had shown her all his pictures.

'That's all right,' said Lord Pomfret. 'Now you've seen them you needn't look at them again. You paint a bit yourself, don't you? My mother used to paint. Ask Lady Pomfret to show you the water-colours she did of the Alhambra. I like to see a woman paint. Not men though – unless they're artists. My father used to have Watts and Leighton and all of them to dinner. Gentlemanly fellow, Leighton. No one paints like that now. None of 'em work.'

Presently an appeal was made to Lord Pomfret by Lady Wimple, a county neighbour, on his right, and Alice was left to Mr Johns. She found him kind, but absent-minded. If she could have seen into Mr Johns's mind this would not have surprised her. That eminent publisher was still digesting the talk he had had with Lord Pomfret in the library before dinner.

Mr Johns's experience of authors was long and varied, but never had he been so entirely at a loss. He had been prepared to angle for his noble author with infinite skill and patience, to hint, to smooth away difficulties, to placate, but before he knew where he was bait, line, reel and rod had been torn out of his hand and he had the sensation of being swept down a very fast river full of rocks, with no possibility of getting advice or help from his partner.

Lord Pomfret, after slamming the library door upon Julian and his piano playing, offered Mr Johns a cigar and a whisky and soda. Mr Johns accepted the cigar, which he knew to be excellent, but refused the whisky and soda, on the grounds that he had lately had tea at Rising Castle.

'Thought all you publishers drank like fishes,' said his lordship, sitting down in front of the fire. 'You *do* publish, don't you?' he added suddenly, glaring at Mr Johns from under his bushy eyebrows. 'I mean books and so on.'

Mr Johns, who was quite accustomed to being confused by the very uneducated people who wish to write books with reporters, printers, literary agents, theatrical entrepreneurs and newspaper proprietors, said he did publish books. As Lord Pomfret would probably remember, he published the novels of Mrs Rivers, and the historical romances of Mrs Barton, as well as many other works.

'Well, if you publish Hermione's twaddle you'll publish anything. Stoopid stuff about old women falling in love with young men. When I was young it was the old men that fell in love with the pretty young girls,' said his lordship with a ribald laugh. 'What do you pay her?'

Mr Johns hesitated.

'I can always ask her if you don't like to tell me,' said Lord Pomfret.

This argument was so convincing that Mr Johns

mentioned the quite considerable sum that he had paid Mrs Rivers for her last two books.

'She told me twice that,' said his lordship, 'so I expect you are speaking the truth. Never knew a woman who could speak the truth about money. Well, you can't offer me less than you give Hermione.'

'I'm not sure if I quite understand you,' Mr Johns began.

'Come, come, you aren't as stoopid as that,' said Lord Pomfret. 'Here's my manuscript, on the table. You can give me twice what you give Hermione and get it polished up a bit by one of your writer chaps and put Hermione's nose out of joint.'

Mr Johns tried to explain to his client that it was not usual to pay a large sum for a work by an unknown author, by an author, he meant to say, who was unknown *as* an author, without having some previous idea of the contents.

'Now, now,' said Lord Pomfret, knocking the end of his cigar and speaking in the voice that he used for farmers who put up too much wire, 'that won't do. You know what it is as well as I do. You were in the library when I mentioned it to the archdeacon. Autobiography. Life of Sporting Earl and that sort of thing. *Punch* would jump at it.'

This view of an autobiography so staggered Mr Johns that he was unable to speak.

'I don't want to hustle you,' said Lord Pomfret. 'Let me know tomorrow. No, tomorrow's Sunday, that won't do. Say Monday.'

Mr Johns said he had a partner, but before he could pursue this subject Lord Pomfret interrupted him.

'I'll tell you what,' he said. 'You pay me twice what

Hermione gets and you can have all the copyright when mine has run out.'

'I don't think you quite understand the position,' said Mr Johns, his brain reeling. 'Copyright is now for a term of years.'

'They've altered all that. Saw something about it in the *Times*,' said Lord Pomfret. 'Now that's settled and we needn't talk about it again. You think it over and say yes on Monday. Help yourself to a drink.' And the earl put on his spectacles, took up the *Stock Breeders' Gazette* and became immersed in its leading article.

'I think I will,' said Mr Johns feebly, and poured himself out a stiff whisky. After he had drunk it he felt a little braver and ventured to suggest to the earl that he should be allowed to read the manuscript, or a portion of it, during the weekend, so that he could form some sort of judgment as to its quality.

'Eh?' said Lord Pomfret. 'Stoke's heifer came first at the Southbridge show again. I wish I could get his cowman.'

His lordship disappeared behind the paper. Mr Johns, cowed, and disheartened, repeated his request in a shortened form.

Lord Pomfret looked up impatiently from the *Gazette*, his angry little eyes appearing smaller and angrier than ever behind his glasses, and asked Mr Johns to say whatever it was he had to say.

'I only thought you might care to let me look at the manuscript,' said Mr Johns.

'Oh, did you?' said the earl. 'Certainly not. *I* know publishers.'

Upon which illiberal and untrue remark Lord Pomfret returned to the *Gazette* so firmly that Mr Johns realised he was only wasting his time, and crept upstairs to dress for dinner.

So it is not surprising that Alice found him distrait during the second half of dinner, so much so indeed that her kind heart was moved to pity and she asked him if he were tired. On hearing that he wasn't, she said sometimes one didn't feel very much like talking, and if he didn't want to talk she wouldn't mind a bit. Mr Johns, ashamed of himself, apologised and said he was rather worried about something, and that was why he hadn't been quite himself. Alice said she didn't suppose it was anything she could help with. Mr Johns said unfortunately it wasn't. It was a worry connected with his visit to the Towers, and he hardly knew where to turn for advice. Alice looked very sympathetic, and Mr Johns, shaking off his moodiness with an effort, had a very comfortable talk with her about how awful it was when you had a book to read in bed and the pages were uncut. This, Mr Johns said, was luckily much rarer than it was in his youth, but he still carried a little paper-knife about with him from old habit. Alice asked, supposing he was in bed and the paper-knife was in his waistcoat pocket and he felt too lazy to get up and find it, what did he do. Mr Johns said he used his finger. For a moment Alice was shocked, but realising that it must be a joke she laughed quite loudly for her, and Mr Johns thought Mrs Barton's girl wasn't so bad-looking after all, and Mr Foster and Roddy, on the other side of the table, were pleased to see her looking so happy.

During dessert it suddenly occurred to Alice that she had

not thought of Julian since she dressed for dinner. Hastening to rectify this omission she looked about to see if he was at the table. It would have been romantic if he had been lying on the open moor, his white face upturned to the night sky, but if he had been there she wouldn't know where he was and would get no pleasure out of it, so it was on the whole with satisfaction that she saw him between Miss Faraday-Home and the archdeacon's daughter, seeing whose bread pellets were the dirtiest. With a loud scream Miss Faraday-Home claimed the prize, but Peter (or Micky) who was on her other side, said she had cheated and used the mascara off her eyelashes, and Miss Faraday-Home put a grape-skin into his port just as Lady Pomfret rose and collected the ladies.

As there was to be dancing after dinner there was no time for games, much to everybody's joy. The furniture in the hall had been pushed back, the rugs rolled up, and the big gramophone moved into the hall, just as Miss Merriman had said. Micky, who turned out really to be Micky, and not Peter, appeared to be something of an authority on records, and took charge of the music. Lady Pomfret established herself on a sofa where she held a little court with the older guests, and Lord Pomfret as usual took his bridge players off to the library.

Alice danced with Mr Johns which was very comfortable, as he moved with the ease of the stout. Then she danced with Professor Milward, which she found rather jerky and uncomfortable. After that she stood with Miss Merriman and watched the dancers. Mr Johns was the moving spirit of the evening, making a good deal of noise in which he was seconded by Miss Faraday-Home, Peter, the archdeacon's daughter and the man with the brick red face. Alice looked for Julian but he was not visible. Presently the sight of Mr Johns executing a few fancy steps with Miss Faraday-Home reminded her of a sad thought.

'Oh, Miss Merriman,' she said, 'Mr Johns said at dinner he was very worried about something to do with the Towers. He seemed rather sad about it. Do you think you could help him if you knew what it was?'

'I expect I could,' said Miss Merriman. 'I don't think it can be the bells, because I spoke to Peters, and Mrs Caxton this morning. If he mentions it again, ask him to let me know. I hope you are having a happy visit.'

'I love it,' said Alice. 'I was rather frightened at first, but Phoebe was so kind. And Julian was very kind showing me his pictures. And Mr Foster is very kind too.'

'He is,' said Miss Merriman thoughtfully. 'I hardly know anyone kinder.'

Guy now came up to his sister. He was in very good spirits and enjoying the dance thoroughly.

'Hullo, Alice!' he said. 'Having a good time? That's right.' And Guy turned away to claim the archdeacon's daughter.

Miss Merriman made no comment on this episode, but her silence had a quality that Alice felt to be slightly depreciatory of Guy. She wanted to make excuses for him, which was a novel feeling, for Guy had always stood above criticism in her mind. But before she could think of the right thing to say, Julian came across the hall.

'I don't suppose you want to dance,' said Julian.

Alice, who loved dancing and was quite ready to begin again, did not know what to say. If Julian didn't want to dance she couldn't make him. Perhaps artists didn't dance. But Micky had set the gramophone going again and Alice's feet were almost dancing in spite of her.

'I brought some of my pictures that you didn't see down to the billiard-room,' said Julian. 'Come along.'

'I don't think there is a fire in the billiard-room this evening,' said Miss Merriman.

Alice could see his lips shaping the word Interference, but he merely repeated 'Come on.'

'I think you had better not take Miss Barton to the billiard-room,' said Miss Merriman. 'Lady Pomfret says she hasn't been well, and it will be too cold for her.'

Alice was divided between disappointment at not seeing more of Julian's pictures, relief that she had not to go and sit in the cold billiard-room, and admiration of Miss Merriman who appeared to take no more notice of Julian than if he were an ordinary person.

'Oh well,' said Julian sulkily, 'come and sit somewhere where there *is* a fire. I want to talk to you about myself.'

At this simple statement even Miss Merriman, loyal as she was to the family, impersonal as she had trained herself to be, could not help smiling. But there was no objection to make if Julian took Alice to a warm room, and Alice was obediently preparing to follow her sun, when Roddy came up and asked her to dance.

'Oh, Roddy, I'd love to,' said Alice, 'but I'm going with Julian. He wants to talk to me.'

'Talk!' said Roddy. 'This is a dance.' And before Alice knew where she was, Roddy had his arm round her and they were dancing up and down the hall to an inspiriting foxtrot.

Alice had danced with Roddy a great deal, at Mellings, at the Wicklows' and at the small dances she had been to. It was one of the pleasantest things she knew. Their steps matched so well, she was so safe, and though Roddy towered above her, she always felt that they were nearly the same height.

Roddy, who was not much given to introspection, had had a few words with himself while he was dressing for dinner. He couldn't make out why he had been roused to such annoyance by young Rivers. It had been thoughtless of Rivers to keep Alice in a cold room while he gassed about his rotten pictures, but that wasn't really reason enough for offering to knock a man's head off. He wasn't going to apologise, but he would take jolly good care to treat the fellow civilly for the rest of their visit. Dash it, one didn't go about knocking chaps' heads off in other people's houses, especially if the other people were one's employer. Full of this virtuous resolve he went down to dinner, and was pleased to see Alice talking so happily with Mr Johns. When the dancing began his code of politeness made him ask the girls who had been near to him at dinner, but as soon as they had been disposed of he hurried to ask Alice. When he found that young Rivers having the impertinence to ask Alice to sit out – Alice, who was one of the lightest-footed dancers he knew – he would have liked to knock his head off on the spot. But as the conventions forbade this simple action, and his conscience was still pricking him about his behaviour to Julian before tea, he had to content himself with carrying Alice off under young Rivers's nose. Looking down on the top of her head as she danced, he felt he had done the right thing, and they had three dances together before he reluctantly went to find other partners.

'I don't often see you smiling, Merry,' said Mr Foster's gentle voice at Miss Merriman's side. 'What is it?'

'It is Mr Rivers,' said Miss Merriman, who never alluded to any of her employers' friends or relations by any but their last name. 'He wanted Miss Barton to look at his pictures in the billiard-room, but I said they had better not, it is too cold. Then he wanted her to sit out, but Mr Wicklow came along and carried her off. Look, there they are.'

Mr Foster looked and saw Alice, her shyness gone for the moment, talking with animation to Roddy Wicklow, while Micky started a new record. She left Roddy for a moment to say something to Mr Johns, then sped back to his arms and into the dance.

'She does look happy,' said Mr Foster. 'You are a brick, Merry.'

'I thought you wouldn't want her to sit in the cold,' said Miss Merriman, 'so I stopped it.'

'I really don't know what we would all do without you,' said Mr Foster.

'You'd do very well,' said Miss Merriman. 'But I must speak about the billiard-room fire. The central heating really isn't enough in this weather.'

To Miss Merriman and Mr Foster the subject of Pomfret Towers was inexhaustible, and they were arranging to do an inspection of the furnaces on Monday when Mr Johns, mopping his face, came up and apologised for interrupting, but said he understood from Miss Barton that Miss Merriman might be able to help him. Mr Foster offered to go away, but

Mr Johns said it was no secret. After saying a great many times that he didn't know if he ought to say what he was going to say, he expounded to his hearers his difficulty about Lord Pomfret's manuscript. He told the story against himself with some humour, and confessed ruefully that he had never been so browbeaten by a client before.

'Of course,' said Miss Merriman when the tale was told, 'I typed Lord Pomfret's book.'

'I thought it was in manuscript,' said Mr Johns.

'So it is,' said Miss Merriman, 'but when he gave it to Lady Pomfret to read, she got me to type a copy. It's about eighty thousand words.'

'Bless you, Miss Merriman,' said Mr Johns. 'Can I see it?'

Miss Merriman at first demurred, but on being pressed by Mr Johns and Mr Foster, who was as eager to see the typescript as Mr Johns, she came to the conclusion that it would do no harm. The typed copy was, she said, in her writing-table in the London house, but she could easily have it posted to Mr Johns, who swore eternal gratitude, kissed her hand, and went back to the dance.

'I hope I have done the right thing,' said Miss Merriman, showing for the first time since Mr Foster had known her slight signs of indecision. 'After all, Lord Pomfret wants the book published, and Mr Johns must see it before he accepts it. If it isn't published now, one never knows what might happen when Lord Pomfret is dead.'

'This is always an uncomfortable thing to say,' said Mr Foster, 'but I think anything that comes into my hands will be safe with me.'

'Oh, I know that,' said Miss Merriman, looking at Mr

Foster, 'but Lord Pomfret hasn't been very discreet, and if Mr Johns doesn't take it, it might be offered to someone else who would exploit it. I think we could trust Mr Johns to have it properly edited.'

She flushed slightly as she finished speaking, and Mr Foster wondered why.

'Yes, I see,' he said. 'I think you are right. But you always are. Merry, how you do all you do I shall never know. You make me feel extremely useless and idle.'

'If you would like to be useful,' said Miss Merriman, 'you can arrange the dinner-table for tomorrow night. The card is here.'

She opened a table drawer and took out a leather-covered card with little slots in it all round an imaginary table to put name cards in. The names of the party as they had been sitting that evening were still in the slots.

'I like that game,' said Mr Foster. 'I'll do the table if you'll let me sit next to you.'

'Very well,' said Miss Merriman, and then she saw Lady Pomfret getting up, and went away to see if she could be of any help. As Lady Pomfret had one or two things to discuss with her secretary about tomorrow's plans, Miss Merriman did not come back to the hall.

While she was listening to Lady Pomfret's plans and making a few helpful suggestions, another part of her mind was wondering if Mr Foster had noticed her stupid slip when she said 'we'. When first Mr Foster had come to the Towers, Miss Merriman, loyally defiant of the heir who was to take the place of the dead Lord Mellings, had kept even more aloof than usual. As her manner was always the same to everyone, no one, and certainly not Mr Foster, would have known that she was privately suspecting, criticising, summing up. It was the first time that she had ever allowed her emotions to creep into any relationship with her employers' friends. Gradually, as she saw more of Mr Foster, who was always invited to the Towers when Lady Pomfret was in England and had also stayed with her in Florence, his natural simplicity and kindness of nature, his diffidence about himself and his courage for others, overcame entirely her original impression. Because she had let herself dislike him, there was a place in her safe, well-ordered mind for thoughts of Mr Foster, and these thoughts had turned into an affectionate devotion. For Miss Merriman, Mr Foster was now part of the family, beyond criticism. They would never be more than Miss Merriman and Mr Foster to each other, but so long as he cared to consult her about the place which would one day be his, so long as she with her power of work and organisation could help him whenever he wanted help, she was content. On one subject her mind was made up. When Mr Foster came into the title she would never remain at the Towers, even if Lady Pomfret, to whom was her first duty, was dead. She knew five or six houses where she was wanted and could rule as absolutely as she did here, and to one of them she would go. To help Mr Foster while he was nobody had been her greatest pleasure in the last two years. Not for anything would she stay on when he was somebody, even if he entreated her. But that he said he would sit next to her at dinner warmed the heart that all Lady Pomfret's friends said Merry hadn't got.

The rest of the evening was a great success. Its crowning

glory was when Lord Pomfret, pleased at having won three pounds from his friends, invited Sally Wicklow to waltz. His lordship's style was of the eighties, but Sally had a good head for fences and swung round joyfully with her host. Alice danced with the man with a brick red face, and with all her other friends, and felt that she was now a real person.

'I say, Lord Pomfret,' said Sally to her host as he whirled her round for the last time. 'Do get those earths stopped in Hamaker's Spinney. I've told Mr Hoare a million times, but he won't hear sense.'

'They'll last my time,' said the earl, amused at her vehemence. 'You ask Gillie. He'll have to learn those things.'

'I did,' said Sally, 'and he said he would. At least,' she added, conscious of having bungled, 'I said if he ever *could* do anything about them – I mean, I'm awfully sorry, I didn't mean to be rude or anything.'

'I don't expect to live for ever if that's what you mean,' said Lord Pomfret. 'Someone must carry on. You can help him, young lady. He'll listen to you.'

'If he won't listen to me, I'll put Alice on to him,' said Sally. 'He'll listen to *her*.'

'Oh, he will, will he?' said Lord Pomfret.

And his lordship looked at Sally, and looked across the hall at Alice and Mr Foster who were talking together, and thought his own thoughts.

7

Trials of an Authoress

There is this to be said for a short weekend, that it leaves less time for an anti-climax. Even so, Saturday evening is often the high-water mark of enjoyment, while Sunday is a slight disappointment. And when the party has begun on Friday, there is even more chance that Sunday will be a little off colour. So far Lord Pomfret's mixed house party had been quite successful. The games on Friday night had been by no means to everyone's taste, but some people had played them and some had very pleasantly avoided or thwarted them. Shooting had occupied a large number of the guests on Saturday, and Lady Pomfret had taken her more intellectual friends to Rising Castle. The dance had pleased nearly everyone, and if Julian Rivers went sulkily to bed at half-past ten, while the rest were happily engaged, that was really his own fault.

But Sunday was going to be a different matter. To begin with there was no shooting. Monday and a meet at Pomfret

Madrigal seemed to the riders infinitely far away. Church would help in the morning and there would be a few people coming to lunch, but a long vista of afternoon and evening stretched before the guests as they opened their eyes on a bleak grey morning with spatters of sleet against the panes of such as were on the north side. To Guy Barton it was peculiarly provoking, because he had left his window wide open and the wind was blowing his curtains straight out into the room and drenching his dressing-table. He got up angrily, shut the window, saw it was only seven o'clock, and got back into bed again. Such a morning was thoroughly annoying because he had planned to go for another walk with Phoebe Rivers, but as he reflected upon his career since Friday evening he felt a compensating glow of satisfaction. He had at once found friends in the party, and had enjoyed the games very much. It was while they were playing games that he had first been struck by Phoebe. Very few girls would have taken him up as quickly as she did about Hengist and Horsa. If it came to that he had been pretty quick about it himself, and it was nice to be able to help Alice. He glowed more than ever as he thought what a pleasant time his sister was having, and of all the help he had been to her. He had been almost annoyed with Phoebe on Friday night when she said he might think more of Alice. That just showed how people didn't really know what other people were really like. Because if only Phoebe knew how much he had thought of Alice, she would be surprised and ashamed. Why, dash it, last night he had gone out of his way to ask if she was having a good time. Some people might have gone to Phoebe and said Look here, I'd just like you to see what care

I take of my sister, but he wasn't that sort. He would let Phoebe find it out for herself, only helping her a bit by telling her exactly what he had done.

His thoughts then wandered to the walk he and Phoebe had taken yesterday, and the talk they had had about stage architecture. From stage architecture his mind, gently dozing, went to Italian architecture and the Renaissance and so by a natural train of thought to his mother's books. It was at this moment that he felt as if an icy hand had grasped his entrails. He had quite forgotten his mother's request to ask Lord Pomfret about the book. His mother had been a bit vague about it, and he was feeling even vaguer, but it was probable that as soon as he got back she would ask him if he had remembered. It was annoying enough that your parents would ask you if you had remembered things, just as if you always forgot; but when you actually *had* forgotten, it was little short of devilish in them to remember about it themselves and remind you. And then there had been his father's appalling breach of good feeling in taking his arm and telling him to do what his mother wanted, in what Guy could only describe as A Voice. For a short time he indulged in a burning sense of being wronged by his parents, but he could not get away from the fact that he had promised, under duress it is true, but a promise is a promise, to ask Lord Pomfret about this beastly book that he couldn't really remember anything about, and in his agony he banged up and down on the excellent springs of the bed till a knock at the door made him hastily recompose himself for the arrival of his shaving water.

Presently he got up and dressed and went down to

breakfast, but the glow of self-satisfaction was gone and a sense of injury took its place, and when he came into the breakfast-room and found he was the first down and that the newspaper had not yet arrived, he felt like rushing out into the sleet and being found dead. But soberer councils, helped by porridge and sausages and bacon, prevailed, and when Mr Johns came in, Guy saw a ray of hope.

'I say, sir,' said Guy, 'you know all about Mother's books. Do you think you know a book about Ferrara that she wants that Lord Pomfret has?'

Mr Johns, who could not understand why Mrs Barton should have to apply to Lord Pomfret for one of her own books, though he could not at the moment recollect one about Ferrara, said he was sorry, but he didn't.

'Oh,' said Guy, rather dashed, 'I thought you would. She said it was a cousin or something of Lord Pomfret's, and I was to ask for some brown paper to put round it.'

'Oh, not one of *her* books,' said Mr Johns. 'No, I'm afraid I don't. Who is Lord Pomfret's cousin?'

'I don't know,' said Guy. 'Some sort of relation, I suppose. I think Mother said he was an Italian.'

Mr Johns said they might ask Professor Milward who had just come in. Professor Milward said that must be one of the cadet branches that had settled in Rome after the Revolution.

Guy asked if that was the French Revolution, because if it was he didn't think that was the one.

Professor Milward, who was used to young men's elliptical mode of expressing their ignorance, said that he meant '88, which caused Guy, a stickler for accuracy, to say he thought it was 1789. Professor Milward very courteously made it clear that he alluded to the year 1688 and the flight of King James II, whose adherent, Eustace Pomfret, a staunch Roman Catholic, had in the following year found it more convenient to leave his native land, and had settled in Rome, where he married a lady of rank and wealth. The family was now, said Professor Milward, very poor and almost extinct; but the present representative, Count Strelsa, whose name was taken from the lands belonging to his Roman ancestress, was a scholar of considerable merit, who had compiled several books on the Renaissance period from old family papers.

By this time Mr Johns had ceased to pay any attention, for Count Strelsa's books were not enough in his line to be worth translating. Guy, though sorely bewildered, was hoping that Professor Milward might drop a word or two that would help him in his difficulty.

'Strelsa?' said the archdeacon, who did not eat what is called a cooked breakfast, but made up with any amount of cereals, hot bread, cold pheasant, cold ham, honey and fruit, 'Strelsa? I met him in Rome two years ago. It is curious how the family type persists. This will interest you, Milward,' said the archdeacon in a slightly threatening manner, so that Professor Milward, who wasn't listening, had to assume a look of intelligence. 'I saw in him a likeness, a distinct likeness I may say, to poor Mellings,' said the archdeacon, in what Guy again mentally termed A Voice. 'None of you knew him, I think, but the likeness was really remarkable. Not in colouring of course, for Strelsa is very dark, and not perhaps exactly in build or feature, but there was something, undoubtedly Something. It may have been the eyes,' said the archdeacon, helping himself to an unfair amount of cream. 'Strelsa of course has brown eyes, and Mellings had blue ones; but blood tells.'

'What's that?' said Lord Pomfret as he came in. 'Peters, get me some coffee and two fried eggs. Not those filthy soft things: properly fried. And some bacon. What's that, archdeacon?' The archdeacon, who hoped very much that Lord Pomfret hadn't heard his last words, remembered that he was, if not a prince, at least a pillar of the Established Church, and said boldly,

'I was saying, Pomfret, that Strelsa had a look of poor Mellings.'

'I never saw it,' said Lord Pomfret. 'And don't say "poor" Mellings. Boy served his country. More than any of *us* have. Peters, these eggs are uneatable. Tell cook if she can't give me decent eggs she can go.'

'Very well, my lord,' said Peters.

The archdeacon, remembering that a soft answer turneth away wrath, and that if it doesn't you may as well try to shift the wrath onto someone else, said that Strelsa had been brought to his mind by something Professor Milward was saying.

'Well, what is it?' said the Earl.

Professor Milward said he had been asked by Mr Johns about the cadet branch of the Pomfret family, and had been doing his best to explain it. The explanation, he said, had been all the easier to make since he had had the privilege of going through the Pomfret papers. But this graceful reference to his kindness did not at all placate Lord Pomfret.

Determined to get to the bottom of things he turned on Mr Johns, and asked him what he had been talking about.

'I was merely asking Professor Milward if he knew anything about your Italian relations,' said Mr Johns.

'Do you know them then?' said the earl. 'Strelsa's all right, but his brother Guido is a blackguard. Been turned out of every gambling hell in Europe. How did *you* come to know him?'

Mr Johns, eager to clear himself from this imputation, and indeed to extract himself if possible from a conversation which was becoming more and more alarming, said that he had never known any of the family, but that Mr Barton had inquired from him whether he knew anything about Lord Pomfret's Italian cousins and that he, being unaware of their existence, had asked Professor Milward, who had given them a very interesting account of the Italian branch, an account which had been supplemented by the archdeacon, who—

But Lord Pomfret, who had only restrained himself so far because he felt that Mr Johns, as a publisher, was of a slightly inferior social order and as such entitled to a forbearance that he would not have shown to his equals, now interrupted. Fixing his angry little eyes upon Guy in a most terrifying way, he said,

'You're Mrs Barton's boy, eh? You keep away from Guido Strelsa. You won't get any good from *him*.'

'I don't know him at all, sir,' said Guy. 'It was my mother She—'

'Well, I suppose she met him in Florence,' said Lord Pomfret. 'He did call on Lady Pomfret once or twice, but I soon put a stop to that. Can't think how your mother could stand him. Women always like bounders.'

'It wasn't about him, sir,' said Guy, floundering wretchedly in the morass of misunderstanding that his lordship had created. 'It was a book by the other one, sir, the Count, and Mother said you'd know which one it was, and,' he added breathlessly, but determined to go through with what had been so ill begun, 'she said would you lend it her and I was to be sure to put some brown paper round it.'

'Brown paper?' said the earl in an unfriendly way. 'Can't you talk English?'

'I mean, to keep it clean,' said Guy, 'and it was about Ferrara.'

Luckily for Guy the arrival of several late breakfasters made a diversion. Lord Pomfret got up, said anyone who liked could drive to church, and went off on his own affairs. Guy finished his breakfast, feeling that he had hopelessly offended his host and would have to return to his mother empty handed. He devoutly wished that it were Monday and he were on his way back to Nutfield and the office. However there was nothing for it but to set his teeth and go through with Sunday.

When the churchgoers assembled, Guy looked for Phoebe and presently found her with his sister Alice.

'Look here, Phoebe,' said Guy, 'oh, hullo, Alice. I say, Phoebe, what about us going over to Plumstead today in your car? I can show you a marvellous fifteenth-century house that we are reconditioning just outside the village.'

Alice, realising from her brother's manner that she was

not included in this invitation, had moved away and was taken possession of by Miss Merriman.

'We might,' said Phoebe, 'if Mother doesn't know. I can see it in her eye that she wants to get me and Gillie alone together this afternoon. The snag is it's her car, not mine. Well anyway he won't have to walk to church with me, the poor lamb. Look!'

Guy looked and saw Lady Pomfret, all furs and pearls, sweeping across the hall to the front door followed by Miss Merriman carrying extra wraps, Alice, and Mr Foster. Alice, who rather wanted to walk with Sally and perhaps Roddy, did not dare to refuse Lady Pomfret's invitation to drive with her, though she felt safer when she found that Mr Foster was to go with them. She tried hard not to sit next to Lady Pomfret, a seat to which she felt that she, as the youngest of the party, had no right, but Miss Merriman with her matter of fact efficiency had her settled and fettered with a fur rug before she could make any adequate protest. Miss Merriman and Lady Pomfret then fell into talk about plans, so Alice and Mr Foster were left to entertain each other during the short drive to church.

'Have you seen the stables yet?' asked Mr Foster. 'We always visit them after church. My uncle likes it.'

Alice looked alarmed.

'You won't have to say anything about horses,' said Mr Foster noticing and interpreting her expression, 'only walk round with the rest.'

'Are you coming?' Alice asked.

Mr Foster said he was, unless his aunt particularly wanted him to drive. Lady Pomfret, emerging from her discussion with Miss Merriman, said she would drive the archdeacon back and Professor Milward if he wished to come, and Gillie must certainly take Miss Barton to the stables, and show her the Madrigal filly, an expression which seemed to Alice very dashing, but calculated to throw one into the depths of ignorant despondency.

'It's all right,' said Mr Foster as they got out of the car. 'I really hardly know which the filly is myself, and I've only just stopped calling her it, but the name is painted over her stall, so you can't mistake her.'

After church, which was chiefly remarkable to Alice from the fact that Lord Pomfret put a pound note into the plate, Mr Foster was as good as his word and accompanied her to the stables. Most of the party were used to horses, and Lord Pomfret and his head groom enjoyed themselves vastly in the appreciation or intelligent criticism of connoisseurs. To Alice the hunters all looked much alike, except that some were even bigger than others, and what pleased her most were the neatly plaited edges of the horses' bedding. Presently they came to a stall over which the name Madrigal was painted on a scroll, so Alice knew this must be the filly which she was to look at. Mr Foster was peremptorily summoned by his uncle to give some point of information about the elegant creature, and Alice realised that he had really known quite a lot about the stables.

'Hullo!' said Roddy Wicklow at her elbow. 'What do you think of her?'

Alice said she thought she was very nice.

The head groom had now led the Madrigal filly out onto the cobbles and was turning her about so that every point might be admired. Julian Rivers, who had only just had breakfast, came strolling into the stable yard and sketched a kind of salute to Alice.

'Horses are all the wrong shape,' he said loudly.

'All the wrong shape, what do you mean?' said the man with the brick red face. 'I've not seen a prettier filly since Leslie's Rush-cutter won the point to point in '35.'

Various voices were raised approving and supporting this statement, but Julian was unimpressed.

'Well, look at that,' he said, jabbing with an artist's thumb just behind the filly's shoulder, who at once reared, dragging the groom off his feet by the unexpected action, and did a few dance steps backwards, scattering the onlookers. Roddy ran to her head. In a moment the alarm was over and Roddy and the groom were leading the justly irritated filly back to her stall.

Mr Foster, who seemed to have eyes for everything, came quickly up to Alice, who was very white, and asked if she was hurt.

'Not exactly,' said Alice, 'but it – I mean she – trod on my foot. It will be quite all right in a minute.'

In proof of which she burst into tears.

'Oh come on, Alice,' said Julian. 'I got trodden on too. You shouldn't stand behind horses. You never know when they'll be vicious.'

'It's a pity she didn't tread on your damned face,' said Mr Foster, with a vigour that surprised all those that heard him. 'Take my arm, Alice.'

Guy, who had seen what happened from the other end of the yard and was really concerned for his sister, came to her help and, half laughing, half crying, she went back to the Towers with them.

Lord Pomfret, who had been talking to one of the stablemen at the moment, now demanded a full account of what it was all about.

'It was Mr Rivers, my lord,' said the head groom. 'The young gentleman can't rightly have been thinking, my lord. He gave the filly a poke, as you might say, all unexpected, and she reared up, and and if Mr Wicklow hadn't of come to her head there's no saying what might have happened. She's quite quiet now, my lord.'

'Boy's a fool,' said Lord Pomfret angrily. 'Hermione's a fool, and I always told George he was a fool to marry her, and the boy's a fool too. And don't let Mr Rivers come near the stables again,' he added to the groom, 'd'ye hear? Come here, Wicklow, and have a look at the bay mare.'

'Yes, my lord,' said the groom, winking at Roddy who had to pretend not to see, and what was even more annoying, had to go after his employer instead of carrying out his threat of yesterday and knocking Julian's head off. But the rest of the company expressed their opinion of Julian's action in no uncertain terms, especially as regarded his profane use of the word vicious. From every side came a strong expression of the opinion that the filly hadn't an ounce of vice in her. The man with the brick red face, who had no imagination and didn't know what the word sensitive meant, and was thus impervious to all Julian's attempts at explanation, and to his deliberate rudeness, took his arm in a grip of steel and explained the way to treat horses to him till the lunch bell rang, while the stablemen nudged each other at a respectful distance.

As they walked back Alice begged her kind companions not to say anything about the incident, alleging a wish not to be conspicuous, but really, it is to be feared, from the very foolish motive of shielding Julian. The matter was hardly referred to at lunch, except by the man with the brick red face, who told Miss Faraday-Home and the archdeacon's daughter again and again that young Rivers was an ass and the filly hadn't an ounce of viciousness in her. Thus it happened that Mrs Rivers did not hear of her son's disgrace, and was able to devote herself during lunch to the diplomat, who would have preferred to talk to Sally Wicklow on his other side.

Mrs Rivers's daughter had rightly diagnosed her mother's plan to throw her and Mr Foster together for the afternoon. Mrs Rivers was already uneasy. Sally Wicklow's immediate friendship with Lord Pomfret's heir she had regarded with dislike and annoyance, but his apparent interest in that little Miss Barton was more disquieting. Mrs Rivers though a conceited was not altogether a stupid woman, and she would have been very stupid indeed if Mr Foster's kindly thought for Alice had passed unnoticed. He was thoughtful for everyone, it was true, but to be considerate of secretaries and servants and dowagers is quite different from attention to a girl whom Lady Pomfret for some reason seemed to have taken up, and for whom one's own son had shown a marked preference. A most unsuitable match was that Miss Barton for either of them, and Mrs Rivers felt that a week-end of dodging from side to side, protecting Julian and Mr Foster against Alice, pushing Phoebe towards Mr Foster, and now, too annoying, having to see that Phoebe didn't spend all her time with that Miss Barton's brother, was more than she could stand. And all the time she wanted to get on with her Work, but what with arranging the games and unsuccessfully chivvying the young people, her heroine was still wandering, guide-book in hand, at Angkor Wat, only too conscious that her heart was blossoming at the sound of the Corsican savant's voice. It was going to be a hard tussle, for the heroine's husband was a little cold, and her children did not understand her, and her marvellous talent as a pianist was unappreciated, but here, in the tent of the Marquis dei Franchi, who never travelled without his Steinway, her fingers, evoking from the upright grand the slow movements of Beethoven's sonatas, would make both hearts beat faster, in a passion that could never, as both too well knew, find its earthly close. And now there was Gillie actually taking that Miss Barton away somewhere, or more probably it was she that was taking him. Mrs Rivers got up and went in pursuit. At the door of Lady Pomfret's rooms Miss Merriman met her.

'Have you seen Gillie?' said Mrs Rivers.

'He has just taken Miss Barton to Lady Pomfret's sitting-room,' said Miss Merriman. 'Lady Pomfret wanted the doctor to look at her foot.'

'Her foot!'

'Yes. One of the horses trod on it this morning,' said Miss Merriman, 'and it is rather painful. I expect Mr Foster will be back very soon if you want him.'

Mrs Rivers returned to the hall, and so persecuted was she by fate that as she entered by one door, she saw her daughter Phoebe, in outdoor clothes, going towards the front hall with that Miss Barton's brother. She hastened her steps and caught them up at the front door.

'Where are you off to, Phoebe?' she asked, trying to conceal her irritation.

'Just going out for a bit, Mother,' said Phoebe.

'Well, I rather wanted you this afternoon,' said her mother. 'People are coming to tea.'

'We'll easily be back by tea, Mrs Rivers,' said Guy. 'We are just running over to Plumstead to see a house.'

Guy had better have held his tongue, for this unconsidered remark gave Mrs Rivers an opening. She looked through a window and saw her car waiting outside.

'Darling, I'm afraid I can't possibly spare the car,' she said.

'But you said you wanted me here because of people coming to tea,' said her daughter.

Mrs Rivers nearly stamped with irritation.

'Well, I'm afraid the car can't go out,' she said. 'I am frightfully sorry, but you and Mr Barton must go another time. Besides, Mr Barton won't want to leave his sister.'

'Oh, Alice is all right,' said Guy.

'No thanks to Julian,' said Phoebe.

Mrs Rivers inquired what she meant.

'Oh, Julian was playing the fool with one of the horses,' said Phoebe, 'and made it back onto Alice's foot. Gillie can tell you about it,' she added, as Mr Foster came along the other corridor from Lady Pomfret's rooms. 'How's the foot, Gillie?'

'The doctor says it is only a little bruised,' said Mr Foster.

While Mrs Rivers was questioning Phoebe about the accident, and trying to persuade herself that Alice had put her foot under the horse's hoof on purpose, Guy drew Mr Foster aside.

'I was going to run Phoebe over to Plumstead,' he said, 'and now her mother won't let her go. She says we can't have the car and she doesn't want it herself. Phoebe'll be awfully sick.'

'Hermione,' said Mr Foster, addressing himself to Mrs Rivers, 'I've got to go out on some estate business. Will Phoebe come with me? My car's in the stable yard.'

Enchanted at this happy turn of affairs, Mrs Rivers hustled her daughter out of the house and went up to her room to grapple in peace with her Work. Mr Foster and Phoebe went round to the stables, where they found Guy sitting on a stone. They all three got into the car, and Mr Foster drove away in the direction of Plumstead.

'Now,' he said, stopping the car at a suitable distance from the house and getting out, 'you take the car wherever you like, Barton. I've got plenty to do in the estate office. Just leave her in the yard when you come back.'

Without waiting for their thanks he walked cheerfully back towards the house, and on his way met Sally Wicklow with Lady Pomfret's spaniels.

'Hullo, Gillie,' said she. 'I'm exercising these little brutes. Julia, or whatever her name is, looks fitter already. I've put the fear of God into Peters and that maid of Lady Pomfret's, and those dogs will get proper food from now on. And what's more Lord Pomfret said I could drop in unexpectedly when Lady Pomfret's away and see that they're not being stuffed. What are you up to? You look a bit peaky.'

'I am a little peaky,' said Mr Foster smiling. 'It's difficult work getting to know all about a place when you aren't a country bird, and Hoare always thinks I want to poison Uncle Giles if I so much as look at a paper in the office, so I have to put in time there when he has gone, and I find some of it perplexing.'

'And you are going there now, I suppose,' said Sally, 'though why you are coming from the lodge beats me.'

Mr Foster told Sally what he had been doing, and his underhand action met with her warmest approval.

'I'll tell you what,' she said. 'I'll hand these little brutes over to someone and come and give you a hand. I don't mean to shove in,' she said hastily, 'but I've been over such a lot of stuff with Roddy, and I really do know the country almost as well as Mr Hoare, and might be able to explain a bit.'

Mr Foster was very grateful for this suggestion. Together they walked back to the house where Sally, who seemed to know most of the staff by name, handed over the dogs to Finch, with instructions to give them to a footman to give to Lady Pomfret's maid.

'And I say, Finch,' said Sally, 'you might tell someone to bring some tea to the estate room. I'm going to work there with Mr Foster.'

Finch said he would, and hurried off at a pace of which the dogs deeply disapproved to tell the lower members of the staff that Miss Wicklow was having tea with Mr Foster in the office, just the two of them. This news, which was very well received, gradually percolated into the upper ranks, so that by a quarter to six, when Peters came to superintend the clearing away of tea, he knew that his master's heir and the assistant agent's sister had been shut up together since three o'clock. But being a discreet man he kept the news to himself, as far as his employers and their guests were concerned, reserving it for the moment when he could bring it out with most effect.

For nearly three hours, with a short interval for tea, Sally and Mr Foster went through papers and looked at maps. Sally was an invaluable guide and was able to supply the kind of information that Hoare would never have thought of giving, though he would have despised Mr Foster for not possessing it. From Sally Mr Foster learnt that Finch's old uncle was one of the worst poachers in the country but would only poach within limits on Lord Pomfret's land; that Mrs Dixon at Starveacres was well known to have been a witch and could spoil a day's hunting by magicking the fox away if she didn't get five shillings on Michaelmas Day, that Wheeler's cousin over at Little Misfit was the only man who really understood the Pomfret Towers chimneys, whatever Mr Hoare might say about the sweep from Pomfret Madrigal.

'I'll tell you what,' said Sally, 'if you like I'll take you round the village and introduce you a bit, if it wouldn't look like butting in. Are you going to be here long?'

Mr Foster said he would be a good deal at the Towers for the next two months, as his Uncle Giles wanted him to meet some of the influential people, political and otherwise, in the county.

'You'll be going into Parliament, I suppose,' said Sally.

'I would rather like to,' said Mr Foster, 'but it's a bit complicated. You see I might stop being a commoner at any moment. Uncle Giles is hale and hearty, but he is nearly eighty. My father is an invalid and he may live for ever or go off at any moment. It's unsettling.'

'I *am* sorry for you,' said Sally, with real compassion. 'I think you behave jolly well, considering. I mean, putting in all this work when you aren't going to have much of a say for ages – at least that's what it looks like.'

Mr Foster said one rather felt one had to.

Sally said yes but people didn't always do what they felt they had to, and it was jolly good when they did.

By now they had tidied up all the papers and Sally said she must go and see how Alice was. If, she added, there was a bigger fool than Julian Rivers in the house, or indeed anywhere else, she would like to see him, whether he were Mr Foster's cousin or not.

'And what's more,' said Sally, 'Alice seems to be getting it into her head that he's a bit of a hero. She doesn't know a thing about people and just because he has long hair and messes about with paints, and is as selfish as they make them, she is ready to fall for him.'

'But surely she doesn't feel like that now,' said Mr Foster.

Miss Wicklow looked at him with kindly pity.

'If you mean because of his making that filly tread on her foot,' said Sally, 'that's exactly where you are wrong. I'll tell you what Alice is like,' said Sally, pausing at the door. 'I once had a spaniel. She was a darling, but an absolute fool, and didn't know a thing, and the more you punished her the more she wagged her tail. That's Alice all over. I'll tell you exactly what she is thinking: that it is rather marvellous to have a horse walk on her foot because Julian made it do it.'

'Poor Alice!' said Mr Foster.

'Well,' said Sally, 'there's nothing to be done about it. Sooner or later she'll get through it. But if I find Julian making her sit in damp attics again, or playing the fool with horses, I'll tell him quite a lot.'

'I believe you will,' said Mr Foster, looking with admiration at her handsome eager face. 'And let me know if I can help. By the way, what did you do with the spaniel?'

'Oh, Roddy took her in hand,' said Sally. 'I can do most things with horses and dogs, but Roddy is a wizard. She got all right with him. Come on, let's get going.'

Mr Foster followed Sally along the passage that led from the estate room to the inhabited part of the Towers, reflecting on what she had just said. It was quite true that there was something in Alice Barton that made an immediate appeal for help and protection, and he could quite understand that with some people, as with Julian, this weakness would be an incentive and encouragement to bully. If Sally, in whose judgment he had great faith, said that Julian's silly behaviour that morning would only make Alice like him more, Sally was probably right. He felt sorry for Alice if she was going to care for his cousin Julian, for whom he had very little sympathy. It was unfortunate that Hermione, presuming on Uncle Giles's family feeling, had made herself and her children more or less permanent residents at the Towers this winter. Nutfield was ten miles away but ten miles are easily covered in a car. He and Sally must do all they could to protect Alice; and Sally would be an excellent watch-dog. What Alice needed was someone to take all responsibility till she could stand on her own feet, someone to treat her with great kindness and enough firmness, like Roddy with the spaniel. Roddy. A thought came into his mind.

'Sally,' he said, as she opened the door into the green drawing-room, 'What happened to the spaniel that Roddy cured?'

He had made up a pretty story for himself about the spaniel, with eyes rather like Alice's, a reformed character and deeply attached to the master who had made her.

'Oh, that spaniel,' said Sally. 'Roddy sold her and got a jolly good price.'

At which Mr Foster laughed aloud, and though Sally didn't see the joke and couldn't know that he was laughing at himself, she was so glad to see him happy that she began to laugh too, and so they both came laughing into the drawing-room.

Mrs Rivers had passed a pleasant afternoon. Her daughter Phoebe was out with her cousin, the future heir to the earldom, and that Miss Barton was safely laid up with a bruised foot. As for what Phoebe said about Julian having made someone or something tread on Miss Barton's foot, she took no notice of what was just a piece of sisterly sparring. Her slight annoyance at that Miss Barton resting by invitation on the sofa in Lady Pomfret's sitting-room was on the whole counter-balanced by the thought that she couldn't get at Julian as she had yesterday and spend the whole afternoon alone with him. Julian himself, after refusing in a very unfilial way to put on a pullover, had retired to his temporary studio, and his mother had devoted an hour and a half to peaceful literary composition. The scene between her heroine and the titled Corsican savant was going well. The air for miles round Angkor Wat was thick with renunciation. Mrs Rivers saw herself clearly in the moonlight outside the great ruins. Slim and alluring she stood in her riding-kit. No one would have taken her for forty-eight. Her intelligence, her mocking wit, her disillusionment with life, all these availed her nought against the overpowering passion of a late flowering love. The Marquis, his long sensitive hands and his fine sensitive face twitching with the control he had to exert, stood beside her. To hide his emotion he described to her in detail the ruins that were before them, but the words faltered on his lips and froze to a magic silence.

It would be at this point that at least twenty thousand middle-aged women of no particular charm or interest (for of such were Mrs Rivers's large public), seeing themselves as Helen Travers (for such was the heroine's name), would turn the wireless a bit louder, take another cake or chocolate, and read eagerly on, hoping that Lady Travers's virtue (for her husband, though cold, was a baronet) would be tempted to the uttermost, yet confident that Mrs Rivers would never allow her white purity to be smirched.

Having written so far she laid down her pencil and went in search of tea. Miss Merriman and Lady Pomfret were not there, so Mrs Rivers, putting resolutely from her the thought of that Miss Barton having tea with them in a select way, was able to take command of the teapot and hot water, and felt like a chatelaine. Professor Milward, a little weary from a day's work on the Pomfret papers, sat beside her and relaxed himself by leading her on to talk of her own books, so that nothing could have been nicer or more comfortable.

After tea some of the younger men went off to the billiard-room where a bright fire was now burning, but most of the party gathered in the green drawing-room. Mrs Rivers brought out her tapestry work and compared it with the work of other ladies, and they all spoke at once, saying how divine each other's work was and how dear Sir Harold at the Museum had let them have a design that *no* one else had been allowed to copy. As Mrs Rivers, partly through long practice at literary cocktail parties, and partly by natural gifts, had a very piercing voice with a tone of intellectual condescension difficult to bear, she easily out-screamed her friends and told old Lady Wimple, who had covered three sofas and forty-five chairs at Wimple Hall, exactly how to put in her backgrounds.

Into this happy scene Peters came. Walking up to Mrs Rivers he paused silently before her in a manner that compelled the attention of the whole room.

'Well, what is it, Peters?' said Mrs Rivers.

'Excuse me, madam,' said Peters, 'but will you come to Miss Phoebe?'

'What's the matter?' asked Mrs Rivers.

'Miss Phoebe has sustained a slight cut on the forehead, madam,' said Peters, enjoying as only an artist can his own subtle approach to what he had to impart.

'Cut herself?' said Mrs Rivers, gathering up her work. 'How?'

'In Mr Foster's car, madam.'

'Has there been an accident? Is Mr Foster hurt?' said Mrs Rivers anxiously.

'No, madam. Mr Foster was not in the car. It was Mr

Barton who was driving, madam, and the car is Piled Up, I understand from one of the men, just by the South Lodge. It *seems* that Mr Barton tried to take the corner too narrowly, madam.'

The whole affair appeared to Mrs Rivers so fantastic that she almost suspected Peters of being drunk. Why Gillie's car, in which she had seen him and Phoebe start, should have been piled up, if Peters were not exaggerating, by young Barton, she could not conceive. Everyone exclaimed and asked questions at once, which Peters answered with courteous patience and the reserve of a man who is conscious of knowing more than other people, when an end was put to their suspense by Phoebe walking in with a piece of sticking plaster on her forehead.

Everyone exclaimed more loudly and asked more questions than before.

'What *have* you been doing, Phoebe?' said her mother. 'Where is Gillie? How could he let you get into an accident? Are you hurt?'

'It's all right, Mother,' said Phoebe. 'I only got a tiny cut on my forehead. I don't know where Gillie is. I haven't seen him for hours.'

'But he took you to Plumstead,' said Mrs Rivers.

'We found Guy wanted to go too,' said Phoebe, lighting a cigarette, 'and Gillie had a lot of work to do, so he lent us the car. Guy took the corner by the South Lodge too quickly and we ditched the car. Some of the men will get it out tomorrow. I must apologise to Gillie. Peters, do you know where Mr Foster is?'

'Mr Foster, miss,' said Peters, who had been living for this chance ever since a quarter to six, 'has been in the estate room with Miss Wicklow all afternoon. They had some tea sent in, miss. Charles, who took it in, said they were studying the papers, miss.'

'Papers? Oh, I see what you mean,' said Phoebe, '*papers*. Thanks, Peters.'

Peters lingered a moment, making a few unnecessary adjustments to the furniture, to have the intense pleasure of seeing Mrs Rivers quite speechless for the moment with mortification. And by a lucky chance, which he attributed later in the housekeeper's room to his birthday being between October the fifteenth and November the sixteenth, a period of time which, so an eminent astrologer in a daily paper foretold, ensures to those born in it a joyful and unexpected surprise, he was still in the room when Mr Foster and Miss Wicklow came in together, laughing.

'Gillie!' exclaimed Mrs Rivers. 'Where *have* you been?'

'Working,' said Mr Foster, in his gentle voice.

'And having tea,' said Mrs Rivers ominously.

Mr Foster, choosing to take this as a question, thanked his Cousin Hermione, and said he and Miss Wicklow had tea in the estate room.

Sally catching sight of Phoebe's sticking plaster asked what had happened, adding that she was awfully good at first aid or broken legs.

'Thanks awfully,' said Phoebe. 'It's only a cut I got, banging my head on Gillie's car. Guy drove it into a ditch.'

'It's just what I'd expect Guy to do,' said Sally. 'He was trying to do something funny, I suppose. Really he's the biggest idiot I know except Julian.'

Mrs Rivers looked horridly at Sally and might have said something, but a diversion was created by Guy, who came in looking very apologetic, and spoke to Mr Foster.

'I'm most awfully sorry, Foster,' he said. 'It was all my fault. I took that corner by the South Lodge too close and went into the ditch. There's no damage, and the lodge keeper said they could get it out tomorrow. But I am really most awfully sorry.'

His contrition was so obvious that Mr Foster at once got over any slight irritation he may have felt, and told Guy he had once nearly gone into the ditch himself at that corner. Mrs Rivers, realising how very useless it would be to make a scene in public, managed to restrain her feelings, but determined to speak to her daughter later on. Thank goodness the Bartons were going next day.

Everyone now lost interest in the affair, for a large house party cannot be expected to concentrate on anything for long, and some of the shooting men and the attendant nymphs who had to leave by the evening train came in to say goodbye. When the tumult had subsided, Mrs Rivers suggested that they should have some reading aloud. Phoebe and Sally on hearing this left the room. Miss Faraday-Home said she *must* go and play the gramophone in the hall if Mrs Rivers didn't mind, and Micky must come and put the records on. When everyone who had no inhibitions about good manners had escaped, and those who had enough presence of mind were pretending to write letters at distant writing-tables, Mrs Rivers said it would be such a treat if the archdeacon would read to them. The archdeacon had no objection. The question then arose of what he should read.

Peter said P. G. Wodehouse was jolly good, and in case anyone had not quite understood him he said P. G. Wodehouse was *jolly* good. There were, said the archdeacon, seizing Peter's words as a text, while ignoring the speaker, unfortunately no humorists among us now who could be compared with Dickens. There was, he said, in modern humour a tendency to what he might call cynicism, which he for his part found deplorable. Where, he said, could one now find anything like the trial scene in Pickwick, or the scene between Mrs Gamp and Mrs Prig. He would much like, he said, to read to them one or two of these passages.

Lady Wimple said that she and her husband had read aloud to each other every evening, when not otherwise engaged, for nearly fifty years. They had formed the habit, she said, while on their honeymoon in Rome, and had never let it drop, though she understood that Rome was much altered now.

The archdeacon asked whether there was a set of Dickens at the Towers.

Professor Milward, speaking to Lady Wimple, said he had been in Rome last year and had been much struck by the new excavations, though he could not but deplore the destruction of part of the seventeenth- and eighteenth-century Rome which it implied. One of the great charms of Rome, he said, was the mixture of classic, mediaeval, Renaissance, baroque, and even later styles. To attempt to revive any one of these styles at the expense of any other was bound to mean as much loss as gain.

Mrs Rivers said she was sure there was a Dickens somewhere about, and began to look along the shelves.

Lady Wimple said she remembered the Coliseum very well, and she did not suppose it had changed much.

Peter said there was a jolly good show at the Coliseum, with a lot of jolly good dancing. A *jolly* good show, he added, to enforce his meaning.

'I don't seem to see Dickens here,' said Mrs Rivers. 'I'd better ask Peters.'

But before she could ring the bell, her son Julian walked in.

'What an awful fug you've got in here,' he remarked, looking intolerantly on the company. 'I've been for a long walk.'

'Sit down, darling,' said his mother. 'The archdeacon is going to read some Dickens to us. Do you know where the Dickens is, Julian?'

Peter said, 'Where the dickens is Dickens?' a remark which was well received by some of his friends.

'This is very interesting,' said the archdeacon, who had also been looking on the shelves. 'Here is a first edition of *Leaves of Grass*.'

As usual, the archdeacon's utterance was of a nature to quell his audience. No one cared if it was a first edition of *Leaves of Grass*, and a great many did not know what he meant. But everyone hoped he would not read aloud from it.

'If you *want* to know where a Dickens is,' said Julian to his mother, 'there's one in the library. At least there was last time we were here.'

'Do go and get Pickwick for the archdeacon then, darling,' said Mrs Rivers.

Most unwillingly Julian went upon his errand. In the library Lord Pomfret was talking with the diplomat and much resented the interruption.

'Well, what is it?' he said to his young cousin.

'Nothing, Cousin Giles,' said Julian. 'Only that Mother wants Pickwick.'

'Good God, boy, take it then, and don't stand there, and shut the door,' said his lordship.

'Where is it?' asked Julian.

'Can't you use your eyes?' said the earl. 'Over there in the corner.'

And he made a sweeping gesture that included at least three walls of the room.

'None of these young men know what they want,' said Lord Pomfret to the diplomat. 'You heard young Barton at breakfast. A child could have made itself plainer. And now Julian coming for a book and not having the wits to find it. Haven't you got it yet?'

'No, Cousin Giles. It isn't where it was last year.'

'Who the devil said it was?' his lordship replied. 'I said it was over there. And shut the door after you. And what I mean to say in the House when the Bill comes up—' he continued to the diplomat, as Julian, baffled and bookless, left the room.

As Julian did not return with the book, the party began to go and lie down before dinner, saying how dreadfully disappointing it had been not to hear the archdeacon read. The archdeacon immediately offered to read something else, but they all said that they couldn't *dream* of imposing on him and pushed each other in a polite way to get out of the room first. Mrs Rivers went up to her daughter's room to expostulate with her, but Phoebe, foreseeing this visitation, had bolted the communicating door and was splashing loudly in Alice's bath, so her mother had to go away.

The dinner party was smaller tonight on account of the people who had left by the evening train. Alice, whose foot hardly hurt at all and who had very much enjoyed being an invalid in Lady Pomfret's sitting-room all afternoon, was much to her pleasure next to Roddy.

'How's the foot?' he said as soon as they had sat down.

Alice said it was nearly quite all right. Not all right for dancing, perhaps, but quite all right. And would he please not say anything to her mother about it in case she worried, and she didn't want her to think it was Julian's fault.

'Whose fault was it then?' said Roddy.

'Well, people oughtn't to stand behind horses,' said Alice. 'You've told me that often, Roddy.'

'People oughtn't to play the fool with horses,' said Roddy, and was going to say more, but Alice looked so unhappy that he refrained, and they talked very comfortably about nothing in particular till Alice was claimed by the man with the brick red face on her other side and Roddy turned to Phoebe.

Phoebe, in the most clinging and bare-backed of gowns, more sophisticated in hair and make-up than ever, was hiding a black fury under her coldly exquisite appearance. Her mother's ways were a perpetual mortification to her. It was bad enough to know that people were laughing at her mother on account of her literary airs, but to be thrown at Gillie's head, as she had been ever since they came to

Pomfret Towers, bitterly wounded her pride. Her brother was no comfort. His egoism made him an insupportable companion, and now he had made an absolute fool of himself in public and hurt that poor little Alice. She knew well that he was entirely unconscious of the dislike with which several of the party regarded him, and wished vindictively that someone would tell him exactly what people thought of him: though even then he would merely despise his dislikers in a very offensive way.

'I say, Roddy,' she said, 'I'd like to murder Julian.'

'Let me do it for you,' said Roddy.

'I wish you would. Sisters aren't very good murderers. I do think Alice is a darling, and Julian is treating her like mud, and she's so sweet-natured that she can't see it.'

'She is a darling,' said Roddy seriously. 'But I think she must see what he's like by now. I mean I know he's your brother and all that, but after that silly ass business with the filly today she can't think much of him.'

'Oh, can't she,' said Phoebe.

Roddy looked at her, a shade of anxiety on his face.

'You see, Julian is very good-looking,' said Phoebe. 'We all are, we can't help it. Look at Mother. And Father's the best looker I know. I don't think much of Julian's style myself, but girls fall tor him like anything. And they think being an artist is romantic. God!' she said bitterly, 'what a selfish, conceited lot artists are. At least Julian's friends are – I don't know any *real* artists. And it doesn't matter how rude and beastly Julian is. Just because he looks like that and smells of paint and is rude to everyone, girls simply adore him. And the ruder he is, the more they like him. I bet you

Alice is thinking how marvellous it is that her foot got hurt because of him. Most women are masochists when they're in love. Alice is a super-charged example.'

'What's a masochist?' asked Roddy, who had not at all enjoyed some of his neighbour's remarks.

'Someone who enjoys being hurt,' said Phoebe.

'I see what you mean,' said Roddy. 'Well,' he added, squaring his shoulders, 'I must do something about that. I can't let her go about enjoying being hurt. I've known her all my life.'

'Good for you if you do,' said Phoebe. 'But don't think bashing Julian's face is going to help, because it isn't. Oh, my God, how sick I am of it all.'

Roddy, putting his own anxieties aside, was so sympathetic that Phoebe unbent a little, and confided to him that she had gone on the stage because her mother would try to marry her off.

'And now it's Gillie she's after,' said Phoebe. 'He's one of the nicest men I know, but we haven't really a thing in common. Now if he fell in love with Alice, there'd be some sense in it. She'd have a splendid time with him, and Mother would leave me alone for a bit. I shouldn't wonder if he had already. He loves being kind to people.'

'Well, it all seems rotten,' said Roddy with much feeling. To hear that one's oldest friend is probably in love with a stinking longhaired ass, and alternatively that the heir to an earldom is ready to lay the reversion of a coronet at her feet, is enough to make any chap think a bit. His thoughts produced such gloom in him that Phoebe turned to Mr Foster and made herself so amusing that Mrs Rivers from across the table felt she had misjudged her daughter, and quite recovered her spirits.

'I wish Alice and Guy weren't going tomorrow,' said Phoebe presently. 'I do like her, and Guy isn't bad.'

'I thought so too,' said Mr Foster. 'I'll ask her if we can go over to Nutfield and see the Bartons.'

'Do,' said Phoebe, pleased that her cousin should show such interest in her new friend. 'Blast, I suppose Julian will want to come too.'

'Oh Lord, yes, he's going to paint her portrait, or what he calls a portrait,' said Mr Foster. 'Well, we must do our best. Merry must ask Julian to paint her, and keep him busy.'

He turned to his next door neighbour.

'Merry,' he said, 'do you think you could ask Julian to paint you? Phoebe and I want to go over to Nutfield and see the Bartons, and we don't want Julian. If he were painting you he couldn't paint Alice.'

Miss Merriman laughed, and said that was the one thing she couldn't do for Mr Foster.

'But if he is going to paint in Miss Barton's studio, it will be better than doing her here,' she said. 'He has put paint all over that walnut cabinet that is stored in the North Attic, and Lord Pomfret will be extremely annoyed when he finds out.'

'I know an awfully good man in London,' said Mr Foster. 'He works for us sometimes. If the cabinet is badly marked, I could get him down for a couple of days, and Uncle Giles needn't know.'

'That would be very kind,' said Miss Merriman.

They then talked about Alice's foot, and Miss Merriman,

seeing how kindly and carefully Mr Foster thought of her, wondered, as she had often done before, about a future countess, but could come to no conclusion. However, if Mr Foster wanted to see Miss Barton, she would do anything in her power to help him: anything, that is, except letting Mr Rivers paint her.

Everyone seemed to Alice to have conspired to make her last evening happy. By Lady Pomfret's orders she reclined on a sofa after dinner, and all her friends took it in turn to come and amuse her. Mr Johns asked her to tell her mother that he would be most grateful if he might be allowed to call at Mellings whenever he was next in the country. The diplomat said a few parting words of condolence so charmingly that Alice on her sofa felt like Madame Récamier. The archdeacon sent kind regards to her father, and the archdeacon's daughter said Alice must come and stay with her at Plumstead. And best of all, the remains of the sporting guests, headed by the man with the brick red face, were loud in their sorrow that she wouldn't be able to get out on Monday. Alice thought at first that they meant her foot would be too bad to let her go home, but luckily before she had exposed her ignorance she discovered that they had thought she was going to hunt, and were condoling with her on her disappointment in missing whatever chances Monday might bring. All this made her feel so gay and happy that she looked quite charming, and even Guy was struck by the improvement, and was not ashamed to own her as his sister.

Only one small cloud marred the evening. Neither Roddy nor that nice Mr Foster were among her courtiers. She supposed Mr Foster found her rather dull, but that Roddy should desert her and deliberately devote himself to Miss Merriman, she could not understand, except that Miss Merriman was very nice and kind, and she hoped Roddy was enjoying himself. The reasons for their absence, if she had known them, were of the addle-pated nature peculiar to men. Mr Foster, pleased to see Miss Barton casting off her shyness and flowering under the attentions of the party, felt that it would be selfish of him to add to the numbers when that very nice fellow Roddy Wicklow would like to be there. Roddy, delighted that Alice looked so full of beans after what might have been a nasty accident, damn that fool Rivers, thought that with so many round her sofa, he would be one too many, and keeping away that really decent chap Foster who evidently liked her very much. It would be funny if Alice were a countess. No, it wouldn't be funny at all, but one mustn't barge in, and this seemed an excellent opportunity to have a good talk with Miss Merriman about Mrs Tucker's three invalid and mentally deficient children down at Starveacres Hatches in whom Lady Pomfret had been interesting herself.

When Lady Pomfret went early to bed she kissed Alice very kindly, and said she would go over and see her mother before long. Mrs Rivers then approached her sofa and Alice, although surrounded by friends, felt rather as Fair Rosamond must have felt when Queen Eleanor's step was heard in the labyrinth. Mrs Rivers's intentions were, however, perfectly pacific. She had had a talk with her son Julian after dinner, during the course of which Julian had said that he did wish people didn't interfere, and he was going over to Nutfield to paint in Alice's studio as soon as possible, and she was a decent sort of girl who didn't make a fuss if a horse, which everyone knew was a stupid kind of animal, just touched her foot. Her face, he continued, was not quite so blatant as some, but that was not her fault, and he would *not* get his hair cut till he felt like it.

On hearing this Mrs Rivers decided that the only way of checkmating Alice's bold-faced advances on her son was to invade the enemy's country herself, so she sat by Alice and asked about her foot with the natural charm that so rarely lifted its head among her literary airs and pretensions. Alice, disposed to think well of everyone tonight, felt that she had misjudged Mrs Rivers, and responded to her advances with shy pleasure. Mrs Rivers said she had wanted for a long time to meet Mrs Barton, whose books she so much admired. Did Alice think her mother would allow her to come to Mellings one day and make her acquaintance.

'Oh yes,' said Alice. 'At least I don't know, but I'm sure she would.'

'I might bring Phoebe and Julian with me,' said Mrs Rivers. 'Julian is going to paint you, isn't he?'

'Oh, I don't know,' said Alice. 'He did say so, but I'm afraid my studio is frightfully untidy and it isn't a north light.'

'I'm sure that won't matter,' said Mrs Rivers, thinking that perhaps after all she had been silly to take seriously Julian's feeling for anyone as stupid as Alice. 'I might come and read aloud while he is painting you.'

'Oh, thank you very much,' said Alice. 'Don't you think it's awfully difficult to listen when people read aloud? I mean one always seems not to be able to help thinking of something else. But I'm sure Mother would like to see you and please do bring Phoebe.'

Mrs Rivers wondered a little whether Alice was really more cunning than she looked, but feeling on the whole reassured she said she would ring Alice up before long. Miss Merriman then came up with tomorrow's plans. The Bartons' car was coming quite early, so that it could drop Guy at the office by ten, and Miss Merriman said she had told the housemaid to call Alice and Sally a little earlier and bring their breakfast at half-past eight. Roddy was staying on to work at the estate office.

'Oh, Mr Rivers,' said Miss Merriman to Julian who was loitering near, 'can I speak to you for a moment? I am sorry,' she said, lowering her voice, 'but Lord Pomfret doesn't want the North Attic to be used. There is the old racket court if you like, which is always empty, and I can have a very good oil-stove put there.'

'All right,' said Julian, who always felt that a mysterious but very real power prevented him from being rude to Miss Merriman. 'I suppose Cousin Giles doesn't want me to paint at all.'

'Not in the North Attic,' said Miss Merriman pleasantly. 'But you will find the racket court very nice, and the oil-stove heats splendidly.'

She then passed on to another guest, leaving Julian a prey to misunderstood genius.

Alice and Sally were sorry that their visit had come to an end. Both had profited. Sally had the promise of a mount in very good country and of a Bazouki puppy, besides the prospect of helping that very nice Mr Foster with the estate work. Alice felt that she was now a woman of the world. A well-known publisher had talked with her, a real artist had offered to paint her, Mrs Rivers wasn't as horrid as she had seemed, and Mr Foster was very nice indeed. And Julian would be coming to her studio perhaps. Julian was a very noble and beautiful name. It was strange how some people had the names that suited them.

Such pleasant thoughts passed through the heads of the two girls as they waited in the hall for Guy. Wheeler had taken Alice's five shillings without throwing it on the floor and spitting on it, the luggage was all in the car, with the addition of two brace of pheasants, one for the Barton and one for the Wicklow family. Guy was saying goodbye to Phoebe and arranging to run her over to Barchester to look at the work the firm had been doing on Hiram's Hospital, when Julian lounged into the hall with what Alice at once recognised as the easy grace of a panther. She had forgotten him since about nine o'clock last night, but now her heart beat fast again.

'Hullo,' said Julian. 'You can give me a lift to Nutfield if you like. I'm going to get my hair cut.'

'There isn't much room,' said Sally tartly, for she shared her brother's feelings about Julian.

'We'll make some,' said Julian. 'Here,' he called to Carter, move some of those things onto the front seat, will you, and I'll go inside.'

Guy now came up, followed by Roddy, and asked Carter why he was moving the bags.

'It's all right as it is,' he said. 'I'm coming outside with you, Carter.'

'Sorry, Mr Guy. It was this young gentleman ordered the suitcases to be moved. He says he's coming inside. He said he was coming to Nutfield to get his hair cut,' said Carter, who like all servants disliked Julian at sight.

'It's a pity he didn't think of that before,' said Sally in a loud aside.

'Don't, Sally,' said Alice in an anxious voice, as Julian put his foot on the running-board.

Roddy saw her face and heard her voice, though he could not distinguish the words. But that she looked afraid, and that he disliked Julian, were enough for him. He took Julian's arm in a powerful grip and pulled him away from the car.

'Good old Roddy,' said Guy and Sally in unison.

Guy got into the car and called to Carter to start. Roddy, still holding Julian firmly, said goodbye to his friends, and told Sally he would see her again at dinner. But to his horror Alice's face at the window showed every sign of misery and disapproval.

'Oh, Roddy, how could you!' was her farewell, in a voice of reproach which made him let go of Julian and stride off to the estate office, there to drown care in work.

Julian, white with rage, was going to pursue Roddy and kill him, when, turning, he saw Peters waiting impassively at the top of the steps with a footman in attendance. His courage oozed away. He mounted the steps as carelessly as possibly and went into the hall, whistling. The footman, who was the young footman that had received the Bartons and Wicklows on their arrival, looked at his earthly lord to see if a wink would be permitted. It was not. But Peters showed as clearly by his want of expression what he thought of his employer's young cousin, as Julian's worst enemy could have wished, and the young footman went away rejoicing to tell the servants' hall how Mr Wicklow had given that young Rivers the Nelson touch.

8

Rash Proposal

Mr and Mrs Barton had had a peaceful weekend, only troubled by a slight anxiety about Alice's welfare. A first experience of a big house party is an ordeal for most girls, and Alice had been about so little. Mrs Barton had felt rather like a murderess when she detached her clinging daughter from her and sent her off to face the unknown. Mr Barton had taken the affair more sensibly, but he knew how cold and draughty Pomfret Towers could be, and hoped that Alice would not get one of her bad colds. However it was no good worrying about what one couldn't help.

Mrs Barton, unable to account for a slight feeling of depression which she had refused to recognise as missing her daughter, had laid down her pen for the weekend and read aloud several chapters of her new book to her husband in the evenings. Mr Barton had driven her over to Plumstead to look at the work there, and she had taken her usual intelligent interest in what he was doing, and Mr

Barton began to hope that this was the beginning of the Golden Age.

This hope was dashed on Monday morning when Mrs Barton said at breakfast that she thought she would have to go to Italy in the spring.

'Count Strelsa has written to say that he has made a most interesting discovery in an unused room,' she said. 'There was a big *cassone* that no one had looked into for years, and he has found a bundle of papers in a box, wrapped up in some curtains. He wants me to come over and see them, because there are several allusions to Ganimede. Would you mind if I went?'

'I would rather,' said Mr Barton. But he quickly pretended that it was a joke, and asked how long she would stay.

'Perhaps a month,' said Mrs Barton. 'It seems a pity not to stay a little when I have got there. I might take Alice.'

'Would she like it?' asked Mr Barton. It was no good pretending that his wife's absence would make a martyr of him, for the excellent staff looked after him as well when she was away as when she was at home. In fact the cook's only complaint to her mistress when she returned from her Italian visits was that Mr Barton dined out so often that it wasn't hardly worth while thinking of savouries. But on former occasions there had always been Alice at breakfast and lunch, and at dinner when he was at home. He very much liked her company, and she was an even better listener than her mother when he told her about his work. It might be a good thing for the child, but it would be dull for him. Guy was a good boy and an excellent worker, but like most young men he preferred his pleasures outside the home. It would be lonely.

'I don't know,' said Mrs Barton, smiling ruefully. 'I sometimes wonder if she'll ever like anything. But she can't spend all her life at Nutfield, and if I am to be away and you and Guy are busy, she would get more wrapped in herself than ever. And she could work at her painting in Florence.'

Mr Barton, who had hoped at least to save a daughter from the general wreckage, said Well they must see, and went and put on his hat and coat to go to the office. In the hall he lingered for a moment, touching the carved balusters with affection, lovingly following with his eyes the fine sweep of the staircase. Then he pulled himself together and went off.

Mrs Barton, having done her household jobs, went to her sitting-room. This delightful room was at the south-east corner of the house, lighted by two windows. From one Mrs Barton could see the drive, the other commanded a prospect of lawn, a lime avenue, and at its end the gardener's cottage with its Parthenon façade. By this window her writing-table was placed, and when inspiration failed, or the convolutions of the illegitimate families of the Italian upper classes in the sixteenth century became too difficult, she obtained great relief from looking at the picture which Repton had composed more than a hundred years ago.

This morning she sat looking out of the window, but without thinking of what she saw. The car, after dropping Sally at her parents' house and Guy at the office, would shortly return with Alice. In a few moments she would know the result of her experiment. Would Alice, as so often, come back from her party almost in tears, having sat in a corner and looked her worst all the time, to creep into her studio and there lose herself in a world of her own, or would she by a miracle have enjoyed herself. If, Mrs Barton reflected, they had lived in the period she knew so well, there would have been no difficulty. Mr Barton, bold, shrewd and unscrupulous, would have married his daughter to a suitable husband, of rather higher rank than their own. The husband, considering the large dowry which the Bartons could well afford to give their daughter, would not have boggled at her retiring ways, and by the time she had two or three children and as many brocaded and furred dresses as she wanted, her problems would be solved. But Mr Barton, good husband, father, and man of business as he was, would never dream of looking for a husband for Alice and would mention the considerable sum of money that he was prepared to settle on her in a deprecatory way, if indeed he ever went as far as mentioning it at all. One couldn't find husbands for girls now. They found their own. And if they were not fitted for the chase, it was difficult to know what to do. Perhaps a month in Italy would help Alice. To see the world was part of education, and a part that Alice as yet had not had. She would take her to Italy.

So deeply was Mrs Barton reflecting on the subject of her daughter, that she did not hear the front door being shut. To a knock on her sitting-room door she said Come in, without troubling to turn her head, thinking it one of the ordinary distractions of a household.

'Oh Mother,' said her daughter's voice, 'Roddy was *awful* to Julian.'

'Darling, I am so pleased to see you back,' said Mrs Barton. 'I was thinking so hard about you that I had quite forgotten you. Kiss me. You look a little bit fatter, I think.'

'I might,' said Alice, 'there was such a lot of food, and I didn't like to say no thank you, so I ate it nearly all. And Julian is going to paint me if you don't mind, only I don't know if he'll come now, because Roddy really was *dreadful* to him. I never thought he could be so awful. Oh, I *am* glad to see you again, Mother. It was rather awful, but I did enjoy it.'

After a slightly suffocating hug had been exchanged, Alice sat down on a hassock before the fire and poured out an excited and very disjointed account of her weekend. From it Mrs Barton gathered that her daughter had eaten off silver plate, that the housemaid had been very nice, that there were simply millions of people there, that Lady Pomfret had been very nice, that Miss Merriman had been very nice, that Mr Foster had helped her to find her shoes and had been *very* nice, that Phoebe had the loveliest frocks she had ever seen and was most awfully nice, that Mrs Rivers was rather horrid, but not really quite so horrid, and that everyone had been very nice indeed.

And, said Alice, in a reverent voice, there was Julian.

Of course Lord Pomfret, she said, was *very* nice, but she did think it was rather unkind of him not to let Julian paint on the staircase, because he painted in a way that was quite different from anyone else, and people didn't understand him, but he was really quite different from other people, and if Mother didn't mind he was coming here to paint her.

'Oh, and Mother,' she exclaimed, 'I never thanked you for my *lovely* rabbit cape. Phoebe liked it *awfully*.'

If a brand-new friend approves of the present that one's mother has chosen with love and care, the present must be good. Mrs Barton quite realised this, and said how very glad she was that Alice had liked it. And who, she said, was Phoebe.

'Oh, Mother, don't you know? Phoebe Rivers. Her mother is that Mrs Rivers that writes books, and Julian,' said Alice, her voice sinking to a low caressing note, 'is her brother.'

'Oh, *those* Riverses,' said Mrs Barton. 'I heard of Mrs Rivers in Florence a few years ago. She amused everyone immensely.'

'Don't you like her, Mother?' said Alice, wondering whether she ought again to reconstruct her view of Mrs Rivers.

'I don't know her at all,' said Mrs Barton. 'She sounded very pretentious. Tell me some more, darling. I'm so glad Lady Pomfret was nice to you.'

Alice gave Lady Pomfret's message to her mother, who said how much she would like it if Lady Pomfret came to lunch or tea one day, and then remembered Mr Johns, and gave his message. Mrs Barton was delighted to hear that the unknown half of her publishers had been nice to Alice, and said she would write to him and ask him to let her know whenever he was near Nutfield.

'And what was the young man like that is going to be Lord Pomfret's heir?' asked Mrs Barton, interested, as everyone must be, in the future earl, for much of the amenity of Nutfield life would depend on the Towers in good hands.

'Oh, Mr Foster. He is very nice, and very kind. He is always doing things for people, like finding my shoes, and picking up my bag at dinner, and he helped me home when—'

She stopped suddenly. Her mother must not know about Julian and the horse, filly she meant. Enough that she knew to whom the slight black mark on her foot was due. That was the ravishing pain that she would hug closely to her heart and let no one share.

'Helped you home?' said her mother. 'Why?'

'I mean, he took me to the stables after church on Sunday,' said Alice. 'The horses were lovely, and I thought the Madrigal filly looked very well.'

Ridiculous, darling baby, thought her mother, pretending you are grown up. But she was glad, as any mother would be, to hear that this Mr Foster had been kind to her daughter.

'We might ask him over one day,' she said.

'Yes, it would be very nice if he could come. He was abroad when he was young because he was delicate, and I expect you'd like him. And I wish Phoebe could come too. Oh, Mother,' Alice said, suddenly jumping up. 'I think I'd better go and unpack my things. I must get the studio ready in case Julian rings up. He can come, can't he, Mother?'

Mrs Barton said of course he could, and Alice ran upstairs. Her mother remained sitting thoughtfully at her desk. It seemed that what she thought so very unlikely had come to pass. Alice had enjoyed her weekend. The child looked different already. Her heart swelled with gratitude to Lord Pomfret for what he had done. She was thankful that she had had the courage to force Alice to go. Evidently people had been kind, and at least two young men, Mr Foster and this Julian Rivers, had made a certain amount of impression on her. It was the first time Alice had ever expressed a wish to ask anyone, except such old friends as the Wicklows, to the house, and her mother was prepared to aid and abet her in every possible way. Visions of dinner parties, of little dances, of garden parties, river picnics, rose before her. Then she laughed. That was looking ahead too much with a vengeance. People's natures couldn't be changed as suddenly as that. But every wish that Alice showed to meet men and girls of her own age should be encouraged, and though it would probably be a nuisance to have this young artist about the house, it was a nuisance that she would gladly face if it amused and pleased Alice. She took a grateful look at the gardener's cottage, thrust her feet into her foot muff, wrapped a rug round her legs and a shawl round her shoulders, her usual preparation for literary work, put on her spectacles, drank a glass of water, and fell back into the Renaissance.

Alice unpacked as quickly as possible, alert for the telephone bell. Then she went up to her studio, looked with a sad disfavour at her own delicate work, and began to clear a space for Julian to paint. She and her mother were alone at lunch, as Mr Barton was lunching with the Mayor, and Guy was away on the Plumstead job. Mrs Barton said she might be going to Italy in a month or so, and how would Alice like to come with her. In a moment Alice was her old self, shrinking with alarm.

'Oh, Mother, need I?' she exclaimed.

'I only thought it might be an interesting change for you,' said Mrs Barton mildly.

'It would be lovely,' said Alice, 'only I don't know if

Julian will have finished. He said it might take weeks, or months, or even years to do a really good picture. Oh, Mother, I can't go away if he needs me.'

'Well, we'll see,' said her mother. 'If it takes weeks we might manage, but months and years seems rather a lot. What was it that Roddy did to Julian? It sounded rather alarming and not a bit like Roddy.'

'Oh, he was rather horrid to him. Rather brutal,' said Alice impressively.

'No, Alice, I can't think Roddy was brutal. Or if he was Julian must have been very annoying.'

'It was only something he had done, not a bit on purpose, and Roddy was angry, and he was *horrid* to Julian,' said Alice with the maddening tenacity of the love-struck.

Mrs Barton, seeing that more had happened than Alice could or would explain, wisely let the subject drop, resolved to find out from Roddy or Sally exactly what had really happened. For the rest of the day Alice could only think of the telephone, annoying Horton a good deal by rushing to it whenever it rang instead of waiting for him to take the message, but none of the calls were for her. The horrid thought struck her that Julian might be ill after Roddy's cruel treatment. Perhaps Roddy had broken a small bone in Julian's arm when he held it so tightly, and Julian was now tossing on a bed of fever. She would have rung up the Towers to inquire, but she was afraid of what might happen at the other end. Peters would probably take the message. If Julian were well he would be told in front of everyone that Miss Barton wanted to speak to him, and Alice went hot at the thought of her affection being thus exposed. If he were on the bed of fever perhaps his mother would come to the telephone, and though Alice had been disposed to think better of Mrs Rivers last night, her mother's rather depreciatory attitude and her own first impressions made her afraid that Mrs Rivers might accuse her of forward, un-maidenly behaviour.

Mr Barton and Guy did not get home till late, so the whole family first met at dinner.

Guy, profoundly uninterested in anyone's doings but his own, discussed the work at Plumstead with his father during soup and fish.

'Who do you think I met at Plumstead, Alice?' he asked presently.

'Whom,' corrected Mr Barton.

'You mean who, Father,' said Guy.

'No, I don't. I mean whom,' said Mr Barton.

'Well, I'm not much good at grammar,' said Guy, 'but I know you don't say, "whom did you meet".'

'*You* don't,' said his father.

'I said so,' said Guy, satisfied but puzzled.

'Well, who was it that you met?' asked his mother.

'There, Mother says who,' said Guy triumphantly. 'Oh, I met a girl called Phoebe Rivers. Alice knows her.'

He did not add that he had told Phoebe at breakfast that he would be over at Plumstead during the afternoon, nor that she had said in the tired scornful way which he found so attractive that she might run over there herself if she could get the car.

'We might have her over some time,' said Guy, who felt no reticence about his affections. 'She's staying at Pomfret

Towers for a bit. Her mother writes books or something, and her brother's an artist, at least that's what *he* says.'

'Guy!' breathed Alice, shocked.

'Well, I haven't an atom of use for him myself, but if you like him that's all right,' said Guy, handsomely. 'Sally and Roddy think he's no earthly use.'

Alice suddenly hated Roddy with a vehemence that surprised her. What right had Roddy, who wasn't an artist and didn't understand things like rhythm and tonality, to have no use for Julian; Julian for whom she was bearing the Mark of Pain on her foot. Let them wait; though who they were and what they were to wait for was not evident. The rest of the evening was uneventful and when Alice went to bed she was sorry to see that the bruise on her foot was perceptibly lighter in colour. She had thought of kissing it, but had to give up the idea because the top of one's foot is practically impossible to reach with one's lips, but to make up she washed that foot more lovingly than the other, and dusted it with some very special powder that she had been given at Christmas.

Life now resumed its normal course. Alice flew to the telephone every time it rang, but no message came from Pomfret Towers. She wrote a handsome Collins to Lady Pomfret, in which she expressed the hope that everyone was well. A sound instinct told her how improbable it was that Lady Pomfret would answer her letter, saying that Julian was in bed delirious, or alternatively had been called away suddenly, leaving no address, but that did not prevent her always being on the spot when the postman came. The studio was kept as though Julian might come in at any moment, but Alice managed to work quite happily at her book cover and found to her own surprise that she was not inclined to sleeplessness or want of appetite.

Mrs Barton, meeting Roddy one rainy day outside the butcher's, stopped him and said he hadn't been to see them lately.

'I thought Alice wasn't very keen for me to come,' said Roddy.

'Nonsense,' said Mrs Barton. 'Why not?'

'Well,' said Roddy, 'I'm afraid I upset her a bit.'

'There are too many people here,' said Mrs Barton, looking round at Mr Bones's Saturday customers. 'Come into the post-office. It's drier there.'

Having got Roddy into the post-office she so bullied and badgered him that she wrung from his unwilling lips the full story of how Julian had first made Alice sit in a cold attic from lunch to tea, secondly made the Madrigal filly tread on her foot, and thirdly been extremely offensive on the Monday morning. Of what the offensiveness exactly consisted of she could not quite make out, but if Julian had done even half of what Roddy said, she had no doubt that his mere existence was offensive. Her indignation against Julian knew no bounds. To keep her dear, delicate child in the cold. To jab horses with one's thumb till they trod on a girl's foot. And then to be offensive on Monday morning. No, it could not be borne. But Alice was apparently bearing it well, and this needed thought.

'Don't worry too much, Roddy,' she said. 'I promised Alice he could come and paint her portrait, but I expect she'll be very tired of him before it's done. Anyway he won't be here for ever. Tell Sally to ask Alice and me to tea one day next week, and then you come in after work and it will be all right again.'

Roddy thanked her and said he would, but he didn't suppose it would do any good. By the way, he said, half the Towers were down with flu. Two of the housemaids had it and a kitchen-maid and a footman, so had Mrs Rivers and Julian and so had Mr Hoare, so he was having to do double work.

'Thank goodness Alice left before it started,' said Mrs Barton. 'Influenza at this time of year would have been the last thing for her. That's why Julian didn't ring up.'

'Was she expecting him to?' asked Roddy.

'Yes, about that portrait. I expect it will all be a great nuisance and horribly bad. Goodbye, and don't forget to tell Sally. Any day next week.'

To the great regret of the post-mistress Mrs Barton then went home, and told Alice that Mrs Rivers and Julian were down with flu. 'Roddy told me,' she said. 'I met him at the butcher's. I told him to tell Sally to ask us to tea next week. Mr and Mrs Wicklow have gone to Madeira on a cruise, so it's safe. Otherwise I'd have to have tea with her while you had tea with Sally.'

Alice said, How nice. Her whole being was ravaged by the thought of Julian having influenza, nailed to a couch of pain, his raven locks lying darkly on his marble brow, his pyjamas, if she might mention them, damp with the sweat of agony. But she continued to put on weight, and in spite of this and of sleeping soundly for eight hours every night, she somehow managed to exist.

Sally duly rang up and invited Mrs Barton and Alice to tea on Saturday. When they got to the Wicklows' house, Wuffy, Chips and Chloe were in the front garden. On seeing the well-known faces of the guests they fell into wild hysterics, at once recognising in them emissaries of the police, the post-office, and the Tramps' Association. Chloe and Wuffy ran madly up and down inside the railings, barking loudly, with occasional fiendish leaps at their bars, while Chips devoted himself to digging a hole in which to take refuge when the invaders should have stormed the gate.

Mrs Barton stopped a small boy who was taking a parcel down the High Street.

'You are Mr Bones's little boy, aren't you?' she said.

The little boy looked blankly at her and muttered Jimmy.

'Well, Jimmy,' continued Mrs Barton, 'I thought you were Alf, but it doesn't matter. Do you know Miss Wicklow's dogs?'

Jimmy was understood to say, as far as the roaring of the dogs would allow him to be heard, 'Two pounds of liver and three of bones.'

'That's right,' said Mrs Barton. 'Now I want you to go in at Mrs Wicklow's gate and shut it after you, and ring the front door bell, and say I want Miss Wicklow to come out. Can you do that?'

Jimmy still looked blank, but a light began to break on him.

'Are you frightened of the dogs?' he asked hoarsely.

'I'm not,' said Mrs Barton, 'but Miss Barton is, and I'm not going in till these dogs have gone.'

Jimmy, without a word, handed his parcel to Mrs Barton,

opened the gate, shut it behind him and walked up to the front door. The dogs recognising in him one of their natural masters or equals took no notice of him, beyond a perfunctory sniff, and continued their work of defending the house and garden. The front door was opened, a parlour-maid appeared, Jimmy spoke to her, she went away, and Sally came into the garden, brandishing the dogs' leads. In a moment they were all captive and Sally came down and let her visitors in.

'I am sorry, Mrs Barton,' she said. 'I meant to shut them up when you came, but I was doing the beagles accounts and forgot all about it. Do go in, and I'll take them round to the back.'

'Have you seen what Chips has done?' said Mrs Barton, pointing to a large hole in the turf with earth scattered round it.

'Chips, you *are* a bad dog,' said Sally in a loving and severe voice.

Chips, choosing to recognise the love rather than the severity, uttered a short bark, pushed his face affectionately into his mistress's hand, and ran round his friends till all their leads were inextricably plaited. Sally unhooked the lead from his collar, picked him up, beat him gently on the nose, and went off, pulling the other dogs after her, in the direction of the stables.

In Sally's sitting-room Mr Foster was seated at the writing-table. He got up as they came in.

'Oh,' said Alice.

'Sally told me you were coming,' said Mr Foster. 'How do you do.'

'Oh, how do you do,' said Alice, looking helplessly from Mr Foster to her mother.

Mrs Barton wanted to tell her daughter to introduce her unknown friend, but it appeared from Alice's expression that any suggestion to this effect might precipitate her into lunacy. Mr Foster said in his gentle way, 'Will you introduce me?'

'Oh,' said Alice, looking in a fixed way in front of her, 'it's Mr Foster, Mother, that was so kind to me,' and backed into the wireless.

Mrs Barton, thinking it best to ignore her daughter, began to talk to Mr Foster. They were both fond of Lady Pomfret, both knew Italy, both liked pictures, and they got on extremely well. When Sally came back she found her guests talking away like old friends.

'I thought you and Gillie would get on,' she said to Mrs Barton. 'He's been helping me with the accounts this afternoon. I thought he ought to know a bit about the beagles if he's going to live down here. He's going to subscribe.'

Alice now summoned up enough courage to ask how everyone was at the Towers. Mr Foster said his uncle and aunt were very well. Mrs Rivers was still in bed and so was Julian. The kitchen-maid and the footman and one of the housemaids were almost well, but the other housemaid had been taken to the Nutfield Cottage Hospital in an ambulance, as pneumonia was feared. Sally said she wouldn't nurse Julian for anything and hoped they had cut his hair off.

'I don't know about his hair,' said Mr Foster, handing cake to people, 'I haven't seen him, but Merry, who goes up every day, says he is a difficult patient. It has been hard work for Merry. Of course we got nurses, but that all means extra organising and a lot of waiting on the bedrooms, when you are shorthanded. But she is a marvel. I think she's coming to fetch me, Sally, on her way back from visiting the housemaid in hospital. Will that be all right?'

Although Mr Foster had spoken in this slighting way of Julian, Alice found it impossible to dislike him because she felt so comfortable with him. Really more comfortable than with anyone; except Roddy, she was going to add mentally, but then she remembered how brutal Roddy had been to Julian, and thought poorly of him.

'What happened to your car, Gillie?' said Sally.

'They got it out next day,' said Mr Foster. 'One of the guards was a bit bent, that was all.'

Mrs Barton asked if Mr Foster had had an accident. Mr Foster said no, it was nothing, but Sally the uninhibited said it was Guy joyriding with Phoebe. These side-lights on her son interested Mrs Barton in an abstract way, and she felt a certain curiosity to see the Phoebe of whom Alice had spoken so warmly. Her wish was shortly granted, for when Miss Merriman, looking a little tired but equable as ever, came in from the Cottage Hospital, she brought Phoebe with her.

Phoebe was at first inclined to consider Mrs Barton in the dual and unpleasant light of a mother and a writer, but Mrs Barton's all-embracing vagueness and her apparent unconsciousness of being a female author gradually won Phoebe's confidence, till she found herself talking about herself quite naturally.

'Do you know my mother?' she asked.

Mrs Barton said she had never met her.

'I thought all the writers got together,' said Phoebe, 'like the theatricals.'

'I hardly ever go to London,' said Mrs Barton placidly. 'Tell me about your theatre work.'

'I loathe it,' said Phoebe violently.

Mrs Barton said she was very sorry, and she did hope Phoebe would come over to Mellings and see Alice, or perhaps stay the night.

'Yes, I'd love to,' said Phoebe, and then added abruptly, 'Do you know why I came here?'

Mrs Barton hazarded that it was to see Sally.

'Mother made me come,' said Phoebe. 'She found out that Gillie was going to help Sally with the accounts, and Merry was going to fetch him, so she made me come too. One can't fight all the time. Can I get you some more tea?'

Mrs Barton judged, rightly, that Phoebe, having made this sudden half-confidence, didn't want to continue it. It was all confusing, especially as everyone's name appeared to end with a Y, but she had gathered from her children's conversation that Mrs Rivers was doing her best to make Mr Foster marry Phoebe, and if that was so she felt very sorry for the handsome, elegant, sullen girl. Phoebe was now talking and laughing with the others, but she smoked incessantly and looked restlessly about. Miss Merriman was giving a vivid account of Lord Pomfret's rage when he found on Monday morning that Mr Johns had gone off by an early train without making an offer for his Life. Miss Merriman said she had written to the London housekeeper to post the typescript to

Mr Johns at once, and hoped he would soon send word about it, for what with that and the influenza his lordship was in a mood that spread gloom all over the Towers.

'And what's more,' put in Phoebe, 'he has been letting Mother talk to him about publishers, and there's going to be some dirty work I should say.'

The door opened. Mrs Barton saw Phoebe's face light up and sink back to indifference as Roddy Wicklow came in. She also saw her own child, who had been talking very happily to Mr Foster, look up with her most delightful smile, and suddenly turn it off like an electric light. Of course it was because Roddy had been brutal, as she put it, to that assuredly odious Julian Rivers. She watched how Roddy went and sat near Alice, how pleasantly Alice talked to him when she forgot, and how suddenly she froze when she remembered. Roddy appeared to have made up his mind to take things as they came, and remained his usual large, safe, comfortable self.

Presently Miss Merriman said she must be getting back. The spaniels, she said to Sally, were doing nicely. Giulia was quite herself again and Lady Pomfret was delighted. This rash remark reminded Sally of her dogs, and she offered the company the great treat of going out to the stable and looking at a litter of five cocker spaniels. Mrs Barton, who did not in the least want to see them, felt she must make some return for Sally's kindness in having caught and imprisoned Chloe, Chips and Wuffy, and she accepted the invitation.

Just as Mr Foster was following the rest of the party Phoebe, who had been looking angrily at some magazines, called him back.

'I didn't want to come here,' she said. 'I suppose you know that. It's all Mother.'

Mr Foster said nothing.

'I think the best thing I could do,' said Phoebe bitterly, 'would be to propose to you. Then you could refuse me and Mother would shut up for a bit.'

'I am so sorry, Phoebe,' said Mr Foster. 'You know I don't like it any more than you do.'

'But you don't have to listen to Mother,' said Phoebe. 'You're an angel, Gillie, and I adore you, but we could never make a do of it. Oh God!' she added inconsistently, 'I'd marry *anyone* to get out of all this.'

'But not me,' said Mr Foster very kindly, but firmly.

'No, no, not you,' said Phoebe. 'Go along and look at Sally's puppies. I'll go and sit in Merry's car.'

She was fighting her angry tears and Mr Foster knew it. He liked his cousin Phoebe very well indeed, but his conviction was strong that they would, in her elegant phrase, never make a do of it. He thought of his cousin Hermione, and felt a strong wish to take a good handful of her well-waved hair and pull it. He laid his arm on Phoebe's shaking shoulders and held her for a moment. She laid her cheek on his hand and he felt that her cheek was wet.

When Mr Foster had gone, Phoebe dried her eyes fiercely and went into the hall. As she opened the front door, a shaft of light streamed out, down the flagged path. Guy Barton came up it.

'Hullo!' he called, with that complacency which his mother found hard to bear. 'I thought I'd find you here.'

'Oh,' said Phoebe who had come out of the house and met him on the porch. 'And why?'

'Because I told you this morning at Plumstead.'

'Did you?' said Phoebe carelessly. 'Well, if you want to know I wasn't thinking of you. I meant to go riding. But Mother knew Gillie was here, and Merry was coming too, so Mother went at me till I came with Merry. That's all.'

'Well, that's all right,' said Guy. 'And now you can talk to me. Come in.'

'I'm going to sit in the car,' said Phoebe.

'Oh, come on,' said Guy. 'I say, you're not crying are you?'

'Shut up!' cried Phoebe. 'Well then, yes I am. I hate everyone. I wish to God I were clever enough to earn my living. The stage is a joke. If I don't get away I'll die. I'd do anything to get away from Mother, anything. I'd marry the crossing-sweeper.'

She pushed past Guy.

'Hold on,' said Guy, catching her by the arm. 'Did you mean that?'

'Mean what?'

'About marrying the crossing-sweeper.'

'Let go of me. I'd marry anyone.'

'Then marry me,' said Guy.

'Oh, all right. I don't care if I do,' said Phoebe.

The whole party, returning from the stables through the house, were able to have a first-rate view of Mr Guy Barton holding Miss Phoebe Rivers in his arms, illuminated by the light from the hall. The same light showed them up excellently in silhouette to anyone going past in the High Street. In fact Jimmy Bones, renowned for always being there when an accident happened, was standing at the gate, printing off impressions of the bars on his face in his eagerness to see the lady and gentleman.

With remarkable presence of mind Roddy strode forward and shut the front door. Everyone, he said, must be dying for a drink, so he herded them all back into Sally's room, and fetched the sherry. When Guy and Phoebe strolled in a moment later, although the room was almost bursting with curiosity, no one made any allusion to the scene they had just witnessed. Miss Merriman then collected her charges and drove them back to the Towers, in silence. Phoebe in the dark reached out a hand to the back seat. Mr Foster took it, patted it in a soothing way, and restored it to its owner. It speaks volumes for Miss Merriman's character that Phoebe never thought of asking her not to speak of what she had seen.

As everyone had been too gentlemanly to discuss the scene which had taken place outside the front door, it was not till they got home, or in the Wicklows' case were alone, that they could discuss it. The first to react was Jimmy Bones, who went straight back to his tea and while eating it told his mother he had seen Mr Barton kissing a lady. His mother very rightly told him not to be a story. Jimmy protested that he wasn't a story and it was just like the pictures. Mr Bones, who had just come in from the shop, said what was all this about, and on hearing that Jimmy was a horrid story and had contradicted his mother, cuffed his son for giving sauce. The threepence with which he was to go to the pictures after tea was then confiscated and Jimmy sent in tears to bed, while Mr and Mrs Bones went to the village whist drive, where Mr Bones, by his excellent play, leading first all his aces and then his trumps, scored the highest marks and received a china cruet composed of three mushrooms with scarlet lids.

Roddy and Sally, drinking sherry when the others had gone, had little to say. Sally, who was two years younger than Guy, merely remarked that he was a young fool. Roddy said he hoped Alice hadn't noticed, which made his sister look at him curiously. They then agreed that it was a shame about Phoebe and that Gillie was no end of a good sort, after which Sally went to feed the puppies and Roddy did some of the extra work that Mr Hoare's illness had forced on him.

Alice went into her mother's room before dinner and fidgeted with the ornaments on the mantelpiece in a way that made her mother ask what it was.

'Mother,' said Alice, 'did you see?'

Mrs Barton, whose ideals of unstained womanhood were not so high as Roddy's, knew at once what her daughter meant.

'I did indeed,' she said. 'I wonder if Guy noticed that we were all there. I thought it very tactful of Roddy to shut the door. I don't think we'll tell your father; it might worry him.'

This was delightful. One was being promoted to gossip about people like a grown-up person. She and her mother were delightfully conspiring against the men of the family. It all came of spending a weekend at the Towers, which enlarged one's mind. For ten minutes she and her mother had a delicious gabble about Guy and Phoebe and whether it meant anything and what fun it would be. Then the gong sounded for dinner. As they went downstairs Alice said, 'I don't think we shall hear anything about it from Guy, Mother.'

'No, I don't suppose we shall,' said Mrs Barton. And she also was pleased and surprised to find an ally in her daughter instead of a creature of no opinions, and again applauded her own courage and foresight in having sent her to the Pomfrets, which had brought her out so much.

At dinner Guy was in a mood of quite odious complacency. As a matter of fact, he had not noticed the party in the hall, his face having been at the moment buried in Miss Rivers's cheek and ear, but he had noticed that the light was cut off and thought it was just as well. Fain would he have made arrangements with Phoebe to get married at once, or failing that to meet her again at Plumstead as soon as possible, but she had wrenched herself away, saying she would telephone some time, and turned back to the house. The front door was never locked except at night, so they went back to Sally's room, as we have before described, and Guy, if he thought at all, thought the wind had blown the door to.

At any rate Phoebe, who was quite the jolliest girl he knew, was going to marry him. It had been no trouble. She had simply fallen into his hand, so to speak. He saw no reason to mention the affair to his parents, who might say something stupid about money, or waiting for a bit, and as for Alice, the kid wouldn't understand if he told her. All this put him in a very good humour, and he talked a good deal, rather tiring his father, and never noticing the occasional conspirators' glances that passed between his mother and sister.

The party at Pomfret Towers was a small one, owing to influenza. Only the family and Miss Merriman were present at dinner, Julian being still in his room. Mrs Rivers was still feeling weak after her illness, though not too weak to make the plans that had goaded her daughter into Guy's arms. As Lord Pomfret was afflicted by a deliberate fit of angry deafness that made him request to have every remark at the table repeated to him, Mrs Rivers could not talk privately with her daughter, but in the drawing-room she lay languidly on a sofa and called Phoebe to her side. One cannot refuse a parent's dying wish, so Phoebe unwillingly took her place by her mother.

'You are looking very nice tonight, darling,' said Mrs Rivers. 'Did you have a nice time at the Wicklows'?'

Phoebe, in whom self-dislike, anger and other emotions that she could not analyse had produced a very becoming colour, said Yes it was very nice. Sally, she added, had shown them the puppies.

Mrs Rivers embarked on a rambling speech in which she tried to convey to Phoebe by hints, how she could depart in peace if she knew that her daughter were happy, and how likely it was that someone would snap dear Gillie up because he was so generous and unsuspecting. She was prepared for Phoebe to shut up angrily; that she would say Gillie had come to the point that afternoon she dared not hope, but what Phoebe did say took her entirely aback.

'Yes, Gillie is very kind,' said Phoebe.

Her mother then attempted to take her hand, but this was too much. On the pretence that the fire was too hot for her she withdrew to a safe distance, and presently Miss Merriman came up to say she was going to see that Julian was all right. Mrs Rivers said she was tired, and going up to bed, so she would come too, and Phoebe was left in peace.

Julian's nurse was just going to bed, and only waiting to report to Miss Merriman.

'Good evening, Mrs Rivers,' she said brightly, as the ladies came in. 'Well, we've tucked your big boy up all nice and comfy for the night.'

Julian, who had come to hate the kind, efficient nurse Chiffinch with a loathing that even his dark soul had never before known, snarled and turned over in bed with his face to the wall.

'Isn't he just like a big baby!' exclaimed Nurse Chiffinch delightedly.

Miss Merriman inquired if everything was all right for the night.

'We're all nice and comfy,' said Nurse, whose use of the editorial we was only one of the few things that had enraged her patient. 'We shan't be needing a nurse much longer now, and it's just as well,' she continued in a mysterious voice, every syllable of which clearly reached the patient, 'because I'm booked on Monday week for Mrs Adrian Coates, the publisher's wife you know. I was with her for her First, and she said she must have me for the Second,' said Nurse, as if Mrs Coates were a charade. 'Baby Coates was such a *dear* little mite, and sometimes the Second comes along quite in a hurry, and I don't want to be caught napping.'

At the conclusion of this speech Julian groaned so loudly that his mother went over to the bed and asked what it was.

'God! Do send that woman away,' said Julian taking no trouble to moderate his voice.

Mrs Rivers feared Nurse would be offended, but she only

remarked, bridling, that it was funny the way gentlemen never could bear anyone in the room as soon as they got better. That was quite a sign, she said, that young Mr Rivers was better, and now she thought it was high time he went to shut-eye.

At this broad hint Mrs Rivers and Miss Merriman left the room, to the sound of Julian saying 'God! God!' in a monotonous drone, as if it were a charm against nurses.

'Good night, Mrs Rivers,' said Miss Merriman pleasantly.

Mrs Rivers had meant to pump Merry, as she put it, about the afternoon's doings, but something in Miss Merriman's cheerful, determined farewell made her feel that it would be pure waste of time, so she said good night and went to bed.

Miss Merriman went downstairs, and seeing that Lady Pomfret was still peacefully embroidering, she went to her own sitting-room to go through some household accounts. Here she found Mr Foster.

'I thought you might be coming, Merry,' said Mr Foster. 'I wanted to talk to you.'

He looked anxious, and Miss Merriman said she hoped she could help.

'It's about Phoebe,' said Mr Foster. 'Hermione is making it all very difficult. Would it be possible to make her understand that Phoebe and I haven't the faintest idea of getting married?'

'I don't think it would,' said Miss Merriman candidly. 'Unless of course you told her what we saw tonight. And even then she would only be angry and think it a stupid joke.'

'Is that what it was, do you think?' asked Mr Foster.

'I don't know at all. Mr Guy Barton seems a nice young man, and he and Miss Rivers have been a great deal together lately, but I don't in the least know if it is serious. I wish you wouldn't worry about them.'

'I must,' said Mr Foster seriously. 'I can't bear to see Phoebe so wretched, and after all she is my cousin. It gets harder and harder.'

'What does?'

'Responsibilities.'

'But Miss Rivers isn't your responsibility,' said Miss Merriman, perturbed that Mr Foster should be shouldering this burden.

'She might be,' said Mr Foster. 'I heard today that my father is much worse.'

'I see,' said Miss Merriman, who knew better than anyone how seriously Mr Foster was taking his future responsibilities, the family and its welfare included. If his father were to die now, he would be a step nearer to the burden that he would carry for the rest of his life. She felt very angry, an emotion from which she had studiously withdrawn herself, with Mrs Rivers, and very sorry for Mr Foster.

'Well, I suppose things will right themselves,' said Mr Foster wearily. 'And that reminds me, I think there's a chance of getting Mrs Tucker's cottage repaired now that Hoare is away. I can't tell you what a help Wicklow is – and his sister too. With you to help what a lot of work we could do.'

'Well, when you are running things here I shall be gone,' said Miss Merriman, full of compassion for the young heir, but determined to keep her own integrity of purpose.

'Too bad,' said Mr Foster smiling ruefully. 'Didn't Alice Barton look well this afternoon.'

Miss Merriman cordially agreed. Then Mr Foster went away, and Lady Pomfret came in to talk, and it was eleven o'clock before she could begin the household accounts. She saw a light under Phoebe's door as she went up to bed an hour later, but made no sign.

Phoebe, restless and angry, was lying in bed trying to read, but unable to follow more than a few lines. Guy had offered her a way of escape and she had accepted it, but what did it all mean? She had found a certain savage pleasure in being held by him, but nothing in her told her to return his embrace. And it was all a little scullery-maidish to be kissed on the front door steps with hundreds of people spying. For Phoebe had been only too conscious of the arrival of the spectators and Roddy's quick action. She would marry Guy at once and get away from her mother and Julian. She certainly wouldn't marry a man who could make her a subject for the talk of her friends. She could still imagine the smell of Guy's coat, her eyes looking over his shoulder at the hall and the people. She hated him and would never speak to him again. So her thoughts battered backwards and forwards till the book fell from her hand, and she lay asleep with the light still on. She slept uneasily till three o'clock when she woke with a start to find her light burning. She switched it off, but not till daybreak did she again fall asleep.

9

Lady Pomfret Intervenes

Let us now visit calmer scenes.

In the Polyanthus Club Mr Johns was having lunch with two acquaintances. One was the brother publisher, Mr Bungay, whom we have heard Mrs Rivers mention as a rival to Mr Johns for her bestsellers. Mr Bungay is the present representative of the house in Paternoster Row founded some hundred years ago by his great-grandfather. In the middle of the last century their most serious rival was the house of Bacon, who made a great hit with three-volume novels by people of fashion, but in 1887 an amalgamation took place, Messrs Bungay taking over all the assets and liabilities of Messrs Bacon, together with their copyright in the works of Arthur Pendennis Esq and other well-known novelists of the day, works for which there is now no sale, and which from lying on twopenny stalls have almost risen to be collector's rarities. The present Mr Bungay exploits freely every shade of passing political and religious opinion that may help his sales and is said to have the largest turnover in London. He admits freely that he publishes a great deal of rubbish, but he adds that he believes in giving the public what it wants.

The other guest, Mr Hobb, was a member of a large literary agency. Both these gentlemen envied Mr Johns his connection with Mrs Rivers and Mr Johns knew it, and they all knew that any one of them would be delighted to do down any other, so the utmost harmony reigned.

'How is Mrs Rivers doing?' asked the agent, a very tall and large man, well-dressed, bald and depressing, with a manner of gliding into his office from a side door without perceptibly moving his feet which had struck terror into many young writers and caused them to accept the lowest terms Mr Hobb could offer.

'Mrs Rivers is doing nicely, thank you,' said Mr Johns.

'I hear you did twenty-five thousand of her last book,' said Mr Bungay.

Mr Johns, evading any direct reply, said the whole business of production was becoming so expensive that he didn't know how he would go on much longer, which remark confirmed his friends in the truth of Mr Bungay's last words.

'I expect she does pretty well out of you,' said Mr Hobb.

Mr Johns asked him if he knew Mrs Morland, who wrote those very successful sellers.

'Our friend Adrian Coates publishes her stuff,' he said. 'He told me a most amusing story about her. It seems that the question of dealing direct with your publisher as against employing an agent was under discussion, and Mrs Morland very wittily defined an agent as someone whom you pay to make bad blood between yourself and your publisher.'

Mr Hobb laughed heartily, as did Mr Bungay, and both gentlemen felt positive that Mrs Rivers, properly approached by an agent of position and tact, might be inveigled into Mr Bungay's parlour.

'By the way, Johns,' said Mr Bungay, 'you were staying at Pomfret's place, weren't you, last week?'

'Yes,' said Mr Johns. 'Mrs Rivers is a cousin of his you know. I had to see her on business.'

'Now a life of Lord Pomfret would be an interesting thing to handle,' said Mr Bungay.

'Yes, indeed,' said Mr Johns, 'but I can't say that I've seen any such thing.'

Now in this he was perfectly truthful, for the parcel which Lord Pomfret's town housekeeper had sent on Miss Merriman's request was still lying in the office safe, and he hoped to find time to inspect the typescript that evening.

'Curious story that of Johns's, about Mrs Morland,' said Mr Hobb to Mr Bungay, when Mr Johns had gone back to work.

'Very amusing,' said Mr Bungay. 'I don't suppose there's much in that talk of twenty-five thousand, but it would be interesting to know.'

'Quite, quite,' said Mr Hobb. 'Of course it does no harm to make an offer. I handle her magazine stuff, you know.'

Both gentlemen were silent for a moment, Mr Bungay feeling that anyone with as good a circulation as Mrs Rivers should certainly be on his list, Mr Hobb reflecting with religious disapproval on the back-sliding of authors who dealt direct with their publishers and so defrauded the agents of their hard-earned ten per cent.

'Well, I'll ring you up before long,' said Mr Bungay.

'I may have something to say to you then,' said Mr Hobb.

And both gentlemen went back to their offices.

At last the tide of influenza began to recede from Pomfret Towers. Nurse Chiffinch got to the Adrian Coateses' in plenty of time and wrote to Mrs Rivers that Baby Coates was a dear wee mite and his little sister was so proud of him and she did hope Mr Rivers was feeling quite himself again as the saying is. The housemaid had pneumonia in the Cottage Hospital and went home to her mother for a rest, but luckily Wheeler's married sister's Esme was able to oblige. Mrs Rivers had to go to Bournemouth alone, because Julian was so disagreeable when the subject of a little change was mentioned that she thought it best to drop the matter. However, at Bournemouth she was able to go on with her Work, and by the time she got back to Pomfret Towers Lady Travers had renounced the Corsican savant and met her husband at Singapore. They met in the lounge with well-bred calm, Laura Travers cool and immaculate in white, her husband thin, distinguished, also in white. Mrs Rivers had the end sketched out in her mind. After dining with the Governor, a cousin of Sir Hugh's (for Sir Hugh Travers was his name), they would return to the hotel. Correctly and impeccably they would go to their rooms. Laura would go out onto her balcony. Sir Hugh would go out onto his. The moon would shine. Striding over the partition (she would verify the exact height of balcony partitions at good hotels in Singapore) he would say, always cool and correct: 'Laura,

I know I have not always understood, but I have needed you.'

'And I, my dear,' she would reply, 'have kept for you what you need.'

Together they would pass into the perfumed darkness of her room. And the same moon that laid silver upon the sleeping sea outside their window (she must see if any of the hotels were on the sea), shone on the Marquis dei Franchi as he worked in his tent at Angkor, knowing that a pale pure face would for ever rise between him and all that might make life divine.

Mrs Rivers was so overcome by the beauty of her own thoughts that she almost felt Sir Hugh's strong arms about her in her second floor front. Yes, she would get the work finished by the end of the month, and armed with it approach Mr Johns on the question of bigger and better contracts. For Mrs Rivers had as perfect a faith in her public as her public had in her, and both were right.

At last Julian did ring up. Alice was out and nearly cried when she got back and found what she had missed. However he rang up again before dinner, when she was in her bath, and left a message that he was coming next day. Alice knew her mother would not approve this cavalier treatment, and rather timidly asked if it would be all right. Mrs Barton, having determined to put no obstacle in the way of Alice's newly developing wish to see some young friends, said certainly, and when was Julian coming, because she would like to see him. As he hadn't mentioned an hour Alice was unable to say. Mrs Barton suggested that Alice should ring Julian up after dinner, and during that meal watched her daughter with amusement and some concern as she nervously sparkled in her looks and talk.

The telephoning was not altogether a success. Julian said it was such a bore to make plans and as his mother hadn't taken the car to Bournemouth he would come over any time. Alice said it would be very nice if Phoebe could come, but when Julian said God! they didn't want a whole crowd of people, she saw how stupid she had been. Anyway, Julian said, Mother would be back next week, so they must get something done or she would want to interfere. He would come over some time in the morning, or if not some time in the afternoon. With this meagre fare Alice was forced to be content, and told her mother what Julian had said.

'I say, you're not having that ass Julian over here, are you?' asked her affectionate brother. 'Why don't you ask Phoebe?'

'I did,' said Alice, 'but Julian said it would be too many people.'

'Oh, Lord,' said Guy, 'isn't there room in this house for anyone's friends but yours? Anyone would think you were stuck on Julian.'

Alice looked wretched and said nothing.

'Don't speak like that to Alice, my boy,' said Mr Barton, who but rarely interfered with his family, usually at the wrong moment, and often without effect.

Guy launched a parent-quelling look at his father, but scorned to speak. Mr Barton, who had retired into the Journal of the R.I.B.A., did not see the look, but Mrs Barton did, and thought it as well to divert the conversation.

'Guy,' she said, by an association of ideas which should be

plain to anyone, 'did you ask Lord Pomfret about that book for me?'

'What book, Mother?' said Guy, adopting a schoolboy's tactics to gain time.

'That book by Count Strelsa about the cinquecento,' said Mrs Barton.

Mr Barton, who had an annoying way of getting behind his book or paper and being deaf if spoken to, but hearing perfectly well conversations that didn't concern him, said he couldn't think why the Italians couldn't say sixteenth century like everyone else and have done with it. Something was wrong with them, he said, when it came to figures. Why had they got to say 'They are the seven' when they meant 'It is seven'?

Guy said if he had seven things, he would certainly say they were seven, not it was seven.

'Your father,' said Mrs Barton, as if her husband were a baby or a lunatic, 'means o'clock.'

Guy said he didn't see why a clock should be they.

Mrs Barton, seeing no end to this philological discussion, asked Guy again whether he had asked Lord Pomfret for the book she asked him to ask for.

Guy said he had, but everyone interrupted so much that Lord Pomfret hadn't seemed to know what he meant and he was awfully sorry.

'Never mind,' said Mrs Barton cheerfully. 'I'll write tomorrow and ask him. And I must write to Mr Johns, Alice. I had a letter from him this afternoon and he will be in Barchester the weekend after next, so I'll try and get him to lunch here.'

It shows how much Alice's weekend at the Towers had improved her, that instead of going scarlet, wringing her hands, twisting her feet, and being stricken with twittering palsy, she merely said with a slight stammer that it would be very nice to see him.

All that evening and all next morning Alice waited for Julian. She had particularly wanted to go as far as the post-office to get a twopenny card of pearl-headed pins, but did not think it safe to leave the grounds. She did at half-past twelve decide that no man was worth waiting for, and made an effort to put this valiant resolve into practice, but when she got as far up the road as the place where the curve prevented you from seeing the Mellings gate, she had to turn back in case Julian had come and she had missed him.

She and her mother were in the middle of lunch when the front door-bell rang. Alice, who had temporarily given up hope, thought it was the post, or a message, and was taking no further notice, when Horton came in and said in a voice of extreme distaste that there was a young gentleman to see Miss Alice, and he had shown him into the morning-room. This alone was enough to show how far below Horton's standards Julian fell, for the morning-room, though so called, was only used in the evening, if the large drawing-room was not in use, and rarely had a fire in it till after tea.

'I suppose that is Julian,' said Mrs Barton calmly. 'If it's Mr Rivers, Horton, you had better ask him to come in here. And bring three cups when you bring the coffee.'

Horton had a loyal nature. However he might disapprove of his employers, he rarely hesitated to obey their commands. With the expression of one who picks a half-drowned fly out of a glass of milk and leaves it on the tablecloth to recover itself, he delivered Julian to Mrs Barton and retired to tell the staff what he thought of Miss Alice's young man.

Julian was in his usual professional garb of dirty grey trousers, an old tweed coat, a bright blue shirt and an orange pullover. Partly owing to shyness, partly to defiance, he was still carrying a bundle of canvases under his right arm, and in his left hand held a bag of painting materials.

'I'm afraid I can't shake hands,' he said.

That would learn Alice's mother what to expect.

'Of course you can't with all those things in your hands,' said Mrs Barton. 'Put them down in the hall, will you. I'm so glad you could come,' she continued when he had reluctantly done her bidding and returned. 'We had quite given you up.'

While she spoke she held out her hand, which Julian shook, after a visible struggle with his better nature.

'And you know Alice, of course,' said Mrs Barton.

'Hullo,' said Julian. 'I say, are you having lunch?'

Mrs Barton, looking at the table on which a delicious treacle pudding was still sitting, said they were and asked Julian if he would like some. Julian, who had meant to come earlier, but forgot to get up till nearly twelve, was human enough to say he would. Mrs Barton rang for another plate and Julian pitched into the pudding like a schoolboy.

'Didn't you have any lunch?' asked Alice, who had not yet spoken.

'No. I ran it a bit fine, so I came here and didn't bother,' said Julian. 'Could I have some more, Mrs Barton?'

Both young people then fell silent again. Julian eating, Alice turning a pretty pink, fidgeting with everything within reach, and from time to time gulping as if she had swallowed something she meant to say. There was no doubt, thought Mrs Barton, that the child was attracted by this good-looking, mannerless youth. How long the attraction would last she could not guess, but as violent delights often have violent ends, she did not intend to interfere.

When Julian had consumed practically all the rest of the pudding, a glass of cider, four biscuits and a great hunk of cheese, a banana, and a cup of coffee, he got up and shook the crumbs on his pullover and trousers from him.

'Come on,' he said to Alice. 'Where's the studio?'

'Are you going to paint?' said Mrs Barton. 'Horton will show you where to wash, and tea is at five.'

So saying, she smiled kindly and went off to do some writing. Horton, seeing his enemy delivered into his hands, took great pleasure in terrorising him into the cloak-room and saying he would wait and show him the way, so that Julian, who believed in honest dirt, was obliged to wash long and loudly, fearing that Horton might ask to look at his hands.

When tea-time came Mrs Barton sent Horton to fetch the young people, and so well did he carry out his mission that by ten minutes past five they were all sitting round tea and toast in the drawing-room.

'How did you get on?' asked Mrs Barton.

Alice looked piteously at her mother. She knew that one didn't talk to artists like that. If one did they were apt to burst out in a scornful way. But much to her relief Julian only embarked upon a lecture on studios. Alice's studio was, it appeared, wrong in shape, aspect, decoration, and atmosphere. But all the same he had managed, he said, to put in some damned, he meant some pretty good stuff.

'I don't think it much matters what a studio is like if you really want to paint,' said Mrs Barton.

Julian said the wanting was everything.

Mrs Barton said she didn't know about that. Some people wanted to paint frightfully, but it never seemed to lead anywhere.

'I used to know a man years ago in Florence,' she said, 'who had a really violent wish to paint, but I don't think anyone ever looked at his pictures. He was one of those Russian émigrés. Bolikoff was the name.'

Julian stared at her as if he were committing her every feature to memory.

'Did you *know* Bolikoff?' he said, picking up his buttered tea-cake.

'Yes. I saw a good deal of him in Florence. He got some of my friends to let him paint them. Just dip your handkerchief in this hot water, Mr Rivers,' said Mrs Barton, pouring some boiling water into the slop basin, 'and rub that butter off your trousers.'

Julian pulled out what looked like a very old paint rag.

'No. That will only make it worse,' said Mrs Barton, concentrating upon the work in hand. 'Alice, get that clean handkerchief out of my writing-table drawer.'

She dipped the clean handkerchief into the hot water and handed it to Julian, who gingerly rubbed the stain on his trousers.

'Now wet it again and rub a rather larger circle,' said Mrs Barton, 'then there won't be a mark.'

'Did you really *know* Bolikoff?' Julian repeated, incredulous, but overawed.

'We all did,' said Mrs Barton. 'He borrowed a great deal of money in small sums and never paid it back. An odious, selfish, conceited little man I always thought – and so dirty,' she added reflectively.

Julian was so stunned by this criticism of one of his gods that he took very little further part in the conversation, gazing with superstitious awe upon the iconoclast. It did not improve his spirits that Mr Barton came in tired and not very ready for unknown young men, and shortly afterwards he rose to go.

'Well, goodbye,' said his hostess. 'You must come again soon.'

'Oh yes, goodbye,' said Julian. 'Oh,' he added, pulling a parcel from one of his coat pockets. 'I forgot. Cousin Giles said to give you this.'

Mrs Barton took the parcel, thanked Julian, and hustled him and Alice out of the room. Then she gave tea to her husband and let him talk till he was soothed. When he began to read the evening paper she opened the packet. In it was Count Strelsa's book and a letter from Lord Pomfret, in which his lordship expressed the opinion that the money that had been spent on her son Guy's education had been entirely wasted, but he, Lord Pomfret, supposed this was the book she meant and she could keep it as long as she liked. A postscript said: 'Send that girl of yours here again sometime. Edith likes her.'

Mrs Barton was pleased and touched by this message and by Lord Pomfret's thought of the book. Later in the evening she gave the message to Alice who looked gratified. Her mother inquired what sort of a beginning Julian had made with the portrait, but Alice hadn't much to say. It had been a thrilling, wonderful afternoon, and Julian was more god-like than ever, but she could not think of any one of his remarks that her mother would really appreciate. As they had consisted entirely of praise of himself and criticism of Alice's studio, she was probably right. She would have liked to have shown Julian her drawings and asked for his opinion, but some mysterious instinct warned her that his opinion would be of an unfavourable, even of a crushing nature, so she refrained.

Julian now came nearly every day, at any hour that suited his fancy, finding Alice's warm studio much more agreeable to work in than the racket court at Pomfret Towers, which the oil-stove certainly did not heat. Mrs Barton, looking down from the Renaissance from time to time, continued her policy of not interfering. The only drawback to Alice's happiness was that she saw very little of Roddy and Sally.

A week or so later Miss Merriman rang up to say that Lady Pomfret would like to come and visit Mrs Barton. Accordingly Lady Pomfret drove over with the faithful Merry, who had some shopping to do in Nutfield and was to join them at tea an hour or so later.

It was a very pleasant meeting. Though Mrs Barton and young Lord Mellings had never been in love they had been very good friends, and Mrs Barton had kept a tender memory of a spring in Florence before Mellings went out to

India and was killed. Lady Pomfret had also kept that spring in her mind and had always thought affectionately of Susan Barton as the girl that might have made Mellings happy. Seeing Alice had reminded her of the days before sorrow had broken her health and driven her into herself, and her wish to see Mrs Barton was very real. There were many things to talk of, many remembrances to share. Mrs Barton found her old friend as kind as ever. Lady Pomfret found in Susan Barton all the warmth and affection of the girl she had befriended, and a serenity that had grown with the years. No tears were shed for what had happened so long ago, but both women were moved by their evocation of the past, and felt a renewing of their old friendship.

Lady Pomfret spoke a little of her own life, blaming herself for having been too easily defeated, for having left her husband to do his duty alone.

'Giles is a good man, Susan,' she said. 'If Mellings had lived, we might both have been easier to each other, but it is rather late now. I have a habit of Italy now that I can't break, but I shall stay here as long as I can, and try to come back again during the year. Giles and I both feel we are getting old, and we want to see Gillie properly in the saddle before we go. I don't think you have met Gillie.'

Mrs Barton said she hadn't, but she remembered Major Foster, his father, at Florence one year, a very difficult, touchy man, she thought.

'Gillie is as nice as his father is odious,' said Lady Pomfret, almost with heat. 'Our great comfort is that humanly speaking Major Foster is likely to die at any moment. As soon as he does we shall feel much more comfortable.'

As Lady Pomfret spoke she reminded Mrs Barton of the handsome autocrat who had ruled half Florence thirty years ago.

'If we could see Gillie happily settled before we die,' said Lady Pomfret simply, 'we should feel the place was in safe hands. A wife is so important, Susan. I once thought you and Mellings might be very happy together.'

'There was never anything,' murmured Mrs Barton.

'Mellings would have told me if there were,' said Lady Pomfret, flashing in the old pride again. 'But if he had lived it might have come to pass. I have been thinking, Susan, that Gillie likes your girl.'

She waited for the words to make their effect. Mrs Barton, genuinely surprised, hardly knew what to say. Alice had certainly said that Mr Foster was very nice, but she had said the same of almost every member of the house party. The child wasn't twenty yet, and she had no wish to see her married for the present. Alice as a countess seemed so absurd that she smiled.

'It wouldn't be a bad plan,' said Lady Pomfret, misunderstanding her friend's smile. 'I'd like to think of your girl at Pomfret Towers, Susan. She is a little shy; that is only natural when she hasn't been about much. I suppose you will be giving her a season? If you wish, I should be glad to present her.'

All this was too much for Mrs Barton to cope with. She said something about Alice liking Mr Foster.

'But I haven't seen him at all,' she said.

'So I gathered from Gillie,' said Lady Pomfret, 'and I took the liberty, Susan, of asking him to come and fetch me this afternoon, so that you may meet. I would like you to be friends. Where is Alice, by the way?'

'In her studio, I think,' said her mother.

'I should like to see her work,' said Lady Pomfret. 'I never drew myself, but my mother-in-law had a remarkable talent for water-colour drawing. You must have seen some of her sketches at Casa Strelsa, the year you were there.'

Mrs Barton remembered well the industrious and lifeless yet faintly distinguished sketches with which the late Lady Pomfret had hung every room in the Casa Strelsa, and said so, though not exactly in those words. It used to surprise her that Lady Pomfret, who had a considerable knowledge of Italian pictures and very good taste, should attach so much importance to her mother-in-law's mediocre productions. But she had come to realise that her old friend had, when she married, taken on the family tradition, and that anything done by a Pomfret would have a special place in her eyes, quite apart from its intrinsic value. She realised that unless the next bearer of the title could cherish the hideous gros point chair covers which her friend had copied from some worked by the daughters of the fourth earl, she could not take her true place in the family. It was this same devotion to a family ideal that was driving Lady Pomfret to make plans for Mr Foster and Alice: and Alice was probably in her studio with Julian Rivers.

'We might go up and visit her,' said Lady Pomfret, rising.

'I think Julian Rivers is there,' said Mrs Barton. 'He is painting her portrait.'

'It is a pity he does not settle down to a profession,' said Lady Pomfret. 'But Hermione always spoilt him outrageously.

It is so disappointing for his father. Giles's cousin, you know. Julian will never get to know the right sort of people if he behaves so foolishly. Now Phoebe is a nice girl, much more like her father. I should like to see her properly married. Hermione has been trying to make Gillie take an interest in her, but Hermione is one of the stupidest women I know.'

They had now arrived at the studio. Mrs Barton knocked at the door, her invariable custom. Julian's voice was heard, and the door was opened a little way by Alice, who only seeing her mother said:

'Oh Mother, please could you not come in, Julian would rather not.'

'How are you, dear?' said Lady Pomfret, bending to kiss Alice. 'I want to see your studio.'

So saying, she pushed the door open and went in. Her young cousin was standing behind an easel, dabbing on paint with concentrated fury. His paints and brushes were lying about everywhere, the room reeked of turpentine and cigarettes. Alice, seeing the disapproval in Lady Pomfret's face, hastened to explain that things were rather in a mess.

'That is Julian's doing, I suppose,' said the countess. 'Julian!' she said sharply.

Julian looked round the easel, saw his cousin, and came forward.

'I should have thought the racquet-court a *much* better place to make all this mess than Miss Barton's studio,' said Lady Pomfret. 'Let me see what you are doing, Julian.'

Alice waited for the heavens to fall, but such was Lady Pomfret's unconsciousness of her atrocious behaviour in actually asking an artist if she might look at his work, that the very heavens were appalled and stayed their hand. In Lady Pomfret's experience artists were not only pleased but flattered if you asked to see their pictures, and she studied her young cousin's canvas with perfect unconcern while he stood sulkily by.

Having finished her inspection in unfriendly silence, she turned to Alice and asked whether she might see some of her work. Alice very diffidently produced some water-colour drawings and pencil sketches which her ladyship inspected, again in silence, but a silence of a warm, sympathetic, approving kind.

'I like these very much, very much indeed,' she announced. 'It is a great pity Julian hasn't your gift for line. Without line he will never get anywhere. You must come and stay with us in Florence, as your mother used to. Tell her to bring you. Susan, you and this child must come to Casa Strelsa in April and Gillie shall come too. Now, Susan, will you give me some tea and then I must be going.'

'Come down to tea, Alice,' said Mrs Barton, 'and bring Julian.'

Alice looked anxiously at Julian, but he vouchsafed no communication beyond the word 'Line!' in a tone of Satanic scorn, followed by an equally contemptuous ejaculation of the word 'Tea!' She was afraid to say anything to him, and followed her mother downstairs, where they found Miss Merriman. As Miss Merriman had been kind to Alice, Mrs Barton was well disposed towards her, and found her a very pleasant, easy person to get on with. Lady Pomfret told Miss Merriman that Mrs and Miss Barton were probably coming out to Casa Strelsa in the spring and Miss Merriman said that would be very nice. No one noticed that Alice said nothing: Lady Pomfret because she belonged to an age when girls were not expected to thrust themselves forward, Miss Merriman because she knew Alice was shy, and Mrs Barton because she was thinking how delightful it would be to visit Casa Strelsa again, and how much work she could get done.

Before they had finished tea Mr Foster came in with Phoebe.

'I may as well say,' said Phoebe, when she and Mr Foster had greeted their hostess, 'that I came with Gillie to keep Mother quiet. She only got back from Bournemouth yesterday and she's on her hind legs already. I hope you won't mind, Mrs Barton. I can easily go round to the Wicklows if I'm butting in. So long as Mother sees me go out and come in with Gillie she'll be quite happy, and I'll invent the rest.'

Lady Pomfret breathed the word 'Hermione!' in a tone that left no doubt as to her feelings about poor George Rivers's wife. Mrs Barton felt very sorry for Phoebe and exerted herself to show her how welcome she was. Phoebe gradually became less defiant, and found as she talked that Mrs Barton knew a good deal about private theatres in Italian palaces and had even seen performances in eighteenth-century settings. The liking that she had felt for Mrs Barton when they met at the Wicklows was now increased by a considerable measure of respect for an authority on her own favourite subject. She said she would like more than anything to go to Italy and see those palaces herself.

Lady Pomfret, who had prolonged her visit because Mr Foster and Alice were talking so happily, now said they must really go. Mrs Barton asked Phoebe to come whenever she liked, adding that Julian came nearly every day. Phoebe repeated her brother's name almost as disparagingly as he had mentioned the word 'Line', but said she would love to come if Mrs Barton really meant it. Mrs Barton would have liked to issue a general invitation to Miss Merriman, but she felt that Miss Merriman would prefer to be approached with more reserve, so she contented herself with a friendly goodbye and a hope for a meeting before long.

'What a very nice tea party,' said Mrs Barton to her daughter when the guests had gone. Alice said it was. She then began to twist her hands and exhibit symptoms so unlike those of a young lady who had enjoyed a nice tea party that her mother's heart sank.

'Do you think Lady Pomfret really wanted us to come to Florence, Mother?' she said.

'Of course,' said Mrs Barton. 'It will be a lovely time of year if it isn't too cold.'

'But—' said Alice.

Her mother felt she could keep her temper better if she said nothing.

'I mean,' said Alice, 'I simply *couldn't* go if Julian wants me.'

'Wants you?' said Mrs Barton, almost coldly.

'The portrait,' said Alice. 'It's so terribly important, Mother. Julian can't possibly finish it if I'm not there.'

Mrs Barton had never shown anger to Alice. For a moment she was so exasperated that she could have told her daughter exactly what she thought of her, and of Julian for that matter. Then she blamed herself for having let Julian have the run of the house, then she told herself the mischief had been done at Pomfret Towers before Julian ever came to Mellings. Then she looked at Alice, a pitiful mixture of anxiety and diffidence, a little defiant too, and remembered how young she was, how ignorant in virtue of her sheltered invalid's life. All this passed through her mind in an instant of time.

'Well, perhaps the portrait will be finished by then,' she answered with a deliberately heartless cheerfulness. 'And by the way, where is Julian all this time?'

Alice sprang to her feet and ran upstairs. The studio was empty. She fled down again full of terror. Julian had been angry at Lady Pomfret's insults and she had not defended him. He had gone out into the black night alone, misunderstood, unfriended. In the hall Horton met her and said Mr Rivers had gone about an hour ago and said he wouldn't have any tea and would be round tomorrow morning. Alice thanked him and went upstairs again quite happily to tidy up the studio against Julian's return.

10

Mr Foster Chooses

Mr Johns had read Lord Pomfret's *Memoirs* and had great hopes of them. Several passages were probably actionable and his lordship's criticisms of his colleagues in a short-lived Government which he had once adorned were unprintable. But if he could get Lord Pomfret's consent to a few alterations and excisions, the book, with Lord Pomfret's name, would have in his practised opinion a very good chance. This delicate matter would best be treated, he felt, by a personal interview, so he wrote to Lord Pomfret saying he would be at Barchester at the Deanery from Saturday to Monday and would, if convenient, come and see him on the Saturday afternoon. On Sunday he was going to lunch with Mrs Barton, so the weekend promised to be one of useful activity. The one drawback was that if Mrs Rivers were still at the Towers, it would be difficult to avoid one of her usual predatory attacks, but he trusted to his host's dislike of his talented cousin to keep her out of the way.

Accordingly on the Saturday afternoon Mr Johns arrived at the Towers with his host, the Dean of Barchester. Canon Crawley was a friend of Lady Pomfret's and intended to pay a call on her while Mr Johns transacted his business. Lord Pomfret was waiting for Mr Johns in the library and lost no time in getting to business.

'Well, Johns,' he said, 'you've been a long time considering. Suppose I told you someone else had been quicker, eh?' and his lordship laughed in a meaning way.

Mr Johns felt very uncomfortable. As he had the only typewritten copy available, and Lord Pomfret had refused to part with his manuscript, he had thought himself absolutely safe. But evidently there had been some sinister agency at work.

'You know Hermione,' said his lordship.

Mr Johns said he did.

'Deuced unpleasant woman,' said Lord Pomfret, 'but she's got a head on her shoulders. You ought to know that.'

Mr Johns with an inward groan said she was undoubtedly a person of great ability.

'Well, Hermione's been at me,' said Lord Pomfret, eyeing Mr Johns keenly, 'about some other publisher chap. Seems he offers very good terms. Question is, are yours better?'

His lordship then lit one of his best cigars, pushed the second-best box across to Mr Johns, and waited for a reply.

If Mr Johns had given way to his feelings he would undoubtedly have banged out of the room, got into the Dean's car, and without waiting for the Dean had himself driven back to Barchester. But the long habit of putting himself aside where the firm's interests were in question came to his rescue, and he answered very civilly that what Lord Pomfret had said rather complicated the question and he had perhaps better consult his partner and write to Lord Pomfret.

'No, no, that won't do at all,' said the earl, alarmed. 'Let's get this settled now. Hermione's had a letter from some literary fellow or other who says he knows a publisher that would give her a better price than you do and she wants me to come in on it. It's not my idea of business,' said the earl candidly, 'but I don't like to see good money going begging. How the deuce Hermione knew I was writing anything I don't know, but these things slip out.'

It had now become clear to Mr Johns that Mr Hobb, in consultation with Mr Bungay, must have made Mrs Rivers an offer. It would be difficult to say with certainty whether Mr Johns, when he had lunch with those gentlemen, had foreseen this. As we know, he and Mr Fairchild had often said they would willingly give up their best-selling authoress for a little peace, but even publishers do not always mean what they say. In any case, willingly and deliberately to lose a very trying author from whom you have already made large profits and who will continue to demand higher advances without regard to the state of her market is one thing; to see a prospective client, and that client an earl, snatched away from under your nose by that author and delivered into the hands of your business rival, is another.

Mr Johns was used to rapid thinking, but for the moment his brain was paralysed. Bitterly did he regret that he had come to Pomfret Towers instead of writing. Even more did he regret it when Mrs Rivers came in, though he obtained a faint comfort from the unwelcoming voice in which her noble relative asked her what she wanted.

Mrs Rivers said she had heard Mr Johns was there, and thought they might have their business talk all together.

'I do believe in frankness, Mr Johns,' said Mrs Rivers, practising one of those smiles that felt so disarming inside her, 'and I am sure you do too.'

Mr Johns didn't, so he murmured something that might have meant anything.

'The fact is,' said Mrs Rivers, 'I have had such a good offer that I feel I ought to consider it very seriously.'

Mr Johns said nothing, and Lord Pomfret watched them both with grim amusement.

'Lord Pomfret rather agrees with me,' Mrs Rivers continued.

'No, I don't,' said his lordship.

'So,' said Mrs Rivers, 'I feel we ought to have a real talk about the terms of my next contract.'

Blackmail, and Hobb at the back of it, thought Mr Johns, but still said nothing.

'Of course I would hate to leave you,' said Mrs Rivers, 'but another two hundred pounds on my advance is a thing I can't afford to throw away.'

'Of course not,' said Mr Johns. 'Perhaps it would be best if you wrote to me, then I could show your letter to my partner and we would see what we could do. That would also give you time to think it over.'

'Oh, but I did think we could settle it now,' said Mrs Rivers. 'A kind of gentlemen's agreement.'

'Don't talk nonsense,' said Lord Pomfret, who had not sat

on County Councils for nothing. 'There's nothing gentlemanly about it. If you want to leave Johns and go to another publisher fellow, that's your business and his. But don't talk about gentlemen.'

'And when you are thinking it over,' said Mr Johns, heartened by this support, 'you will doubtless take into consideration the fact that if you accept what is I am sure a very tempting offer and decide to deal with another house, we shall not of course be able to take the same interest in your older publications as we have hitherto done, which will not be good for your cheap editions. Also, I would suggest that you should consider the scale of royalties, which may not be as generous as ours, and the further fact that ten per cent of this offer will have to go to the firm by whom it was made.'

This was a shot in the dark, but evidently it went home, for Mrs Rivers looked startled.

'I hadn't thought about royalties,' she said.

'Few authors do,' said Mr Johns, now feeling much more master of the situation, 'all they think of is advances. I think, Lord Pomfret, we had perhaps better settle the rest of our business by letter.'

He rose to go, but Lord Pomfret raised his hand.

'Stop a bit,' he said. 'If Hermione goes to this other publisher fellow, you mean to say she'll have to pay him ten per cent?'

'Not him,' corrected Mr Johns. 'The agent, whoever he may be, from whom this offer came.'

'And would I have to, too?' asked his lordship, beginning to glower like one of his own prize bulls.

'Certainly, Lord Pomfret, if the business is done through an agent.'

'You never told me that, Hermione,' said Lord Pomfret. 'Never deal with agents, always with principals. That's what I've always done. Stoke sent his agent over here to see me once about a mare. 'Tell his lordship,' I said, 'that I'll do anything he likes within reason if he comes himself.'

'Did he?' asked Mr Johns, attracted by this divagation.

'Of course he did,' replied his lordship with a chuckle, 'and I twisted him round my little finger. Couldn't have twisted the agent. Clever man *he* was.'

Without stopping to ponder the particular applicability of this story, Mr Johns said goodbye to Lord Pomfret in a firm voice.

'Don't be in such a hurry,' said his lordship, who was rummaging in a drawer. 'Here, take this,' he added, handing a large untidy bundle of papers to Mr Johns. 'You give me what you give Hermione, and no hanky-panky about ten per cent, and you can do what you like with it.'

Mr Johns had sometimes in his younger days dreamed of a scene like this, but never before had it come to pass. He was well aware that what the earl had said was a gentleman's agreement in the best sense of the word and that however Lord Pomfret might resent the pruning of parts of his manuscript he would abide by what he had said. He determined on his side that whatever Mr Fairchild said, the earl should have the same advance as Mrs Rivers and the best publicity a long course of lunches to critics could buy. The reader will doubtless like to hear, though it is outside the scope of this modest work, that *A Landowner in Five Reigns* by the Rt

Hon The Earl of Pomfret K.G. etc., with a decorative jacket that called down such abuse from the author as no one had yet been privileged to hear, was published in the following autumn. In spite of its unattractive title it had one of those waves of popularity for which there is no accounting, was serialised in a Sunday paper, and ran into so many editions that even Mr Fairchild was appeased. Lord Pomfret gave all his royalties to the Nutfield Cottage Hospital, and got as much real pleasure out of his success as an author as he had got from anything since his son died.

But all this is hidden in the future, and we must return to the library at Pomfret Towers. Mr Johns thanked Lord Pomfret, picked up the manuscript, and again said goodbye, but the earl, glowing with the consciousness of being an accepted author, insisted that he should come and see Lady Pomfret. Ignoring Mrs Rivers, he led his publisher to her ladyship's room where she was giving tea to the Dean.

'Well, Crawley,' said Lord Pomfret, 'glad to see you. Edith, you remember Mr Johns. He's going to publish my book.'

Everyone was pleased and interested. Lord Pomfret unwittingly made his publisher's path much easier by telling him to ask Miss Merriman anything he wanted to know. Mr Johns exhibited the manuscript, which he was fondly carrying under one arm, and both he and Miss Merriman felt relieved that their conspiracy need not be known.

Mrs Rivers, a little dejected but by no means disheartened, did not say much, but determined to look up her last contract with Johns & Fairchild and remind herself what the scale of royalties was.

Presently the Dean said he must be getting back to Barchester.

'By the way, Lady Pomfret,' he said, 'how is your nephew?'

'Gillie? Oh, very well,' said Lady Pomfret. 'I don't know why he isn't here. He has been working in the office with Mr Wicklow, our very nice under-agent whom you must meet sometime. Poor Mr Hoare has not been at all well this winter and I expect he will be retiring soon. We are really very lucky to have Mr Wicklow to take his place.'

'Lucky to have Miss Wicklow too,' said Lord Pomfret. 'I've seen her riding a lot this winter. Girl's got the best hands in the county. Nearly as good as yours were, my dear,' he added to his wife, who flushed a little. 'She knows the country inside out, that girl. Put me right about old Finch's lease the other day. Head on her shoulders.'

All this was very annoying to Mrs Rivers. Sally had often spent an afternoon in the estate room lately, giving a hand to her brother in Mr Hoare's absence. The earl had approved, so there was nothing to be said, but Mrs Rivers strongly felt that Gillie needn't spend his time down there too. If only Phoebe would be more sensible. But Phoebe was very difficult to talk to at present and Mrs Rivers felt they could not prolong their stay at the Towers. Lady Pomfret would be going out to Italy shortly, the Towers would be dust-sheeted, and her very good two months' let of her London house would be up. And where was Phoebe this afternoon? Not out again with that Barton boy? Mrs Rivers nearly stamped with annoyance.

Mr Foster and the Wicklows had put in a good afternoon's work. The matter of old Finch's lease had been adjusted and the office was now in apple-pie order. Mr Hoare had let things get slack of late and Roddy had the difficult job of straightening out an older man's work without making the improvements too obvious.

'Well, if Hoare comes back in March as he says,' said Roddy, 'he'll find plenty to grumble at, but I think he'll find it all right.'

'Thank you very much indeed,' said Mr Foster; 'both of you. I've learned a great deal.'

'Rot,' said Roddy, 'I mean thank *you*. It means a lot to have the boss taking an interest.'

Mr Foster looked unhappy and was going to say something when a footman came in and handed him a salver upon which lay what Roddy and Sally could see to be a cable.

'Wait a minute,' said Mr Foster to the man. 'There may be an answer.'

He read the cable and put it in his pocket.

'No answer, thanks,' he said.

The footman went out. Roddy and Sally felt that something had happened and had a good guess what it was.

'Your father?' Sally asked.

'Yes,' said Mr Foster. 'He died in a hospital at Cape Town. It might have happened any time. We weren't friends particularly but I suppose one feels it all the same.'

Roddy, with a man's fine instinct to get away when no practical help can be offered, said he was awfully sorry and he ought to go down to the stables about that drain, but he'd be back for Sally in ten minutes. In case he hadn't been sympathetic enough he embarrassed himself and everyone else by shaking hands with Mr Foster and quickly escaped into the early dusk.

'Would you like me to go?' said Sally, who would dearly have liked to follow her brother, but felt a genuine compassion for her friend.

'I would very much like you to stay, if you don't mind,' said Mr Foster. 'We might just look at the map again. I'm not sure where those earths are in Hamaker's Spinney.'

He walked over to the estate map and pulled it down.

'There,' said Sally, putting her finger on the spot. 'Oh – Gillie – do you mean—?'

'To stop them?' said Mr Foster, pulling the cord that rolled the map up. 'Yes. I suppose I can now. Uncle Giles said he would leave it to me.'

He sat down again at the table. In the glare of the electric light (and Sally made a mental note, even as she looked pityingly at him, that Roddy simply must have some decent reading lamps in the office), his face looked worn and unhappy. He dropped his head into his hands and said nothing. Sally, always impatient of inaction, felt wretchedly uncomfortable and didn't know what one ought to do when people's fathers that they really didn't care for died. She sat down opposite Mr Foster, wishing heartily that she could cheer him up. As he still made no movement and no sign she began to feel some anxiety, a feeling which she scarcely knew and of which she thought but poorly.

'I say, Gillie,' she said, 'I'm most awfully sorry about your father. I'd no idea you'd mind so much.'

'It's not Father,' said Mr Foster's voice, speaking into his hands in a hollow and gloomy way. 'I'm being selfish as usual. It's myself.'

'Don't talk rot,' said Sally sharply. 'Of course you aren't selfish. You never are. Never were. Never will be.'

'It's all this,' said Mr Foster, still covering his face. 'I know I oughtn't to grumble, and I'm jolly lucky to be coming into all this and be able to look after people like old Finch a bit. But it's a lot to face all at once.'

'Cheer up,' said Sally. 'Lord Pomfret mayn't die for ages.'

'I hope he won't,' said Mr Foster fervently. 'I hope he and Aunt Edith will live for years. But I can't get away from Pomfret Towers and the Pomfret possessions ever again till my dying day. Oh, Sally!'

'You poor old thing,' said Sally, in tones of purest compassion, stretching her hands across the table to him. 'I know, it's awful. I felt like that when I'd taken the beagles on. Never mind, Gillie, we'll make a do of it.'

Mr Foster lifted his head and took Sally's hands.

'Do you mean that, Sally?' he asked.

'Of course, I do,' said Sally. 'Anything I can do, just mention.'

Mr Foster looked at her. To Sally's indignation she felt the blood rushing to her face. Mr Foster then kissed both her hands very gently, and stood up.

'I expect Uncle Giles will be pleased,' he said.

Sally sat motionless, looking first at her hands, then at the future Lord Pomfret.

'Lord Pomfret pleased?' she said. 'About your father, do you mean?'

'Yes, he'll be as pleased as Punch about my father,' said Foster, 'but I wasn't thinking of that. I was thinking of you.'

Sally stared at him. The self-possession that Mr Foster had never seen ruffled was shaken to its depths. Her eyes filled, her mouth began to tremble.

'Oh, Gillie, Gillie darling!' she cried, with a kind of yelp, as every one of her manly standards went down, and she was left defenceless before the newcomer whom she had aided and defended. Mr Foster strode round the table and took her in his arms with a thoroughness that left no doubt as to his intentions. For a second Sally stiffened, then she turned and flung her arms round Mr Foster's neck and gulped and sobbed on his shoulder as she would have scorned to do even for the death of a dog. This peculiar method of accepting a proposal did not at all disconcert Mr Foster, who continued to hold her fast and murmur to the top of her head endearing things that surprised her almost as much as they surprised him.

'How annoyed Hermione will be,' said Mr Foster suddenly, in the middle of his transports.

This struck Sally as so extremely funny that she yelped again, laughed, choked and developed every symptom of hysteria. Mr Foster undid her arms from round his neck and got from the office filter, relic of the Victorian era, a glass of water which she managed to drink with a good deal of spilling and slopping.

'Now you'll do nicely,' said Mr Foster. 'We might as well get married quite soon. I suppose I'd better go and see your people.'

'Oh, they never mind what one does,' said Sally, 'and

anyway they're on a cruise. We'll send them a cable. I suppose we'd better tell Lord and Lady Pomfret too.'

'I did always think,' said Mr Foster pensively, 'that if I got married it should be very quietly by special licence, or in a registrar's office. Would you mind?'

'Love it,' said Sally and then her face fell. 'Sorry Gillie,' she said, 'it can't be done. I mean the people would all be so frightfully disappointed if we didn't have a proper wedding at Pomfret Madrigal with tea for the school children and a tenants' lunch.'

'I see,' said Mr Foster. 'You see, Sally, I'd have gone wrong again without you. My blessed darling, how could I live without you.'

These passionate words were uttered just as Roddy came back. His mind, though not agile, was powerful and sensible, and grasped almost at once what was happening.

'Well, good luck, Sally old girl,' he said and smote his sister affectionately. 'I'm jolly glad it's Foster. I had an idea he was keen on Alice.'

He then held out his hand to Mr Foster. Just as they were shaking hands they both remembered the funeral handshake that they had exchanged a short time before, and both began to laugh.

'I say,' said Roddy, suddenly becoming serious, 'Mrs Rivers.'

A short conference was held, at which it was decided that Lord and Lady Pomfret should be told at the first suitable opportunity and Mrs Rivers and the rest of the family later.

The three conspirators went back to the Towers and as they came into the hall they met the Dean and Mr Johns on their way out, accompanied by Mrs Rivers. Mr Johns was valiantly defending himself against a suggestion by Mrs Rivers that he should come over again and see her. He merely repeated, politely, that he was unfortunately engaged all Sunday and had to catch the early train on Monday morning. If Mrs Rivers would write to him, he and Mr Fairchild would give their very best attention to the matter. He then quickly got into the Dean's car and was driven away. Mrs Rivers saw the future Lord Pomfret with his under estate-agent and his sister and felt annoyed.

'Gillie,' she called.

Mr Foster politely came towards his cousin.

'Have you seen Phoebe anywhere?' said Mrs Rivers, with an unfriendly look at the Wicklows. 'She is left alone so much that she goes off by herself and I am quite anxious about her.'

'I have been in the office all afternoon,' said Mr Foster. 'Have you rung up the Bartons? She might be there.'

Mr Foster had no idea where Phoebe was, except that he thought it was somewhere with Guy Barton, and only said this to tease his cousin Hermione, who with an exclamation of annoyance, went off to the telephone.

'I think we'd better get this over,' said Mr Foster. 'Would you mind, Roddy, if Sally and I left you? I could drive her back later.'

'I expect Lord and Lady Pomfret will want you,' said Roddy. 'I'll sit in the blue room, there'll be nobody there, and you give me a call when you are ready.'

Accordingly Mr Foster and Sally, having ascertained from one of the footmen who came by with a tray that his lordship and her ladyship were in her ladyship's sitting-room, made their way there.

Mr Foster had rapidly prepared a little speech in which he proposed to explain to his uncle and aunt that while he wished to do everything they could desire, there was one thing in which he was determined to have his own way, but he had every hope that in this important matter his desires and their wishes might unite in one object; upon which he would produce Sally and leave the rest to their good judgment. The only thing he was doubtful about was the surprise, for a shock might upset them, and he did not at all want to celebrate the day of his betrothal by making his aunt faint, or causing his uncle to have a stroke. But if he had heard what his uncle and aunt were saying before he came in, he would have been saved much mental anxiety.

As soon as the Dean and Mr Johns had gone, with Mrs Rivers in pursuit, Lord Pomfret took up his position on the hearthrug.

'I've been wanting to talk to you, Edith,' said Lord Pomfret, 'about Gillie.'

Lady Pomfret laid down her embroidery and prepared to attend.

'He ought to marry,' said Lord Pomfret. 'It's no joke running a place like this alone, and there's Belgrave Square and Guestings and all the properties. I couldn't have done it myself when my father died if it hadn't been for you, my dear.'

Lady Pomfret sat very still, thinking how little she had helped since Mellings died.

'We can't last for ever,' Lord Pomfret continued, 'and if

we saw Gillie with a good wife and some children, I think we would feel more comfortable.'

'I was saying the same thing to Susan Barton the other day,' said Lady Pomfret.

'Nice girl that of hers,' said her husband.

'She is nice,' said Lady Pomfret. 'I have thought that Gillie rather liked her.'

'Nonsense,' said the earl, 'nonsense. She'd never do. She's a nice girl, but she's a delicate girl.'

'She is quite well now, Giles.'

'That may be, but we don't want any of that sort of thing. Gillie had to live abroad when he was a boy. He's all right now, but what he wants is a wife with plenty of good health and good sense, someone who will look after the place. The sort of wife we would have liked Harry to have,' said Lord Pomfret, who rarely spoke his dead son's first name.

'You may be right, Giles,' said Lady Pomfret, 'but we can't choose for him, and I still think he is attracted by Alice Barton.'

'I am sure he must like her. She's a nice girl. But it's Wicklow's sister he's after.'

'Mr Wicklow's sister?' said Lady Pomfret, with what for one in her position was almost a gasp.

'Wicklow's sister,' the earl repeated. 'I'll put my money on her. Do you remember the bet we had on the Derby just before you said you'd marry me, my dear?'

'They were very good gloves. I have one pair still,' said Lady Pomfret, again flushing a little.

'Well, Edith, if Gillie proposes to Alice Barton, I'll give you a dozen pairs as good as that,' said Lord Pomfret.

'Done,' said Lady Pomfret, just as Edith Thorne had said it to young Lord Mellings. And as she said it Mr Foster came in with Miss Wicklow.

Lord Pomfret gave the couple a searching look.

'Afraid you've lost your gloves, my dear,' he said to Lady Pomfret.

Mr Foster stared for a moment. Then, seizing the situation, he began to laugh, as did his uncle. Lady Pomfret and Sally, knowing men and their unaccountable ways, waited till the creatures had finished their joke.

'I am so sorry, Aunt Edith,' said Mr Foster, seeing his aunt's grave perplexity, and realising that a slightly formal approach would be the best way of pleasing her, 'I do hope that you and Uncle Giles will approve of what I propose to do, which is to announce my engagement to Miss Wicklow.'

The earl looked with amusement at the scene. His wife cast an appealing glance at him.

'It's all right, my dear,' he said. 'I'm sorry about your gloves, but it's one of the best things that could have happened.'

Lady Pomfret was not a quick thinker. Her first thought was of regret that Gillie had chosen this girl whom she knew so slightly. She wished she had not spoken to Susan Barton, and hoped Alice knew nothing of what she had said. Then she looked at her husband and saw his evident pleasure in what had happened. If he was glad, the least she could do was to be glad with him. Perhaps not a very adequate way of making up for so many years' shirking of her duties, but all that was demanded of her at the moment. She rose and went to Sally.

'I am glad to welcome Gillie's future wife,' she said taking Sally's hand in both her own. 'I have never had a daughter. I hope you will let me look upon you as a very dear one.'

Sally, quite overcome by the kindness of Lady Pomfret's words, could only say, inarticulately, how grateful she was and how she would do her best.

'Of course you will,' said Lord Pomfret. 'And I suppose you and Gillie will have those earths in Hamaker's Spinney stopped before a week's out.'

At this the young couple looked at each other a little guiltily.

'You've arranged it already, I expect,' said his lordship in high good humour. 'Well, Sally, my dear, if you make Gillie half as happy as Edith has made me, he'll be a lucky young man. Now we will keep this to ourselves for a couple of days. I can't stand people fussing, and Hermione's bound to fuss. We'll send a cable to Mr and Mrs Wicklow, and I suppose we'd better send one to your father, Gillie, and I'll have it all in *The Times* on Monday. I must say,' said his lordship in an unusual burst of confidence, 'that to see Hermione when she hears the news will be a great pleasure.'

'Oh, I quite forgot to tell you, Uncle Giles,' said Mr Foster, 'that I had this just now,' and he took the cable from his pocket and gave it to Lord Pomfret.

'So your father's gone,' said the earl. 'Can't say I'm sorry. Well, this means you and I will have to work together for good, Gillie.'

Lady Pomfret civilly expressed her regret.

'Tell you what,' said Lord Pomfret. 'We'll put the engagement in *The Times* on Monday and your father's death on

Tuesday. And remember, we keep the engagement to ourselves till Monday. I'd like to let Emily know,' said the earl, who was fond of his delightful, unaccountable sister, Lady Emily Leslie, 'and one or two of the family. Not Hermione.'

'There's one person I want to tell, Uncle Giles,' said Mr Foster, 'that's Merry.'

Lord Pomfret quite agreed that she ought to know and Mr Foster said he would find a moment to speak to her after dinner. Lady Pomfret kissed Sally very kindly, and then her Italian maid came in to ask if her lady was coming to rest before dinner, so Lord Pomfret and the young people went away.

'What about that brother of yours?' he said to Sally. 'I suppose he knows.'

Sally said she could answer for Roddy not mentioning her engagement till he was given permission, and called to him through the door of the blue room to come out.

'Well, Wicklow,' said Lord Pomfret, 'I've congratulated my nephew. Your sister has got the best hands in the county.'

'Yes, sir,' said Roddy. 'Thank you,' and the earl went away.

As they neared the hall doors Peters materialised to let Miss Wicklow and her brother out. No sooner had the door closed behind them than he almost hastened to overtake Mr Foster.

'May I presume, sir,' he said, 'to offer my very respectful congratulations?'

'How the devil did you know?' asked Mr Foster, quite startled out of his generally placid demeanour.

'One generally does, sir,' said Peters pityingly. 'Miss

Wicklow, sir, is very highly thought of in the Room, also in the Hall if I may presume to mention it.'

'Well, thanks very much, Peters,' said Mr Foster, 'but please don't say a word till Monday. Lord Pomfret wants to have it in *The Times* and no one's to know till then.'

'If anyone was to presume to ask me, or mention the subject, sir,' said Peters, 'I should Discourage him, and Mrs Caxton would do so to any of the female staff.'

'Oh, Mrs Caxton knows, does she?' asked Gillie.

'She had been Drawing Conclusions, sir,' said Peters.

Mr Foster thanked Peters again and went off to dress for dinner, wondering if it would be really necessary to put the engagement in *The Times* at all.

Dinner passed off quietly. Mrs Rivers had been told from Mellings that Miss Phoebe had just started home, and Phoebe appeared at dinner, looking tired. Mr Foster did his best to talk to her, to his cousin Hermione's evident gratification, but before he came to the drawing-room Phoebe had gone, saying she had a headache, and discouraging a suggestion from her mother to come and see her in bed.

Mr Foster had a short talk with Lord Pomfret when they were alone over their port, and was surprised by his uncle's generous intentions in the matter of settlements. All Lord Pomfret asked was that the heir and his wife should live as much as possible on the estates which would probably soon be theirs, and was evidently relieved when Mr Foster said that he and Sally felt they ought to do so. When Mr Foster came into the drawing-room his aunt called to him and asked him to give a message to Miss Merriman. Mr Foster went to his aunt's sitting-room and tapped on the door. Miss Merriman, who was doing some of Lady Pomfret's letters, called to him to come in. He delivered his aunt's message, and then lingered.

'I want to tell you something, Merry,' he said.

'Yes,' said Miss Merriman, putting down her papers and turning her pleasant smile upon him.

'Only Uncle Giles and Aunt Edith know,' said Mr Foster, suddenly finding what he had to say a little difficult, 'but I told them you must know too. It's about Sally and me.'

'My very warmest congratulations,' said Miss Merriman, in a voice of whose sincerity there was no doubt. 'You couldn't have done better; nor could she.'

'Thanks awfully, Merry,' said Mr Foster. 'It's to be a secret till Monday, but I felt you must know. It's a good thing for the place that she will be here, and of course I do love her quite dreadfully. I hope we shan't have to live here, in the Towers, for a very long time, but we'll do our best when we have to.'

'Of course you will,' said Miss Merriman. 'And I am sorry about your father's death. Lady Pomfret told me.'

'So am I, in a way,' said Mr Foster. 'I suppose it's a bit selfish, but as long as he was alive I felt fairly safe. Now I've got to get into harness. Oh, Merry, I do wish you were going to help me.'

Mr Foster had no idea with what difficulty Miss Merriman said she was indeed sorry but she would be with Lady Pomfret. Of course, she added, if she could ever help in any small way he need only ask her, or write if she were in Italy. Now, she said, she must go to Lady Pomfret's bedroom in case she had any directions to give, so she would say good night and again give Mr Foster and Miss Wicklow her very heartiest congratulations.

'Thank you very much, Merry. You are a dear,' said Mr Foster.

Miss Merriman went to Lady Pomfret's bedroom, received one or two directions about Sunday's plans, and then went to bed. How she passed the night was, like the rest of her private life, only her own affair. But she was down to breakfast as usual next morning, smiling and pleasant, and Mrs Rivers for one certainly never thought of asking her if she had had a bad night.

11

Happy Ending

If Miss Merriman had lain awake with her own thoughts, so had Phoebe. And Mrs Barton, who rarely let trouble disturb her rest, also passed an uneasy night, caused by the very trying behaviour of her son Guy and Miss Phoebe Rivers on the previous day.

The rash, unconsidered proposal that Guy had made to Phoebe, and her equally unconsidered acceptance of it, had not brought much happiness to either. Undoubtedly they were attracted to one another, but each, while giving way to the attraction, at the same time resented it. Guy, uneasily conscious that he would depend for the present on his parents' goodwill for such supplements to his salary as would make marriage possible, felt that the least Phoebe could do was to go down on her knees in gratitude for what he hadn't got to offer, and fall in with his every wish. Phoebe, despising herself because she had not the courage to break loose from her home, or the talent to make her living if she did, vented much of her harassed feelings on Guy, and was all the more aloof and contradictory, to punish herself for having once yielded. So their delightful meetings at Plumstead and elsewhere, though they served the useful purpose of keeping Mrs Rivers in the dark, were little but bickering. If they could have kept to impersonal topics they might have done well enough, for Phoebe was genuinely interested in Guy's work, but the fatal 'You did', 'I didn't', of lovers' quarrels seemed to permeate every subject. Guy, although not over-sensitive, was getting angry at Phoebe's chilly attitude, while Phoebe was wearing herself into a state of irritability in which she felt it would be a pleasure and relief to say every cruel thing she could think of to Guy.

Their meeting on the Saturday when Mr Foster chose his future countess had been more than usually exacerbating. Among the beams and rafters of the house that Barton and Wicklow were remodelling they argued fiercely about their engagement. Guy wished to tell his parents, Phoebe to conceal it from hers, at any rate till her mother had left the Towers and could not badger her about Gillie every day. Guy found it impossible to believe that a girl of today could be so much in fear of her mother, and told Phoebe so.

'If I were you, I'd simply tell her straight out that you and Gillie never want to see each other again,' he said. 'She can't hurt you.'

To which Phoebe, slim in tweeds, perfectly turned out, contemptuously smoking with a very long holder that Guy detested as swank, said he was only a boy and couldn't understand.

'All right, I can't,' said Guy. 'I certainly can't understand you. You said you'd marry me, and now you do nothing but nag. If you don't care for me, say so, I don't mind.'

As Phoebe only shrugged her shoulders and walked away across a pile of shavings, Guy followed her, catching the leg of his trousers on a nail as he went, tearing it and swearing, and kissed her violently. Her apparent want of interest in this high-handed proceeding was even more annoying than her nagging.

'I say,' said Phoebe when he had released her, and speaking as if nothing had happened. 'Let's go and have tea at your place. I'd like to see Alice.'

'Have it your own way,' said Guy, getting into the car.

'And don't drive on the wrong side of the road,' said Phoebe, getting in after him and slamming the door. 'It's a stupid habit.'

To this Guy's only answer was to drive home at lightning speed, taking all the corners on the wrong side, and only by a miracle getting safely across the narrow Nutfield bridge. Phoebe, who enjoyed driving like that, said nothing at all. When they got to Mellings she walked into the house without taking any notice of Guy, and asked Horton if Miss Alice were in. Horton said she was in the drawing-room.

'Thanks, I'll go in,' said Phoebe, in so unsteady a voice that Horton thought Miss Rivers and Mr Guy might have been celebrating, and retired to his pantry to meditate upon the Sins of Society.

Alice was sitting by the fire reading when Phoebe came in. At the sight of her kind friend she jumped up and came forward to meet her. As they kissed she felt that Phoebe was trembling from head to foot. Thinking she was cold, she led her sympathetically to the sofa, put another log on the fire, and asked how she was.

'I'm all right,' said Phoebe, taking her hat off and squeezing it as if it were an enemy in the form of a bath sponge. 'I wish I were dead, that's all. I can't stand it. It's hell.'

Alice, alarmed at this sudden outburst from a friend upon whom she had always looked as the incarnation of self-confidence and poise, took her hand and begged her to tell her what it was.

'Guy,' said Phoebe. And wrenching her hand away from Alice she opened her bag and made up her face.

'Guy?' said Alice. 'Oh, Phoebe, he hasn't been—'

Making love to you, was what she meant, but to her sensitive mind no words were delicate enough for her friend's wounded pride.

'We're engaged,' said Phoebe, in a hard, unpleasant voice that Alice hardly knew. 'We got engaged a little while ago. Guy asked me to marry him and I said yes. He only liked me because I'm smarter than the girls round here. I said yes to get away from Mother. But it's all wrong. We do nothing but scrap. I hate him.'

Alice was appalled. To add to her embarrassment she knew that her parents were in the study next door. She tried to soothe her friend, but Phoebe, losing all control, was pouring out the accumulated grievances, some real, some fancied, of the last weeks, blaming Guy for everything. On her wild speech Guy came in. Alice, courageous for Phoebe, waved him to go away, but he took no notice.

'What the dickens is the matter?' he said. 'I say, Phoebe, do shut up. Everyone can hear you.'

'Guy, you mustn't talk like that,' said Alice. 'It's all your fault, and you know it is.'

That his gentle, submissive sister should turn against him was more than Guy could bear. In his real anxiety for Phoebe he spoke roughly to Alice, telling her to go away, or get some water, or be useful, instead of bleating. Phoebe by now was quite out of her own control and reciting her wrongs in a shrill, monotonous voice. Mr and Mrs Barton, who had been wondering what the extraordinary noise in the drawing-room was, came in from the study to find their son using very ungentlemanly language, their daughter looking distraught, and what was apparently a maniac on the sofa. What added to Mr Barton's bewilderment was that he had never seen Phoebe before, and hadn't the faintest idea who she was.

'What *is* going on?' said Mr Barton.

'Do for goodness' sake shut up, Phoebe,' said Guy, urgently and quite vainly.

'Oh, Father,' said Alice, all indignation for her sex, 'Guy and Phoebe are engaged, and Guy is being *beastly* to her.'

Mrs Barton, taking command, sent Guy for water and sal volatile out of her medicine cupboard, and sat down by Phoebe.

'How do you do Mrs Barton I'm awfully sorry but I can't help it,' said Phoebe, all in one breath.

'Of course you can't,' said Mrs Barton kindly. 'Now, just stop, and then you'll be able to help it quite nicely.'

At this illogical but somehow helpful command, Phoebe was suddenly silent. Guy returned with a tray of bottles and glasses, and Alice, to her intense interest, actually saw a heroine taking sal volatile.

'As soon as you are better we will have tea,' said Mrs Barton. 'It will be here in a moment.'

Phoebe, who had felt no shame in behaving badly in front of her host and hostess, pulled herself together at the thought of servants. Horton brought the tea, taking as everyone thought an unconscionably long time over it, and at length retired, leaving them to themselves. Phoebe was by now so quiet that Guy hoped the whole thing was only a nightmare, and he might find it had never happened at all. But he had reckoned without his father. When everyone had finished tea Mr Barton lighted his pipe and said, 'Now, what is all this?'

Alice, having delivered her testimony before, did not feel called upon to speak again, but she took Phoebe's hand.

'I was very silly,' said Phoebe, not this time withdrawing her hand, but looking straight in front of her. 'Guy and I thought we liked each other and we don't. I'm sorry. I think I'd better go home.'

'Would you mind waiting a moment,' said Mr Barton. 'Now, Guy.'

Guy had the strongest views on parents interfering, the one subject on which he and Julian Rivers would have seen eye to eye. But deeply as he resented his father's judicial attitude, he had to admit unwillingly that he was very glad to be able to lay his troubles before someone who could deal with them with authority. He looked round for support. His mother was gazing at the fire. Phoebe was still looking into the distance, and Alice's eyes were fixed on Phoebe.

'I did ask Phoebe to marry me,' he said at length. 'I didn't like to tell you and Mother, because I thought you'd think

I was too young or something, and Phoebe didn't want to tell Mrs Rivers because she thought she'd be ratty, because Mrs Rivers seems to have an idea that Phoebe might hit it off with Gillie. It's a rotten idea of course, because anyone could see with half an eye—'

'I think if you would stick to the point, we'd get on faster,' said Mr Barton. 'Do I gather that you asked Miss Rivers to marry you without anything to marry on?'

'Lots of people do,' said Guy.

'I would rather you were not one of them,' said Mr Barton. 'I cannot see any reason for this secrecy. I am very glad to know Miss Rivers, whom your mother already knows and likes. If you will take my advice – you needn't of course – you will both consider that this engagement never took place.'

'Do you mean not be engaged?' said Guy, incredulous, hardly knowing whether to fell his father to the ground for the insult, or kneel to him in gratitude for the happy suggestion.

'Absolutely not to be engaged!' said Phoebe, showing her first sign of any human interest.

'Absolutely,' said Mr Barton.

'Well, that's OK by me,' said Phoebe.

'If you say so,' said Guy.

Mr Barton, gathering from these words that his son and Miss Rivers were expressing their cordial agreement with his suggestion, said to Guy that he had better come and look at the blueprints for Hiram's Hospital, which he had brought home with him. Guy, with an assumption of indifference to hide his inward tremors, got up to follow his father. Phoebe looked pitifully at him, but he pretended not to see.

'Say goodbye to Phoebe now,' said his mother. 'I'm going to send her back to the Towers with Carter. She looks tired.'

Guy turned, and Phoebe, reaching up over the back of the sofa, took his hand in both her own.

'Darling Guy, I did love you, I truly did,' said Phoebe, holding his hand tightly.

'That's all right,' said Guy. 'We'll have another stab at it sometime. You've been jolly decent.'

He then went into the study, expecting a homily from his father, but Mr Barton, keeping his son to the matter in hand, checked any attempt of Guy's to explain, and the matter was not raised again.

When left alone with Mrs Barton and Alice, Phoebe, encouraged by their sympathy, began to talk about herself. Alice was grieved and shocked that her elegant, worldly friend could be made so wretched by Guy, who was after all only one's brother and had lost by his recent conduct some of the glory with which she had surrounded him. Mrs Barton was sorry for the child who had such a difficult home life that she felt even Guy would be a refuge. She liked her very much, and thought Guy would be lucky if he could try again and earn her esteem as well as her love.

'I am taking Alice to Italy in the spring,' she said presently. 'We shall be in Florence and shall probably spend a week or so at Casa Strelsa. I wonder if your mother would let you come with us. I have a good deal of work to do, and it would be fun for Alice.'

Phoebe said gratefully that she would adore it, but fell

back into despondency when she thought of her mother, whose consent she must get.

'I'll tell you what,' said Mrs Barton. 'Your mother is coming to lunch tomorrow. I'll speak to her about it.'

'But I thought Mr Johns was coming,' said Alice.

'Yes he is. When he said he wanted to come on Sunday I had quite forgotten about Mrs Rivers. But your mother won't mind meeting him, will she, Phoebe?'

'I shouldn't think so,' said Phoebe. 'She always likes talking about her books.'

Mrs Barton felt pained by Phoebe's bitter voice, but made no comment. Presently the car was announced and Phoebe got up to go. Somewhat to Mrs Barton's surprise, her guest suddenly flung her arms round her neck and kissed her fervently.

'Do make Mother let me come,' she said.

When Alice came back from seeing Phoebe into the car, she found her mother looking pleased.

'I think it would be a very good plan to take Phoebe to Italy with us. Don't you, darling?' she said.

Alice said, 'Yes, Mother,' but with such marked want of conviction that Mrs Barton looked anxiously at her. Of course; it was that Julian Rivers. Mrs Barton did not press the point, but trusted devoutly that during the next few weeks Alice might manage to get through or get over her attachment to her uncouth acquaintance, for friend Mrs Barton did not like to call him, and admirer he certainly was not.

Family dinner was not altogether comfortable after this, but Mr and Mrs Barton worked heroically, helped by Alice, and gradually Guy was able to talk quite normally. But Mrs Barton did not feel at ease. First Alice and Julian, now Guy and Phoebe, and the one affair seemed to her as foolish as the other, and as unlikely to lead to any result.

When the children had gone away, Alice to bed, Guy to work, Mrs Barton asked her husband what he thought of Phoebe. Mr Barton, having once asserted himself, did not in the least wish to incur any further responsibility, especially, he said, in the matter of a girl whom he had never seen before, who was having hysterics in his drawing-room, and who didn't appear to have any sense.

'Not that you had much sense when you married me, Susan,' said Mr Barton, 'and we hadn't much to marry on either. I daresay it will be all right. Thank goodness Alice doesn't trouble us with calf-love.'

After all this it is not surprising that Mrs Barton was awake for longer than she liked.

Spring had by now set in with its accustomed severity. As Mr Barton sat at breakfast on Sunday morning in his warm dining-room, he was able to observe how a fierce east wind sent the almond blossom scudding across the window, while such stunted crocuses as had pierced the dry, hard earth were being tweaked to pieces by a few unemployed sparrows, and he again congratulated himself on the central heating.

'Do you think Alice had better go to church this morning, Susan?' he asked.

But Mrs Barton reassured him, saying, which was perfectly true, that they really must stop looking upon her as an invalid, and would he speak to Horton about the wine for lunch, as Mrs Rivers and Mr Johns were coming, and the Wicklows, which would make them eight.

After church Mrs Barton collected the Wicklows and asked them to walk back with the family and have a glass of sherry before lunch. Sally said she and Roddy would love to, when Chloe suddenly came bursting into their midst, trailing a broken lead behind her. Mrs Barton looked for Alice, prepared to do battle with Sally and the lurcher on her daughter's behalf if necessary, but to her gratified surprise Alice, though she certainly got very close to Roddy, said 'Good Chloe then. Down then,' in quite an assured voice. Mrs Barton thought Roddy was looking down at Alice with a very pleasant mixture of pride and protectiveness.

'Isn't she a lamb to come after her mother, then?' said Sally. 'Clever girl, she's bitten her lead in two. But she knows she oughtn't to be out just now, doesn't she?'

On hearing these ominous words Roddy offered to take Chloe back, but Sally said she wouldn't be a minute, so Mrs Barton waited for her, letting Roddy and the rest of the family go on ahead. When Sally joined her they walked quickly down the High Street, for the wind was sharp. Sally's conversation was very vague. Mrs Barton asked her about the new litter, and whether she had sold all her last litter but one, but Sally gave such stupid answers that Mrs Barton came to the conclusion she was thinking of mating Chloe again, a business which always occupied Sally's mind very fully, as the lurcher did not see eye to eye with her mistress about husbands, preferring natural worth to Norman blood.

'I beg your pardon, Mrs Barton,' said Sally at last. 'I

honestly wasn't listening to a word you were saying. I think I'd better tell you, though it's really a secret, or you'll think I've gone dotty or something.'

As she stopped here, appearing to think this sufficient explanation, Mrs Barton begged her to go on, especially, she said, if it was a secret.

'Well, only till Monday,' said Sally. 'And anyway Roddy knows, and Lord and Lady Pomfret, and apparently Peters, so I really don't see why you shouldn't.'

'Are you selling a puppy to Lady Pomfret?' asked Mrs Barton.

'Oh no,' said Sally, 'it's Gillie,' and her face assumed an expression of beatific foolishness. 'We're engaged you see.'

So Alice won't be a countess now, was Mrs Barton's first thought. And thank goodness, was her second. Her third, only thoughts come so fast that it was there almost as quickly as the first, was of very great pleasure, which she lost no time in expressing.

'Dear Sally, I never was so glad,' she said, pressing Sally's arm. 'You will be such a success, and I liked Mr Foster so very much the only time I saw him. I really can't tell you how glad I am. May I tell Alice? Or do you want to tell her yourself? It is all too delightful and exciting. Are the Pomfrets pleased? But I'm sure they are.'

'I hope so,' said Sally. 'I think so. They were very nice to me. Yes, please do tell Alice, because she really oughtn't to know till Monday, and if you tell her it won't seem like telling.'

Mrs Barton laughed and said she would, and asked how soon they were to be married.

'Oh, I quite forgot,' said Sally. 'Gillie's father is dead. He got a cable yesterday. But no one seems to mind very much, so I daresay it won't make much difference. Oh, Mrs Barton, Gillie is absolutely perfect!'

Thus pleasantly talking they arrived at Mellings, and while they were taking off their hats and furs for lunch, Mrs Barton told Alice about the engagement. A shade of anxiety had crossed her mind as to whether Alice would feel a little pang, but the news appeared to afford her daughter unmitigated satisfaction.

'Oh, Mother,' she said, 'how lovely! The two nicest people I know getting engaged. Gillie is so nice. He was so kind to me at the weekend. Perhaps if Lady Pomfret hadn't asked us all to the weekend, Sally wouldn't have got engaged. Isn't it wonderful!'

And she became silent, reflecting upon the astounding ways of Providence. If only Providence had seen fit to make Julian be there too, everything would have been perfect, but having accidentally trodden upon a tube of rose madder while stepping back to get the general effect, Julian had become a prey to despair and gone away, not proposing to resume the portrait till Monday. However all such private gloom must be forgotten in the cause of friendship, and if Alice's face and voice of awed rapture when she spoke for a moment to Sally were assumed, the mask would have deceived the closest observer.

Downstairs they found Mr Barton entertaining Mr Johns, who had arrived a little early. Roddy and Guy were helping them to drink sherry. The meeting between Mrs Barton and Mr Johns was accomplished. Mr Johns expressed his acknowledgement of the pleasure he had in meeting one of his most distinguished authors; Mrs Barton said she must thank Mr Johns very much indeed for all his kindness to her daughter. Mr Johns said he had very much enjoyed meeting Miss Barton, and was particularly looking forward to seeing some of her drawings. He accompanied these words by a knowing look at Alice, who blushed furiously and made a face of such despair that Mr Johns changed the subject. Mrs Barton felt some curiosity at this by-play, but the sound of the front-door bell changed the current of her thoughts.

'By the way, Mrs Rivers is lunching with us,' she said to Mr Johns. 'You know her well of course.'

A number of suitable answers sprang to Mr Johns's mind, but he thought it better to say simply that he did, heartily wishing that he were safely back in the Deanery.

Mrs Rivers advanced into the room with the smile that so well (she felt) became her. She was as much surprised to see Mr Johns as he was to see her, and far more pleasantly. To write to her publishers was always difficult, because one didn't always know exactly how to say what one wanted to say, and they had an annoying habit of taking one's letters literally. The gentlemen's agreement, whatever she may have thought to be the meaning of that useful phrase, was still in her mind, and she felt that she could now corner Mr Johns and cajole him into giving her a large extra advance on her next book. She could then refuse Mr Hobb's offer, and go about telling everyone how she had stuck to her publisher in spite of all temptations. Her mind was at ease about her family for the moment, for she had left her daughter Phoebe in close conversation with Mr Foster in a corner of the yellow drawing-room, and though she did not know what they were talking about, Mr Foster's earnest manner and Phoebe's look of delight made her feel that at last things were coming right. As for Julian, he had expressed himself so cuttingly on Friday night about houses where people left footstools for you to trip over and walk on your best rose madder, that she had great hopes that his interest in that little Alice Barton was waning, and as he had gone up to town for the weekend, she felt really free to enjoy herself.

She shook hands with Mrs Barton, said how nice it would be to have a long talk with her, and after a condescending though kindly greeting to the younger people, proceeded to fascinate Mr Barton, to such effect that he made up his mind never to be in to lunch again if Susan asked that woman. But Mr Barton was hardly enough for Mrs Rivers, so ignoring Roddy who was on her other side, she prepared to spread her conquests further.

'Do tell me, Mrs Barton,' she said across the table, in that cultured, piercing Englishwoman's voice that spreads dislike wherever travellers can go, 'something I am longing to know. How do you deal with your fan mail?'

'My fan mail?' Mrs Barton repeated.

'Can you manage yours?' said Mrs Rivers. 'I find I simply *have* to have a secretary for that. Not always, of course, but for a month or two after publication. I can't bear to leave anything unacknowledged.'

Mrs Barton said she always tried to answer letters by return.

'But when there are so *many*,' said Mrs Rivers. 'I often have twenty a day, and all from people I have never heard of.'

'No, I don't think I get letters from people I don't know,' said Mrs Barton, considering. 'Except begging letters and advertisements.'

'But you must have had lots of letters about your last book,' said Mrs Rivers. 'Everyone was trying to get it from the library.'

Mr Johns was on tenterhooks, sensing Mr Barton's annoyance at this assumption by Mrs Rivers that his wife was on her level, and not a little apprehensive at Mrs Barton's baffling replies. But Guy broke in.

'Mother only had three letters about her last book,' he said, 'one from Professor Marston, and one from Cardinal Boccafiume, and one from the Duke of Monte Cristo.'

This was a deliberate piece of impertinence on Guy's part, for even if Mrs Rivers was not familiar with the name of Professor Marston, who knew so much about the Renaissance that his monumental books consisted almost entirely of footnotes, she could not help knowing the names of Cardinal Boccafiume, himself boasting the blood of the Borgias, and of the Duke of Monte Cristo, that cosmopolitan, doyen of that diplomatic world.

'But they were only friends,' said Mrs Barton apologetically.

'Well, I must say it is wonderful to have all those *unknown* friends,' said Mrs Rivers, bravely defending her supporters, 'and I think their praise is so much more valuable than the reviewers'. Don't you agree with me?'

'I don't read reviews,' said Mrs Barton, 'but I'm sure they are; I mean it is.'

'Oh, but you must,' said Mrs Rivers. 'I can put you onto

a very good press-cutting agency. They never miss a thing and aren't at all expensive.'

'Thank you so much,' said Mrs Barton, 'but Mr Johns likes press cuttings, so he collects them and I don't read them, like division of labour.'

Mr Johns's suspicion that Mrs Barton knew quite well what she was saying and how provoking she was being, was now a certainty. Mr Barton had also come to the same conclusion and much to the disappointment of Guy and Roddy, who had hoped for a show-down as they expressed it, he asked Mrs Rivers whether she was going abroad again soon. She at once swallowed the bait, and told him about her plans to visit Ceylon and how she wanted to take her daughter, but Phoebe didn't seem really interested in any of the vital things of life. What these things were she did not explain, nor did Mr Barton trouble to inquire. Meanwhile Alice prattled away happily enough to Mr Johns, and Guy exchanged badinage with Sally. Mrs Barton, released from her guest's importunities, sat brooding peacefully, exchanging an occasional friendly word with Roddy, both of them quietly watching Alice. Roddy's gaze, bent upon Alice, disturbed her for a moment, and she turned her head to give him one of her brilliant smiles. Roddy smiled back, and thought what an excellent thing it was that Foster was going to marry Sally: nothing could be better.

Before lunch was over Horton opened the dining-room door, and with every mark of protesting displeasure on his face announced Mr Julian Rivers, whose arrival gave considerable annoyance to all of the party but one.

'Where did you come from, darling?' asked his mother,

pleased to see her boy, but finding it quite unnecessary that he should have come to Mellings.

To this maternal inquiry Julian's answer, given in an off-hand way, was, we regret to say, 'Nowhere.'

Everyone felt very uncomfortable for Mrs Rivers, which made them, against their better natures, be much nicer to Julian than they need have been.

'The light looked good, so I didn't stay in town, I came down here,' said Julian, addressing himself to Alice. 'We can get a couple of good hours in.'

Alice was on the point of rising when her father said, 'We have not finished lunch yet. Sit down, Rivers, and have some port.'

Julian recognised the voice of authority, disliked and resented it, and sat down where Alice had made a place for him. As he did not dare openly to defy Mr Barton, he made up for it by so snubbing and browbeating his mother that even Alice felt he had, under very great provocation, gone a little too far. Mrs Rivers, who was secretly afraid of Julian's hard selfishness, lost some of her confidence, which made her talk more piercingly and egotistically than ever. It was obvious to the elders that Mrs Rivers had not the faintest control over her son, but they couldn't very well speak to him before her as they would have liked to, so Mrs Barton, sick of it all, said in a very cowardly way that they would go and have coffee in Alice's studio. She meant that she would take Mrs Rivers and Sally and Alice up there, and the men might follow later, but Mr Barton had no wish to be left in charge of the ungracious monster.

'Good idea,' he said. 'Come up, Johns, and see some of Alice's work.'

Julian, muttering something about spoiling people's afternoons, followed them, with Roddy and Guy making hideous faces at him and each other behind his back.

'What a delightful room,' said Mr Johns. 'What is the date of this part of the house? About the middle of the eighteenth century I should say.'

Mr Barton, enchanted by this appreciation of his beloved house, gave Mr Johns a short account of its development, and promised to take him over the old part later.

'Is that your picture of Alice?' Mrs Rivers asked her son, looking at an easel which stood with its back to the company.

Alice could have told her that you mustn't ask artists anything about anything, but even so she felt the scowl with which Julian greeted his mother's inquiry to be overdone.

'And now,' said Mr Johns, 'may I see the drawings we were talking about, Miss Barton?'

Anyone who had known Alice earlier would have been struck by the very limited extent to which she twisted her fingers and legs. Without looking like a mad hare, or becoming crimson and tearful, she opened a drawer and took out a portfolio.

'Could I just show them to Mr Johns only,' she said. 'It's rather private.'

She carried the portfolio to the window and opened it. Mr Johns looked carefully at what she showed him.

'Is it any good?' she said.

'Very nice indeed,' said Mr Johns. 'It's a new line. I believe, Miss Barton, we'll make a hit with this.'

'Make a hit?' said Mrs Barton, who heard the last words.

'Rather,' said Mr Johns. 'It'll knock anything of Bungay's clean off the map.'

'What's all this?' said Mr Barton, diverted from his efforts to be entertained by Mrs Rivers.

'I wanted it to be a surprise,' said Alice, half laughing, half inclined to cry. 'I thought if I could do a dust jacket for mother's new book and some end papers, it would be a surprise. Oh, Mother, *please* like them.'

'A very good piece of work,' said Mr Johns.

All Alice's friends crowded to see the dust jacket, which we need not describe, as every bookshop was full of it last Christmas, and one of the leading booksellers told Mr Johns's traveller that Mrs Barton's new book was selling fifty per cent on the jacket. This was of course entirely untrue, but as Mr Johns's traveller said afterwards when giving an account of his interview to Mr MacGregor the general manager, straws show which way the wind blows as they say. Its charming mock Renaissance design, its good lettering, its gay colour, are known to all those who bought it, for of those base spirits who merely go to the library, and so never see the jackets, we will not speak. The end papers with their delightful procession of the figures in the book are not so well known, for very few readers look at the beginning or end of a book, and if they did would usually find blank paper; but they are equally attractive.

'I'm going to buy that,' said Mr Johns. 'Will you take five pounds for it, Miss Barton?'

'Oh!' said Alice.

'That wasn't an affirmative,' said Roddy, 'it was only a noise. Alice, you need an agent. Make it ten, Mr Johns.'

'All right, ten,' said Mr Johns, amused, and thinking he had made quite a good bargain.

'Oh, Roddy!' said Alice, still quite bewildered, but full of admiration for what was obviously a remarkable business deal on Roddy's part.

'Are you sure you like it, Mother?' Alice asked, with a return of the old self-depreciation, but Mrs Barton said she was with a full heart, and Alice kissed all her family violently, including Sally, and nearly including Roddy because there he was.

Julian was naturally the first to introduce a discordant element by saying he didn't want to lose all the daylight and they should have seen Bolikoff's jacket he did for Sasha Menski's *Worm that Eateth the Flesh*. Mr Johns, who knew his facts and figures, said it was no good at all, and a jacket like that never sold a copy. Julian argued that Bolikoff never wanted his jackets to sell copies.

'I'm sure he didn't,' said Mrs Barton. 'He was quite the most selfish, unpleasant man I ever came across. That is just the kind of bad turn he would have done a friend.'

In face of this crass Philistinism Julian was powerless, and began to move his easel about, disturbing people a good deal.

'Wait a bit, Rivers,' said Mr Barton, good-naturedly enough considering how trying his uninvited guest had been, 'till we've gone down. Then you can get on with your sketch.'

Mrs Rivers saw her son taking such dire offence at the

word 'sketch' that she hastened to placate him by suggesting what fun it would be if he did a jacket for her next book. Julian looked at her with cold dislike and made no answer at all. Mrs Rivers bit her lip, and those of the party who saw her face were shocked and uneasy.

'Oh, Mrs Rivers,' said Mrs Barton, quickly trying to change the atmosphere, 'I wonder if you would do me a real kindness. I am taking Alice to Italy soon, and as I shall be very busy, I wondered if you would let Phoebe come with us. It would be so nice for Alice to have a companion. I'd take great care of her.'

'That is very kind of you,' said Mrs Rivers, seeing a chance of getting a daughter who refused to take an interest in vital things off her hands while she went on her cruise to Ceylon. 'I know Phoebe would love it. The only thing,' she continued, speaking in a lower voice to Mrs Barton and Alice, 'is that there might be a change. Gillie was talking to her this morning, and—'

'Oh, has he told Phoebe? I *am* pleased,' said Alice. 'I thought it was a secret, but now it's all right. Isn't it perfect? Sally told me before lunch and I could hardly bottle it up.'

Sally and Roddy both began talking at once to hide this blunder, but Mrs Rivers was used to domineering the literary cocktail parties she frequented and easily made her voice heard.

'Miss Wicklow, I don't understand,' she said. 'Has Phoebe told you anything?'

Sally could find nothing better to say than that she hadn't seen Phoebe since the meet on Wednesday.

'But Miss Barton said you told her before lunch—' Mrs

Rivers began, and then stopped, with a premonition of disaster.

Mrs Barton, who bore Mrs Rivers no malice for her behaviour, and was sincerely sorry for what had to come, said, 'Sally was telling us about her engagement to Mr Foster before lunch. I do hope you won't feel hurt at our knowing first, but Sally is one of Alice's oldest friends.'

There was a difficult silence. Mr Barton, Mr Johns, and Guy, having seen or been told of Mrs Rivers's hopes, did not like to voice their own pleasure. Then all that was finest in Mrs Rivers, the strong pride that had turned to sham intellectual arrogance, the breeding that she so often used only to insult and wound, the practice in the world that she had long used for no better purpose than gaining popularity among the cheaper literary circles, all these rose from the past and rallied to support her. She congratulated Sally very charmingly, and said she wished she had known sooner, so that she might have expressed her pleasure at once, and that she was sure nothing could give Cousin Giles and Cousin Edith greater satisfaction. She even managed to convey that Sally hadn't done so very well; that to her aristocratic heights a future earl was but as other men. The Bartons and Mr Johns admired her more than they would have thought possible, and were very sorry that this discomfiture had chanced to fall on her in public. Roddy suspected, by reason of his innate kindliness, that unhappiness was there, though he did not realise its full implications, and Guy wondered vaguely why they couldn't get on with it.

'Well, congratulations and all that, Sally,' he said, thus considerably relieving the tension. 'And mind you make

Gillie pull down that awful Towers and I'll build you another.'

'And now,' said Mrs Rivers, 'I really must be going. Julian, are you coming with me? I've got the car.'

'Oh, my God, can't one be left alone for one moment,' said Julian to the world at large, following this appeal by a muttered remark about blasted interference.

Mrs Rivers went quite white. She walked over to the window and stood looking down at the vista of the gardener's Periclean cottage. Everyone knew she was struggling not to cry.

Alice was appalled. Mrs Rivers had never been nice to her, but that didn't matter. Everyone knew she wanted Gillie to marry Phoebe, and it must be horribly disappointing, but as Gillie and Phoebe didn't want to be married at all, it was just as well. But what Julian had done was beyond the bounds. It was true that his mother had been very horrid to him, persecuting him and asking questions and not understanding artists, but to be as rude as that to one's mother, before strangers, was a thing Alice could never have imagined, the most horrible thing anyone could do. With blazing indignation, and entirely carried away by her sympathy for Mrs Rivers, who, making no sound, was standing in such mute misery as should have touched even a son, Alice forgot all her shyness.

'How dare you, Julian!' she said. 'How *dare* you talk to Mrs Rivers like that. Please take that portrait away and I think it is very bad and stupid and I hope I'll never see you again and I don't wonder no one likes you. How dare you!'

'I think Alice is right,' said Mr Barton. 'I don't suppose

you will want to finish that portrait, Rivers. I will have all your things packed up and sent to you at Pomfret Towers.'

Julian again recognised the voice of authority, disliked and resented it even more than before, and felt thoroughly wronged.

'I couldn't have done much with it anyway,' he said. 'I'd better go back to town if there's going to be all this fuss.'

He then ostentatiously dipped a large brush in the remains of the rose madder and with equal ostentation smeared the paint across the canvas, in such a way that he would have but little trouble in removing it.

'That's a jolly good idea,' said Roddy with quiet approval, and taking the brush from Julian he rapidly laid a criss-cross of lines over the painting, using some of every paint on the palette.

'I didn't know I had it in me,' said Roddy, stepping back to view his handiwork with considerable satisfaction.

'Goodbye, Julian,' said Mrs Barton, not unkindly.

Julian mumbled goodbye to her, and went out of the room, ignoring everyone else.

'Oh, Roddy, how could you!' said Alice.

But not in the tone of shocked reproach with which she had admonished him for pulling Julian off the running-board of Mr Barton's car after the weekend: in a voice of pure hero-worship that made Roddy almost burst with humble gratitude. In fact for a moment Roddy, the good, dependable Roddy whom they all liked and all took for granted, became a Greatheart in everyone's eyes. Their feelings were neatly voiced by Sally, who hit him on the back and said she had never been so glad to be in at a kill. Having said this, she wished she hadn't, for there was Mrs Rivers, so quiet that they had almost forgotten her. Mrs Rivers turned round and held out her hand to Mrs Barton.

'I'm afraid Julian is too temperamental,' she said, in an uncertain voice. 'It is *too* naughty of him, but all young people are like that. Thank you so much for a delightful lunch, Mrs Barton, and if you really want Phoebe I'm sure she will love to come, and I'll be most grateful.'

Mrs Barton could only say goodbye. Mr Johns did the same, adding that he would look forward to hearing from her.

'Oh, that,' said Mrs Rivers. She put her hands to her eyes for a moment and then said, 'I'm feeling too stupid for business, Mr Johns. It's this wretched influenza. Do you mind if we leave things as they were? It's rather nice to deal with people who will be . . . nice to one.'

'Of course, of course,' said Mr Johns soothingly, but by this time Mrs Rivers was quite unable to control her voice or face. Mrs Barton took her hastily away to her own room, said little, brought a hot water bottle and eau-de-Cologne, drew the curtains and left her in the dark to rest.

Mr Johns was amazed at the way Providence intervened on behalf of the house of Johns & Fairfield. Only the day before Mrs Rivers had been flourishing offers from Hobb – he knew it must be Hobb, and also Bungay – and putting a pistol to his head. Today, by pure luck, she was glad to remain with the firm, who he must say had always treated her well, on the old terms. What a story to tell to Fairfield. And how Hobb and Bungay would gossip over it, and try to guess how much he really made out of her. Nothing could have fallen better. So Mr Johns said goodbye to Mr and Mrs

Barton and Alice, whose drawings he took with him, and drove back to the Deanery. And if he reflected that he had often prayed to be delivered from his most trying author, he realised that one must pay a price for everything in this world, and so went his way.

The young people, sobered by this awful occurrence, sat talking in the studio, chiefly about a dog that Roddy was training for shooting, avoiding all reference to what had happened, for they were still young enough to be horribly shocked and outraged by the sight of a grown-up person in distress. Mrs Barton, having seen that Mrs Rivers was resting, went to the drawing-room and sat by the fire. She was tired by the emotions of so many people and must have gone to sleep, for suddenly Horton was in the room, turning the lights on and announcing, 'Lady Pomfret, madam.'

'Susan, my dear,' said Lady Pomfret, 'I don't know if you have heard our news, but I felt I must tell you myself, before it is in *The Times*.'

She was more agitated than Mrs Barton had ever seen her, and her manner was almost apologetic.

'Sally told us after lunch,' said Mrs Barton. 'She said it was a secret, but we are such old friends of hers that I'm sure you and Lord Pomfret won't mind. We are all, every one of us, more delighted than I can say.'

'I used to think of you and Harry,' said Lady Pomfret. 'I have been thinking of Alice and Gillie. I am a foolish, presumptuous old woman.'

Mrs Barton begged her old friend not to say such things. Alice, she said, thinking plain speaking the best, was as delighted as any of them.

'Dear Alice,' said Lady Pomfret, pressing Mrs Barton's hand. 'I am sure I shall love Sally very much. She has been perfectly wonderful with the dogs. Giulia looks a different being already. Of course Alice must be a bridesmaid. We mean to have the wedding at the end of March, before I go back to Italy. It will have to be rather quiet, because of Major Foster's death, but we shall have tea for the school-children, and a lunch for the tenants, and a ball for the servants. Giles is perfectly delighted about it all.'

Mrs Barton recognised with amusement that her friend intended to run the whole wedding herself, and that Mr and Mrs Wicklow would have very little say. Also that the whole ceremony appeared to be planned for the tenants and servants rather than for the bride and bridegroom, though she didn't think they would see anything wrong in this.

'I am taking Phoebe to Italy with Alice,' said Mrs Barton. 'She and Guy had a silly kind of semi-engagement. It is all over for the present, but if they are going to take it seriously I'd like to know Phoebe better, and Alice is so fond of her. By the way,' she continued, thinking it best to get everything over and minimise it as much as possible, 'Mrs Rivers is upstairs. She didn't feel very well after lunch, and Julian came here in one of his trying moods, so as soon as he had gone back to town I made her lie down. She was perfectly charming to Sally about the engagement. Alice stupidly let it out, but as it is all to be public tomorrow I don't suppose it matters.'

Lady Pomfret was not deceived by this, and Mrs Barton knew it, but she approved Mrs Barton's methods and said she would drive Hermione back with her if she was rested, and one of the men could come over and fetch Hermione's car. Mrs Rivers came down just then, and hearing what had been arranged, said she felt quite well again, but would be so grateful to Cousin Edith for a lift, as she really didn't feel quite up to driving.

'And thank you so much for being so sweet to Phoebe,' she said to her hostess, 'and I must let you have the address of my press-cutting agent. He is really marvellous.'

Mrs Rivers was herself again, and Mrs Barton accepted the situation, knowing that they had seen something they should never have seen and would be truly kind to forget. Lady Pomfret kissed Susan Barton with great affection and trailed away, carrying Mrs Rivers with her.

Mr Barton and the younger people now came in for tea, and there was a delightful talk about Sally's wedding. Alice on hearing that she was to be bridesmaid said, 'How lovely, Mother, what can I wear?' and her father and mother exchanged grateful glances. She wasn't grown-up yet, she would not yet shed altogether her disastrous timidity, but that she could enjoy the thought of having a new dress and walking up an aisle where several people were bound to see her, was an improvement that a short time ago they would never had dared to hope.

Presently Sally said they must be off, and Guy said he would walk back with them and see the puppies.

'You needn't go yet, Roddy, need you,' said Mrs Barton. 'I've got some letters to write, but you won't disturb me.'

So Roddy stayed on, while Guy and Sally went off together, Guy not altogether displeased at escorting a future countess to her home.

Mr Barton said he had some work to do. But instead of going straight from the drawing-room to his study, he went out into the hall. There was an address that he wanted to look up in the London telephone book. He took it from its place and began to turn the pages. Then he laid it down and looked out of a window at the cold, hard spring twilight. The wind was lashing the almond tree more furiously than ever, but the sparrows had gone, leaving mangled saffron petals on the lawn. Guy and Phoebe. What a foolish tearing of their own hearts and their parents' feelings, and all for nothing. What a good, intelligent, hard-working boy Guy was in the office, and what, to put it mildly, an infernal nuisance he had been in the home. Mr Barton found himself wishing that Guy and Phoebe could get married at once, and give each other the trouble they were giving their elders. Both of them might do worse, and he found himself calculating how much he could allow them for a start. If Guy could stand Mrs Rivers for a mother-in-law, and that young Rivers as a brother-in-law, he could stand anything.

And how funnily and pluckily little Alice had flown out at young Rivers, like a very small kitten attacking a mastiff, and with the same ridiculous success. What a lot of good her little incursion into society had done her. Perhaps she would dine out with him sometimes now, when Susan was away, and they could even have one or two small dinner parties. No: Susan was taking Alice with her. Well, it would be good for the child to see Italy and miss the long English spring, and he would get on very well by himself, with occasionally Guy's company when that young man was not dining elsewhere.

Mr Barton walked over to the staircase and lovingly felt the large pineapple on the lowest of the balusters, with its comfortable patina of two centuries. His eye followed the stairs up to the second floor and found nothing but beauty in their lines. Behind him the two perfectly proportioned windows of the hall were framing the last of the daylight, their frames sharply silhouetted against the sky. The lease of Mellings would see him through his lifetime, and while Mellings was there, the world was not entirely empty. He looked up his address and went into his study.

Hardly had he left the hall when Horton came through it to the drawing-room and removed the tea-things. Mrs Barton established herself at her writing-table and went on with a long letter to Count Strelsa about the research she proposed to do that spring.

'Sit down and be properly comfortable,' said Roddy, pushing Alice gently into the largest chair by the fire. Horton had switched off the wall lights, and all was very warm and peaceful with the light of a reading-lamp and the glow of the flames. Roddy sat down on the heavily padded arm of Alice's chair and pulled out his pipe.

'Would your mother mind?' he asked.

'I shouldn't think so,' said Alice. 'Father always does.'

Roddy lit his pipe very slowly.

'Tired?' he asked Alice.

'A bit. It was a funny day, wasn't it.'

'Not a bad day,' said Roddy. 'Why not be comfortable?'

He put his arm quietly round Alice, so that she rested in a warm nest of peat-scented tweed, very tired, but with a sense of relief and well-being that she did not try to account for. Mrs Barton, looking up from her letter, saw her daughter looking so peaceful and safe that her heart beat in gratitude. There, under her eyes, might be the shelter that would let that timid creature grow in strength and courage. But not yet, not yet. Their voices reached her, muted to the low sound of the fire, and by a desire, she knew, not to disturb her as she wrote.

'I say, Alice,' said Roddy, 'I was talking to Jim at the kennels yesterday. He's looking for some people to walk the puppies. Do you think you'd like to have one in the summer, when you're back from Italy? They're decent little fellows.'

'Do you think I could?' said Alice, pleased but anxious.

'Of course you could. I'll give you a hand.'

'Oh, Roddy!' said Alice, and sighed with pure happiness.

VIRAGO MODERN CLASSICS

HIGH RISING

Angela Thirkell

Successful novelist Laura Morland and her boisterous son Tony set off to spend Christmas at their country home in the sleepy surrounds of High Rising. But Laura's wealthy friend and neighbour George Knox has taken on a scheming secretary whose designs on marriage to her employer threaten the delicate social fabric of the village. Can clever, practical Laura rescue George from Miss Grey's clutches and, what's more, help his daughter Miss Sibyl Knox to secure her longed-for engagement?

Irresistibly entertaining and witty, *High Rising*, originally published in 1933, was the first of Angela Thirkell's celebrated classic comedies.

'A terrific holiday story'
The Lady